O'Marie, Carol Anne.
The missing Madonna
M

DATE DUE

JAN 2 2016			

THE
MISSING
MADONNA

THE MISSING MADONNA

Sister Carol Anne O'Marie

Delacorte Press

Published by
Delacorte Press
The Bantam Doubleday Dell Publishing Group, Inc.
666 Fifth Avenue
New York, New York 10103

Library of Congress Cataloging in Publication Data

O'Marie, Carol Anne.
    The missing Madonna / by Carol Anne O'Marie.
        p.   cm.
    ISBN 0-440-50040-0
    I. Title.   C.L
PS3565.M347M57   1988
813'.54—dc19   88-15349
                                                             CIP

Manufactured in the United States of America

December 1988

        10 9   8   7   6   5   4   3   2

                        BG

With love
to my nieces and nephew,
Caroline, John, and Noelle Benson,
who can finally see their names in print
and
prove to their friends we are related!

Author's Note

The Older Women's League (OWL) is a real (and wonderful) organization founded in 1981, in Oakland, California, by Tish Summers and Laurie Shields. It should be emphasized, therefore, that all characters in this story are wholly fictitious and bear no relationship to any actual members of the organization, living or dead.

Tuesday, May 1

Feast of St. Joseph, the Worker

Sister Mary Helen grabbed the handrail of the Down escalator to steady herself. She peered into the late-night crowd at Newark Airport, hoping to spot their escort.

"Over there." Nudging her, Sister Eileen pointed at a silver-haired woman holding a large printed sign that read OWLS WELCOME.

Mary Helen adjusted her bifocals. Sure enough, her friend Eileen was right. That was no doubt Mrs. Taylor-Smith, the woman who was to meet them and drive them to New York City.

"I feel downright foolish standing under a sign marked OWLS," Mary Helen muttered out of the side of her mouth. "What in the world do you suppose people think?"

"I'm surprised you give a hoot." A grin spread across Eileen's wrinkled face.

Mary Helen laughed in spite of herself. "You're beginning to sound just like Lucy Lyons," she said, looking up the escalator at Lucy and their three other OWL companions, all chatting happily.

Quickly, the six OWLs cut through the crowd and stood in a circle around Mrs. Taylor-Smith.

"Welcome to New York." She bobbed her beautifully styled head of hair. "And welcome especially to our annual OWLs convention. I don't have to tell any of you how important our political clout is or how happy I am to see you here. Our San Francisco chapter is one of our most influential."

Mrs. Taylor-Smith paused, pursed her lips, and tilted her head. *Like an expensive cat.* Mary Helen had just come across that description in the English mystery she was reading on the plane. The woman fit the description *purr-fectly.* Good night, nurse! Lucy Lyons is contagious! she thought, patting her pocketbook to make sure she had remembered the paperback. Sure enough, it was there, wrapped in her faithful plastic prayerbook cover.

Their escort continued, "And San Francisco is also one of our most unusual chapters." Smiling, she nodded toward Sister Mary Helen and Sister Eileen.

Mary Helen could feel her backbone stiffen. It was hard to tell if Mrs. Taylor-Smith was being patronizing or complimentary. Deciding to give the woman the benefit of the doubt, she smiled back.

"I'm sure it is," Erma Duran spoke up. "And I know much of it is due to the presence of our dear Sisters." Cocking her curly gray head, Erma smiled first at Mary Helen and then at Eileen. Finally, like a teacher about to present her prize pupils, she addressed their escort: "Why, where else would you find two older nuns carrying picket signs protesting the cuts in social security?"

Mary Helen winced, remembering Eileen and herself walking in a wide circle, freezing cold, in front of the Federal Building. HONK IF YOU LOVE YOUR MOTHER their large signs had read. Secretly, she had to admit she had been thrilled each time she heard a honk.

"And we are so pleased they could come with us," Erma

That was why she had been especially thrilled when Erma Duran had suggested she join the OWLs. In addition to doing some good, she'd be keeping her mind active and maybe even her waistline thinner.

"With your history background, you'll be a wonderful asset," Erma had insisted.

Mary Helen had been impressed. After all these years, how had Erma remembered her major? She couldn't recall if she had even declared one yet, in that long-ago summer session.

"And, of course, we want Sister Eileen too. With her vast knowledge of reference materials." So, it wasn't memory at all! She had pumped Eileen.

* * *

"If that's all right with you, Sister?" Erma's voice brought Mary Helen back to the present.

Mrs. Taylor-Smith, pewter eyes unflinching, looked at her expectantly.

"Oh, yes," Mary Helen answered. If good old Erma said something was all right, she'd bet even money that it was.

Everyone smiled pleasantly—everyone, that is, except Eileen, who looked puzzled. Mary Helen would ask her what she had agreed to as soon as they were alone in the hotel room.

Meanwhile, she watched while Erma introduced the other OWLs to Mrs. Taylor-Smith.

Beside her, Caroline Coughlin removed a glove and extended her hand. The feather on the wide-brimmed hat covering her champagne-colored hair quivered ever so slightly as she inclined her head. Caroline's deep blue eyes smiled, but she curved her lips just barely, so that not a wrinkle creased her subtly made-up face. In Mary Helen's opinion, this woman was the closest the OWLs would ever come to meeting a royal princess or, at Caroline's age, a queen dowager.

Rumor had it, though, that when provoked, the genteel Mrs. Coughlin, who had outlived two husbands, could sing a song of swearwords guaranteed to make a stevedore blanch.

Whenever she had accidentally let one slip in front of the nuns, Mary Helen noted, she had the uncanny knack of making it sound like the height of refinement. Yes, indeed, she thought, observing her charm Mrs. Taylor-Smith, Caroline Coughlin was, as they say, "to the manner born."

Lucy Lyons, whom Erma introduced next, was blessed with another attribute. *Born with the gift of laughter and the sense that the world was mad.* That inscription over the door of Yale's Hall of Graduate Studies fit Lucy perfectly. These two qualities had been her only patrimony, yet they had served her well. Short, plump Lucy Lyons probably had more money than all her other companions put together.

Mary Helen watched their escort's pewter eyes examine Lucy. They began at the top, where a hastily plaited braid coiled around her head like a thick gray snake. With disdain they wandered from her horn-rimmed glasses down her jersey off-the-rack suit to her sensible black pumps. They flickered only for a moment when they focused on the diamond in its Tiffany setting on Lucy's left ring finger. The stone was the size of a small marble. Her husband, Jimmy, had given it to her a year or so before his death.

"A token of his *affliction,*" Lucy always said when asked about the ring. Jimmy was the type, Mary Helen had been told, who could sell snow to the Eskimos. As a matter of fact, he had started out selling purses. "There's a lot of money in purses," Lucy often quipped.

With his ability and her sense of fun, the couple had amassed a fortune, bought a palatial home in San Francisco's St. Francis Wood, and sent four children through college. Yet Lucy never lost her simplicity. Her one flaw was her terrible addiction to corny jokes and puns. She just couldn't seem to resist them. Mary Helen sincerely hoped she would not be able to think of one until Mrs. Taylor-Smith had safely deposited them at their hotel.

"Hello. I'm Noelle Thompson." Looking over her half

glasses, Noelle extended her hand before Erma had the chance to introduce her. Noelle, a spinster, was probably the most intelligent or at least the best-educated member of the group. Surely she was the most assertive. The woman had held several important positions with the federal government and often acted as its spokesperson. Noelle Thompson had been the OWLs' unanimous choice for president of their chapter.

"It's nice to meet you, Alice," Noelle said. Mary Helen had forgotten that Mrs. Taylor-Smith's name was Alice. From the way the woman was blinking, she wondered if Mrs. Taylor-Smith might have forgotten too.

Adjusting her blue leather shoulder-strap purse, Noelle picked up her matching blue carry-on case. She straightened the jacket of her blue-plaid wool suit. Everything about Noelle Thompson was blue or had a touch of blue, even the light rinse in her white hair.

"The color picks up and intensifies her blue eyes," Eileen had commented when Mary Helen first noticed it. "I read about it in *Vogue,*" she said with authority. "Many women choose a color to highlight their eyes. It commands attention."

Dumbfounded, Mary Helen had stared at her friend. "What in the world were you doing reading *Vogue*? Don't tell me, at our age, you're going glamorous on me!" She smoothed her own navy-blue skirt, wondering just how out of style it was.

"Glory be to God, Mary Helen." Eileen's eyebrows had shot up. "It will take more than one article in *Vogue* to make a pacesetter out of the likes of me. If you must know, the truth of the matter is that *Vogue*—and an old issue, to boot—was the only magazine in the dentist's office." She paused to let that sink in. "I did, however, find it an interesting idea. Don't you?"

Mary Helen had mulled over the idea briefly and decided against ever trying it. Her own hazel eyes showed such a myriad of color that choosing a hue to highlight them would be more trouble than it was worth.

Sister Mary Helen didn't realize how tired she was until the six women had finally snuggled into Mrs. Taylor-Smith's stretch Cadillac, hired, Mary Helen suspected, for the occasion.

Her eyes burned. She closed them. She'd be glad to get to New York City and into bed. Let the other girls carry on the chitchat on the way there. She would just rest her eyes. She took a deep breath. No wonder she was tired. It was just a little more than two weeks ago, right before Easter, that she had unexpectedly run into Erma Duran at the college.

"What in the world are you doing here?" Mary Helen had blurted out the moment she saw Erma. "I'm surprised to see you," she had added quickly, realizing just how rude her question sounded.

Apparently good old Erma hadn't noticed. "Not as surprised as I am to be here," she had answered. "A couple of weeks ago Lucy talked me into signing up with her for one of your Senior-Enrichment classes. She thinks it will be good for both us. Luckily it's on Monday, my day off."

Grimacing, Erma had unfurled the college brochure in front of Mary Helen and pointed to a blurb about an intensive journal-writing workshop.

Mary Helen was just about to say that she never thought of Erma as the journal-writing type, intensive or otherwise, when Lucy rounded the corner.

"Hi, Sister," she had called. "I'm so glad we ran into you. It saves me a phone call. Jimmy used to say that when I died they would have to get the damn thing surgically removed from my ear."

Mary Helen had laughed. Although she had heard Lucy say that at least two dozen times, she still enjoyed it. "What's up with you two eternal coeds?" she had asked.

Lucy had demurred in favor of her friend.

"Well, we've been talking among ourselves . . ." Erma's brown eyes had sparkled with the excitement of finally being able to tell a secret. "And the four of us—Noelle, Caroline, Lucy, and me"—she had counted the names off on her chubby fingers—"are going to New York for the OWL convention. We would all be delighted if you and Sister Eileen would come along with us. Actually," she had said with a quick smile, "it wouldn't be the same without you."

Surprised by the invitation, Mary Helen had hesitated.

"Now, Sister, if it's the expense, don't you worry for a moment." She cocked her curly head toward Lucy. "We talked about that, too, and the trip will be our treat."

Mary Helen had gulped. She had a hunch that Erma had done most of the talking, and her good friend Lucy would do most of the treating. Not that Lucy would mind. And not that Erma wouldn't do what she could—perhaps even more than she could.

In Mary Helen's opinion, Erma Duran was sometimes generous to a fault. For example, since they had become reacquainted she had discovered that after graduation Erma Mc-Sweeney had forgone her own plans in order to take care of her aging parents. She was more than thirty by the time she felt free to marry Tommy Duran.

According to Eileen, who had been at Mount St. Francis for so many years that she was considered the walking *Who's Who,* Tommy had been a handsome devil. According to some others, he had been one of those dashing fellows who meant well but never seemed able to do as well as he meant. It was believed by all that, to his dying day, Erma had supported him as well as their three children. In fact, she was still working.

At first Mary Helen had felt a little sad for her old friend. Yet as far as she could tell, despite or maybe because of what life had dealt her, Erma had aged into one of those salt-of-the-earth women.

"To look at her, you'd think she had the world by the proverbial tail," Mary Helen had remarked to Eileen after one OWL meeting.

"Erma's made of sturdy stock." Eileen had nodded her head knowingly. "She's full of faith, a real survivor.

"Besides"—she winked at Mary Helen—"she has a touch of the lace-curtain Irish in her, so she would never let on otherwise."

*   *   *

Eileen nudged her. Mary Helen opened her eyes with a start. She must have been dozing.

"We are about to enter the Lincoln Tunnel," Mrs. Taylor-Smith sounded like a high-class tour guide. "But before we do, ladies, over there." She tilted her head.

"Look, Mary Helen." Eileen pointed across the darkness to the magnificent skyline. Mary Helen drew in her breath.

On the horizon New York looked like a clear, well-taken photograph. Thousands of lights blinked. A phrase from a Hopkins sonnet popped into her mind—"O look at all the fire-folk sitting in the air." She wanted to pinch herself. It didn't seem possible that she and Eileen were actually here. It had been so unexpected.

After meeting Erma at the college—yes, that was exactly what she had been thinking about when she dozed off—after Erma's invitation, they'd barely had time, what with Holy Week services and Easter Sunday, to make the necessary arrangements at the college, pack a small bag each, and purchase a few traveler's checks.

"Disneyland for adults." That's what Sister Cecilia, the college president, had called New York when the two Sisters told her they'd be there for a few days.

Cecilia had looked pleased. Too pleased, if you asked Mary Helen.

"I'm so glad you two have the opportunity," Cecilia had said. "It's a perfect time for you to go before graduation and the start of summer school."

"We'll be gone only three days," Eileen reminded her.

"Oh, don't hurry back," Cecilia added quickly. "Stay as long as you like. We'll manage without you."

"That was nice of Cecilia, don't you think?" Eileen had remarked when they left the president's office. "She seemed genuinely thrilled we could go."

Not only thrilled, downright eager, Mary Helen thought. If I didn't know better, I might even think she was happy to be rid of us.

Mrs. Taylor-Smith pulled to an abrupt stop at the corner of Seventh Avenue and Fifty-third Street. A doorman dressed like a deserter from the French Foreign Legion held the car door open. In a matter of seconds, he had summoned the porter for their luggage, opened the front door of the Sheraton Centre, and escorted them into the plush forest-green and red lobby of the hotel.

While Eileen spoke to the desk clerk, Mary Helen gazed sleepily around. On one wall, by the curved stairway leading to a small cocktail lounge, she spotted a waterfall, the basin of which was full of coins. CONTRIBUTIONS FOR ST. MALACHY'S stated a printed sign nearby. Mary Helen was wondering how she could persuade the Fairmont or the Mark Hopkins in San Francisco to install a waterfall to benefit the scholarship fund of Mount St. Francis, when Eileen pulled her sleeve.

Still drowsy, she followed her friend into the elevator, then out and down the narrow fourth-floor hall to their double room.

"I was a bit surprised when you agreed so quickly to pronounce it," Eileen called from the small closet where she was hanging up her clothes.

Mary Helen sat on the edge of the bed, removing her shoes. She was too tired to unpack.

"I agreed to . . . ? What are you saying, Eileen?" She yawned and unbuttoned her blouse.

"Agreed to pronounce it. I thought you didn't like to speak in public." Eileen stood with her hands on her chubby hips.

"What in the name of all that is good and holy are you talking about?" Mary Helen adjusted her glasses and blinked at her friend. "When did I agree to . . . ?" Suddenly she remembered: In the airport, when she had let her mind wander. She cleared her throat. "What did I agree to?" she asked, feeling a little foolish, not to mention apprehensive.

Eileen sat on the adjoining bed. "Just as I suspected. You haven't the foggiest clue what they were asking you."

"Good night, nurse! Eileen! Get on with it. What did I agree to do?"

"To pronounce the benediction at tomorrow's opening breakfast meeting, Mary Helen. From what I gathered, it is rather like a solemn high grace before meals."

Groaning, Mary Helen climbed into bed. From the street below she heard taxis honking and car tires squealing. Streaks of light angled in between the slits where the heavy draperies failed to meet the windowframe. They moved along the ceiling of the darkened room, making grotesque shadows slide down the wall.

"Can't you sleep?" Eileen whispered from the next bed.

"No."

"Why not?"

"Because I'm thinking about what I'm going to say at the breakfast tomorrow, of course."

"Have you any ideas?"

"Not yet."

"You'll think of something, old dear. You always do." Eileen grunted consolingly and turned over.

Mary Helen stared at the shadow-etched ceiling. She didn't have the heart to tell Eileen that, at the moment, the only grace she could think of was one she had learned from a mischievous third-grader.

"Rub-a-dub-dub. Thanks for the grub. Yeah, God" was the way it went. Somehow, she didn't think that it would do.

Wednesday, May 2

Feast of St. Athanasius, Bishop

The luncheon speaker, a stately-looking woman, paused to entertain questions. How in the name of all that's good and holy do you *entertain* a question, Mary Helen wondered, glancing down at the convention program. Answer, maybe; ignore, possibly. But entertain?

Running her finger down the program schedule, she checked her watch. The session should be over in about ten minutes, unless some long-winded participant commandeered one of the four floor microphones. From the restless stirrings of the five hundred conventioneers seated at round tables, it didn't seem likely. The OWLs had sat long enough. She could feel a stretch in the air.

Right after lunch there was to be a minisession for new members. The rest of them were free to sightsee, shop, or nap. All around her Mary Helen could hear the pop of lipstick tubes and the click of powder compacts. Obviously, most of the OWLs were not going to rest.

Before they had left their bedroom this morning, Eileen and she had agreed to meet after lunch in front of the waterfall in the hotel lobby. It was a good thing, too, because they hadn't seen each other since.

As soon as the group was dismissed, Mary Helen followed the arrows marked LOBBY, planted herself firmly in front of the waterfall, and searched the milling crowd for her friend. Quickly, she spotted Eileen elbowing her way across the crowded lobby, with Lucy Lyons and Erma Duran trailing in her wake.

Erma hung behind the other two, and even from this distance, Mary Helen thought the woman looked distressed. What's wrong, she wondered, watching Erma stop at the main desk. She couldn't remember ever having seen her upset before. Erma said something to the man in a morning coat behind the desk.

The gentleman smiled brightly, checked the slots behind him, then shook his head. The thick mane of gray hair bounced from side to side, making him look, Mary Helen thought, for all the world like a friendly lion. He picked up the phone receiver, spoke briefly, then shook his head again.

Erma clutched her cloth purse to her chest. For a moment her shoulders drooped, but only for a moment. Running her hand over her gray-streaked hair, she pushed a stray curl behind her ear. She straightened up, smiled at the gentleman, then bent forward to pat his hand. She wouldn't want him to feel bad. As he gaped, she turned and bustled across the crowded foyer.

"Congratulations on the remarkably erudite blessing you gave this morning," Eileen said before Mary Helen could wonder what that was all about.

Eileen's gray eyes twinkled. "You do amaze me!" she said. "We've been friends for more than fifty years and I've never heard you say the Prayer of St. Cyril of Jerusalem used in the Coptic Orthodox Church." She moved closer. A group of women going to the Café Fonda squeezed around her. "To tell the God's honest truth, I hadn't the ghost of an idea you even knew any Coptic Orthodox prayers. Where did you manage to dig up such a thing?"

"You're not going to believe this," Mary Helen said.

"That was a lovely grace, Sister." A stout woman touched Mary Helen on the shoulder. "Very inspirational."

Mary Helen smiled and nodded. "Thank you," she said. The woman paused to exchange pleasantries with Erma and Lucy.

"Come clean, Mary Helen." Eileen was not to be put off.

"It was printed on the back of the plastic bookmark I stuck in my murder mystery," she whispered. Mary Helen was happy that Erma and Lucy were busy chatting.

"And there are those among us who dare to doubt the luck of the Irish!" Eileen rolled her eyes heavenward. Mary Helen not only doubted that the Irish had an edge on luck, she had her doubts about the rest of Eileen's superstitions as well. She was just about to say so when Lucy turned back to the group.

"Did I hear *Irish*?" she said. "Which brings to mind St. Patrick's and Fifth Avenue. What kind of devilment can we get into this afternoon?" Her eyes twinkled behind her horn-rimmed glasses.

"What exactly did you have in mind?" Mary Helen asked.

"I can't hear myself think in here, which probably is no great loss." Lucy leaned in toward the group. "But I can't hear you either. Can we talk outside?"

"Where are the other two?" Eileen shouted over the crowd.

"Noelle is introducing the speaker in one of the minisessions," Erma explained, "and Caroline has a childhood friend living in an apartment on East Fifty-sixth Street whom she promised to visit."

Outside the hotel, New York City was having a sparkling spring day. The sky above the tall buildings was a clear, picture-postcard blue and the air had a snap to it.

The noontime crowd bustled along in all directions. Taxis honked at trucks, cars, and pedestrians alike. A tight group of young men with yarmulkes and earlocks dashed across Seventh Avenue against the light. Businesswomen in smartly tailored wool suits and tennis shoes rushed past one another on the crowded sidewalks.

Although Mary Helen had visited New York City several times in her seventy-plus years, she never seemed to get over the sense of excitement she felt whenever she was there. There was a certain verve in the air that could not be denied.

"Shall we head for St. Patrick's Cathedral first?" Erma's brown eyes snapped with eagerness. "I've always wanted to see it."

They all nodded. Who would have the heart to say no, Mary Helen wondered. Lucy led the way and the others followed her, zigzagging single file across West Fifty-third Street to Fifth Avenue. Sister Mary Helen brought up the rear.

"We must look like a string of gray-haired ducklings," she shouted to Eileen, who was just ahead of her. She was not sure her friend had heard her. She wished Eileen would wait. She wanted to tell her about Erma looking worried and stopping by the front desk of the hotel. She also wanted to ask Eileen if she had any idea why, but they had reached St. Patrick's before she caught up.

The four women stood for several minutes, looking up at its Gothic splendor. Then they threaded their way through groups of people seated on the entrance steps, having lunch, chatting, or just leaning back to enjoy the sunshine.

Skirting the bronze doors, they entered the vestibule. Once inside the cathedral, Mary Helen paused while her eyes adjusted to the cool dimness of the immense structure. Behind her on the west wall, the rose window, framed by the thousands of shining pipes of the great organ, shed muted light on the nave.

The group moved reverently down the side aisle past the altars of St. Anthony, St. Anne, and St. Monica. They stopped for a moment at the shrine of Elizabeth Ann Seton, the first American-born saint.

Mouth open, Erma pointed to the cardinals' hats hanging from the ceiling hundreds of feet above them. Craning their necks, the women stared up at the four round, flat red dots, with their clusters of dangling tassels.

"These cardinals!" Lucy whispered after a few moments. "They really have their heads in the clouds."

Mary Helen had wondered how long it would take her to say it.

"But they do keep on top of things," Eileen whispered back. Egad! Lucy Lyons was rubbing off!

The group decided to split up. Mary Helen and Eileen would attend the one-o'clock Mass in Our Lady's Chapel, drop by the elegant old Scribner bookstore, and then simply windowshop. Lucy and Erma intended to shop in earnest: Saks, Gucci, Tiffany, F.A.O. Schwarz. The four agreed to rendezvous at quarter past three at the Lexington Avenue entrance of Bloomingdale's.

* * *

Mary Helen didn't realize how sore her feet were until three-ten, when Eileen and she were seated on two hard chairs next to the fine-jewelry department in Bloomingdale's. From where they sat they had a perfect view of the store's glass doors and the three or four steps leading to the old revolving door that opened onto Lexington Avenue. No one could get in or out without their noticing.

She and Eileen had bought a Big Apple T-shirt to take back to Sister Anne. The shirts were so cute. But in Mary Helen's opinion, Anne was the only nun at Mount St. Francis College young enough and thin enough to wear one. They had picked out a large box of Fanny Farmer chocolates to bring home to the others. Which calories they didn't need, they both had agreed.

Right on time, Lucy and Erma arrived, smiling and laden

with brightly colored shopping bags. They had just greeted one another when a piercing cry echoed from the entryway. The milling shoppers stopped, momentarily stunned. Mary Helen could feel the hair rise along the back of her neck.

She strained to see. A thin redheaded woman grabbed at her throat, paled, then burst into tears. In front of her a sinewy teenager in jeans and a maroon velour shirt turned and bolted down the steps. Hitting hard against the revolving door, he whirled out onto the crowded street. He was fast, but not so fast that Mary Helen didn't see a piece of thin gold chain dangling from his clenched fist.

The weeping woman, pale and shaken, slumped onto the steps. Before Mary Helen fully realized what had happened, a broad-shouldered black man, who looked like a college full-back, burst from the jewelry department. He spoke into a walkie-talkie. Seconds later, three men came running from different parts of the department store, and streaked past them. Taking the steps in one leap, they shot out onto Lexington.

"Glory be to God!" Eileen was the first to get her voice back. "Glory be to God!" she repeated, her brogue unusually thick. "We've seen a mugging!"

Stunned, Mary Helen nodded her head. Beside her, Erma's pudgy hand shielded the gold medallion hanging around her own neck. "I don't know what I'd do if anything ever happened to this," she whispered. Clearing her throat, she stared sympathetically at the shaking woman now being comforted by the fullback. "I tell you, girls, I would be absolutely inconsolable."

Shoving her bifocals up the bridge of her nose, Mary Helen studied the filigree-edged medal hanging around Erma's neck. It was Our Lady of Perpetual Help. The Byzantine image of Mother and Child dangled from a gold chain.

"My husband, Tommy, gave it to me a year or so before he died," Erma said quietly, her brown eyes suddenly filling. Embarrassed, she looked away.

Pretending not to notice her tears, Mary Helen took the medal in the palm of her hand. "It's lovely, Erma," she said. And it was. Even though the medal was small, in the raised image the Mother looked sad; the Child, terrified. It was no wonder, Mary Helen thought, that this was the most famous of what were called the Passion Madonnas.

She turned the medal over, noting with surprise the 24K stamped on the back.

"It's valuable." Erma, now fully recovered, nodded. It was as if she could read the old nun's mind. "But its real value to me is sentimental. Tommy knew I had special devotion to Our Lady of Perpetual Help."

No doubt, being married to Tommy Duran, poor Erma had needed all the help she could get. Mary Helen let the medal slip from her hand.

*   *   *

The cab ride back to the Sheraton was silent. Each woman clung to the edge of the seat as the cab swerved and screeched through the traffic. Each was lost in her own thoughts. They arrived at the hotel just in time to go to their rooms and freshen up before the four-o'clock session.

As she crossed the hotel lobby, heading for the elevator, Mary Helen noticed Erma out of the corner of her eye. The woman had stopped at the main desk again.

Thursday, May 3

Feast of Sts. Philip and James, Apostles

The schedule for the final day of the annual OWLs convention was chock-full, so full in fact, that even that morning Mary Helen had not yet decided which workshops to attend.

"Do you know which sessions you're going to?" she asked Eileen while the two were still dressing in their hotel room. It wasn't that she wanted a suggestion, but rather reassurance. She'd feel a great deal better knowing she wasn't the only one who couldn't make up her mind.

Eileen stuck her head around the bathroom doorjamb. "Oh, my, yes," she answered brightly, or at least as brightly as she could with a mouth bubbling with pink toothpaste.

She rinsed. "But it took some doing," she added diplomatically. Mary Helen realized her face must have fallen.

"Which topics did you decide on?" she asked, this time from pure curiosity. How in the world had Eileen been able to choose among such stimulating subjects as Nursing-home Reform, Job Discrimination, and Arms Control?

"I'm going to hear the paper on Pain-free Arthritis," Eileen said, "and then the ones on Elderhostel and How to Age Happily."

Mary frowned. "But, Eileen"—she tried not to sound critical—"you don't have arthritis, do you?"

Eileen ran a comb through her wiry gray hair. "No, but Sister Therese does!" she answered, with a bit of logic that eluded Mary Helen.

"I see" was all Mary Helen could think of to say. Immediately she decided against asking, Why Elderhostel? Or remarking that Eileen couldn't be aging any more happily if she tried. Right then Mary Helen made up her own mind to attend the session dealing with pending bills affecting older citizens. Legislation was one of the few things more complicated to follow than Eileen. Snatching her navy wool jacket from the closet, she quickly left their double room.

*　*　*

The final reception that afternoon took place in the hotel's convention center. Waiters circulated through the crowd, serving expensive wine in tulip-shaped glasses. More waiters followed with trays of unusual-looking hors d'oeuvres harpooned with colored toothpicks and artistically arranged on frilly white doilies.

Helping herself to several pieces of what she felt surely must be chicken, Mary Helen moved slowly around the room, greeting other conventioneers and wondering where they had dropped their used toothpicks.

Noelle Thompson stood in the corner, chain-smoking. Through the blue haze of smoke, she listened intently to a group of women clustered around her. Even from a distance Mary Helen could see her snapping blue eyes peering over her half glasses. "Don't agonize—organize!" she heard Noelle remind the group. That was the organization's motto and a good one too. Although Caroline Coughlin had once remarked that "Do it, damn it!" would be more to the point.

Against the far wall she couldn't help noticing Erma Duran

and Lucy Lyons nose-to-nose in conversation. Craning her neck, she could see that the usual smile was missing from Lucy's round face. In fact, she was frowning slightly. Behind horn-rimmed glasses, her eyes were fixed on Erma.

One glance at Erma's expression told her that whatever they were discussing was bothering them both. Erma seemed distraught. Odd, Mary Helen thought. In all the time she had known Erma she could not remember ever seeing her upset. Now . . . twice in two days? What was going on? Not that Erma didn't have plenty to be upset about. It couldn't be easy, Tommy dying and leaving her—to use the old phrase—less than well provided for. And her children! If you could believe what you heard, they fell a little short of the Waltons! But the Erma she knew had always seemed so solid and optimistic about everything.

Curious, Mary Helen watched Erma anxiously fingering the medal around her neck, then stopping just long enough to push a straying curl back in place.

What in the name of heaven is going on, she wondered. She watched Erma's face pucker as if she were about to burst into tears. Something was definitely wrong, and Mary Helen intended to find out what it was.

Slowly, she began to thread her way across the crowded convention room. She had moved only a few feet, when she felt a firm hand on her elbow. Who in the name of goodness . . . ? Whirling around, Mary Helen came face-to-face with Alice Taylor-Smith. Mrs. Taylor-Smith arched her long, slender neck and smiled her cat-smile.

"I have so enjoyed meeting you, Sister dear," she purred.

Mary Helen could feel herself bristle. Being called *dear* at seventy-plus was only slightly less offensive than being called *honey.*

What was it about Alice Taylor-Smith that affected her this way? The woman meant no harm. Mary Helen was sure of that. But there was something in her manner, something that gave the impression she thought herself—what was Eileen's old Irish saying?—"just a cut above" the rest of us.

It took Mary Helen several minutes to exchange pleasantries with Mrs. Taylor-Smith and settle on their departure time for the next day. This business concluded, she turned to find Lucy and Erma gone.

"Pshaw!" she muttered.

"Pshaw, indeed! Be careful you don't date yourself, old girl." Eileen was right behind her.

Mary Helen spun around. "What would you suggest I say instead?"

Her friend paused for a moment, as though pondering a weighty issue. "*Shucks* would bring you forward two or three generations at least. And you'd have such a nice out-West ring. Like a regular Gary Cooper."

"Good Lord, Eileen!" was all Mary Helen could think of to answer.

"What were you *pshawing* about, anyway?"

"Erma. Something is definitely wrong with her."

"What do you mean *wrong*? Is she ill?" Eileen craned her neck to see if she could pick Erma out of the dense crowd.

"No, not sick. She's disturbed or distressed, or something. I saw her across the room talking to Lucy. Everything about her said she was upset." Mary Helen nodded her head. "Yes, definitely upset!" she emphasized.

"You saw her across this packed room and could tell she was upset?" Eileen gestured a bit too dramatically for Mary Helen's liking. "Glory be to God, Mary Helen, you must give me the name of your optometrist. Whoever he is, he's a regular miracle-worker."

Eyes narrowed, Mary Helen faced her. "You know blasted well Dr. Van Houten is my eye doctor. And I tell you, Eileen, the woman is upset!"

Eileen was not to be cowed. "They could be talking about

anything at all. For instance, maybe they're discussing arthritis. Now, *that* is upsetting!"

She paused and looked hard at Mary Helen. "The point I'm making is, don't be searching for trouble. There's an old saying back home . . ." To Mary Helen's astonishment, Eileen could always dig up an old saying from "back home." She often suspected her friend made them up to fit the occasion. " 'Don't trouble trouble till trouble troubles you.' And from what I've noticed, trouble troubles you soon enough!"

It is not my fault, Mary Helen wanted to say but refrained. It sounded too much like a whine. If there was anything Mary Helen detested almost as much as a bore, it was a whiner.

"Humph" was all she said. Turning on her heel, she squeezed her way across the crowded room. Where in the world had Erma and Lucy disappeared to? She checked her wristwatch. Four-thirty. The women had agreed to meet at six for a final fling. Their four traveling companions had planned to treat them to dinner at a place they'd found in the Three A's tour book, before a quick walk over to West Forty-fourth Street and the eight o'clock performance at the Majestic Theatre.

Maybe Erma and Lucy had gone to their hotel room to start dressing for the evening, or perhaps to sneak in a short nap. Suddenly Mary Helen realized how tired she was. A short nap sounded heavenly. Maybe she'd sneak one in herself. It had been a long day. But first she'd stop by Erma's room and make sure everything was all right. Grudgingly she admitted to herself that she'd do well to take Eileen's advice and leave well enough alone. Absentmindedly, she pushed the elevator button.

* * *

The fourth floor of the hotel was plushly carpeted, dimly lit, and deadly quiet. The line of thick wooden doors, like so many rabbit hutches, were shut tight against any intrusions.

Mary Helen stopped in front of Erma's door and leaned

forward to listen. She had just poised her hand to knock when she heard the pathetic sound of muffled crying.

"Shush, Erma. Stop it." Even through the thick door she heard Lucy's high-pitched voice pleading. "You're working yourself up to an absolute frenzy. And about what? Money!" She spat out the last word almost as if it were an obscenity.

Erma muttered something unintelligible and cried all the harder.

"Damn it, Erma! You'd drive a preacher to cuss," Lucy shouted, but her tone was not angry, just helpless. "Better yet, to drink. And I think I will pour us both a short one." There was a long pause, but Mary Helen thought she heard Erma sobbing quietly.

"Please don't worry," Lucy said as if she were comforting a small child. "Here, drink this. Worry is not going to solve a thing," she went on. "It'll only ruin the little time off you have. I tell you, Erma, everything will work out. We'll make sure it does. And in the meantime, I'd be happy to help out. You know that."

Mary Helen heard what she thought was Erma blowing her nose and hiccuping softly.

Suddenly she shifted, embarrassed. She was intruding on a private conversation. Well, she'd never let on for one moment that she'd heard a thing. Straightening up, she decided against even knocking. Whatever was bothering Erma, she and Lucy would work it out. We'll make sure it does, Lucy had said. Mary Helen had heard that.

Besides, it was really none of her affair. To be very truthful, she had probably heard too much already. Eileen was absolutely correct. Why go looking for trouble? It was bad enough that she seemed to stumble into it even when she wasn't looking. She would go straight to her hotel room, put her feet up for a half hour or so, see if she could nap. And if she couldn't, she'd just relax and read a chapter or two of her murder mystery.

Squaring her shoulders, Mary Helen turned away from the door, adjusted her bifocals, and began to walk down the thickly carpeted hall. She was very glad she had, too, for just then the elevator door opened and out stepped Eileen. She would not, for one tiny moment, want Eileen to think that she would stoop to eavesdropping.

May 7

Monday of the Fourth Week of Easter

On Friday evening Sisters Mary Helen and Eileen had arrived back at Mount St. Francis College, where they spent the weekend recuperating. The other nuns were happy to have them home. Or so they said. Eileen staunchly denied that Sister Cecilia's face fell when they'd arrived in the community room on Friday after supper and announced they were home.

"You are terrible!" Eileen said. "Besides, it is just not true. Her face did not change one iota when she saw us. If anything, she smiled."

"Barely," Mary Helen conceded.

"Glory be to God, give the woman credit. She's the college president. Even if she wasn't completely happy to see us, she never would have let on. After all, she has had years of practicing the fine art of pretending to be happy to see people. The poor thing probably just had a hard day."

"Maybe it wasn't her face. Maybe it was something in her eyes." Mary Helen stopped to let that sink in. She considered herself an expert on eyes.

Eileen didn't dignify the remark with an answer.

"But what really made me wonder was when she looked up from her crossword puzzle and said, 'I need a seven-letter word for *disturbance*,' glanced over at us, and said '*trouble*.'"

"You are the living limit" was all that Eileen said.

There was no doubt young Sister Anne had been glad to see them back. "It's Dullsville around here without you two," she said, giving each of them a warm hug. The Big Apple T-shirt they brought home for her was a hit. At least Anne wore it the very next day.

"How do you like it?" she had asked at breakfast, blinking naively behind her purple-rimmed glasses. Mary Helen cringed.

Sister Therese, who preferred her name pronounced *trays,* sniffed and answered for the group. "I do think something from the shrine of St. Elizabeth Seton might have been more appropriate." She rolled her dark eyes toward Mary Helen, then heavenward. "However," she added, with a little jab in her voice, "it does match the blue jeans and those sandal-like shoes you insist on wearing."

Mary Helen could tell from Anne's face that the young nun took the remark as a compliment. Mary Helen knew better.

"Do you feel as if you have just been accused of contributing to the delinquency of a minor?" she asked Eileen, out of Therese's earshot. Although Therese was slightly deaf, her hearing had an uncanny way of suddenly improving. Not taking any chances, Eileen answered with a wink.

There was no question about the Fanny Farmer chocolates they brought home. The candy was an overwhelming success. By Sunday noon the whole box was empty, except for the marzipan piece that no one liked. Mary Helen knew from experience that before much more time passed someone's sweet tooth would get desperate and that piece, too, would disappear.

At first everyone had asked about their trip. At Sunday

supper, however, Mary Helen noticed that although the other nuns listened politely, their eyes were beginning to glaze over whenever someone mentioned New York.

Monday morning Mary Helen had gone over to her office late. All day long she had fully expected Erma Duran to call so they could hash over the trip. Actually she was disappointed when Erma didn't get in touch. Somehow, reliving the adventure was half the fun.

In fact, she had called Erma's apartment once or twice, but there was no answer. Monday was Erma's day off, and Mary Helen was beginning to get a bit concerned.

"Don't be silly," Eileen said when Mary Helen mentioned it to her at dinner. "The poor woman is probably dog-tired. Maybe she's just not answering. Anyway, isn't today the day she comes up here for her class?"

Mary Helen tried to remember whether or not it was a Monday when she had met Erma and Lucy at the college, but she couldn't recall.

"If that were the case, don't you think the two of them would have dropped by to see us?"

"They are probably exhausted, jet lag and all," Eileen had answered sensibly.

Mary Helen nodded. Her friend was most likely right. Lately she noticed that she was able to develop a case of jet lag on a trip between San Francisco and Los Angeles.

She had just settled down in a comfortable chair in the community room and switched on the six-o'clock news when the phone rang. She could hear Therese's short staccato steps echo down the parquet hallway to the phone booth. She answered it on the third ring.

Mary Helen could have laid odds that she would. In fact, she was secretly working on the theory that Therese, despite her deafness and arthritis, could catch the phone on the third ring from any spot in the entire convent. She was so good at it,

Mary Helen speculated, that with a little backing, Therese could make phone-answering into an Olympic event.

"It's for you," Therese called from the doorway, a little out of breath. "It's your OWL friend. That Caroline Coughlin."

From the way she emphasized *that* Mary Helen could tell that she must have been privy to some of Caroline's profanity.

"Hello, Caroline." Mary Helen didn't have a chance to say anything more.

"Have you heard from Erma?" Although Caroline's voice was still controlled and polished, Mary Helen could hear an undertone of worry.

"No, I haven't. Not since we came home." Mary Helen felt a flicker of dread in the pit of her stomach. "Is anything the matter?"

"Noelle and I think there is. Lucy keeps saying that we are probably just missing her. Calling when she steps out and not calling when she is home. But you know Lucy—she doesn't want to worry anyone."

"Has anyone talked to Erma?"

"No, Sister, that's my point. Nobody has heard from her all weekend. Lucy dropped her off at her apartment on Friday. She called her daughter that night to say she was home. But neither of them has heard from her since."

"Has anyone been to her apartment?" Mary Helen winced, reliving for a moment the awful scene she had discovered last December in the apartment of her secretary, Suzanne.

"Yes. According to Lucy, her daughter dropped by on Sunday morning and let herself in. She found no Erma, no note, nothing that would indicate where her mother was."

That was a relief!

"But in my opinion, Sister," Caroline continued, "her daughter is about as effective as a pimple on an elephant's ass. Excuse me."

For a moment, Mary Helen was taken aback. Said with

Caroline's finishing-school voice, that last little vulgarity sounded like poetry. She swallowed a laugh.

"Today Noelle called the man Erma works for, but he was vague. He said something about her mentioning visiting relatives in St. Louis. But it does seem preposterous that she would leave again so soon."

"St. Louis! I thought she was born and raised here."

"That doesn't mean she couldn't have relatives in St. Louis," Caroline answered reasonably, leaving Mary Helen feeling somewhat foolish.

"You're our last hope," she said. "We thought perhaps she might have called you or said something."

"No." Mary Helen could feel her dread growing. "As a matter of fact, I was just beginning to wonder myself. It's just not like Erma not to have called today to chat."

"Not a bit," Caroline agreed.

In her mind's eye, Mary Helen could see her nod her head of beautifully coiffured champagne hair. She wondered crazily if Caroline was wearing her hat and gloves.

"And what is more, it is not a bit like her to leave without saying something to her family and friends. She just isn't that kind of person, unless . . ." Caroline left the sentence unfinished.

"But you say Lucy isn't worried?" Mary Helen asked, trying not to overreact.

Caroline hesitated. "If you ask me, she's pretending not to be. You know, today is the day the two of them are supposed to go to class up there at Mount St. Francis. When Erma didn't call, Lucy tried her, but there was no answer."

Unexpectedly, Mary Helen's heart turned over, but she said nothing.

Caroline continued, "She says she is sure Erma has just forgotten today is Monday and has gone somewhere. She thinks we will all feel foolish for having made such a fuss. But

I can tell by the way Lucy's talking that she's starting to worry too. Why, we managed a whole conversation without even one pun or one of her atrocious jokes. Now that shows worry, if you ask me!"

"What do you think we should do?" Mary Helen asked.

"Lucy said she will try to get in touch with her the first thing in the morning. I am of the opinion that if we haven't heard anything by tomorrow evening at the latest, we should get together and do something about it."

"Maybe we should call somebody this evening," Mary Helen said, thinking immediately of her friend Kate Murphy. Although Kate was an inspector in Homicide, and so far this was, at most, a missing-person case, she knew Kate would know how to help them find their friend.

"We have called everyone we can think of. Unless you mean the police department." Caroline's voice rose a notch. She was frightened, Mary Helen could tell. No wonder Lucy was playing it down. No good would come of getting everyone upset. They'd all be better able to function intelligently if they kept calm.

"No, I didn't mean the police. I meant her relatives or other friends." Mary Helen fudged a little, hoping the end justified the means.

"Oh, yes, then we have called everyone we can think of." Caroline sounded a little calmer. "In my opinion," she said, "if the woman cannot be located by tomorrow, we should go to her apartment and have a look around. We may stumble across a letter or note or something that will tell us where she is, or at least that she is all right. Are you game to go along, Sister?"

Game? Mary Helen was absolutely dead set to get involved. She was extremely fond of good old Erma Duran, and she was still curious about that upset she had noticed while they were in New York. What was the problem she had overheard Erma and Lucy discussing? What would they "work out"? Could there be some connection between that and Erma's seeming disappearance?

Get involved? Of course she would! It was the only decent thing to do. Furthermore, it was more than a matter of decency. It was a matter of conscience.

May 8

Tuesday of the Fourth Week of Easter

On weekday mornings the college began serving breakfast at seven. Even though she had already been to the alumnae office, Mary Helen was one of the first in line. She felt in her jacket pocket for the slip of paper with Erma's address. She double-checked: The Mission District, 400 block of Sanchez.

Taking her toast and half a grapefruit into the dining room, Mary Helen searched the tables hoping to spot her friend Eileen. She found her sitting with Sister Cecilia near a set of windows overlooking one of the college's formal gardens. Outside, the morning was already beautiful. The spring sun was just beginning to touch the row of funnel-shaped petunias that bordered the lawn. A row of sweet alyssum ran behind them, their grayish leaves glistening with drops of early-morning fog. A bed of yellow and gold marigolds circled the marble statue of the Blessed Virgin. Above, the sky was a bright, cloudless blue. All in all, it was a perfect day for an attack of spring fever and a perfect opening for Mary Helen.

"I feel like playing hooky," she said, sliding into the chair across from Eileen. "It's much too nice a day to stay home. We should go somewhere."

"We just came back from somewhere." Eileen eyed Mary Helen's grapefruit.

Since she found it nearly impossible to eat grapefruit without squirting those around her, Mary Helen put it aside for later. She wanted nothing to distract Eileen's attention. Much to her surprise, it was Cecilia's attention she aroused.

"You're absolutely right, Mary Helen." The president smiled nervously. "It is much too nice a day to stay home. Where are you thinking of going?"

"Oh, just for a little ride. Sightseeing, maybe, as if we were tourists. Visit someplace we seldom go, like . . . say"—she paused for effect—"like Mission Dolores . . ." Mary Helen let the phrase ride on the air.

Eileen looked at her perplexed. "Mission Dolores? Why on earth? Besides, we have jobs, old dear. Remember?"

"What a grand idea!" It was Cecilia who seemed enthusiastic. "I'll bet it's beautiful out the Mission today." Her eyes glowed. "I was born and raised in the Mission," she said.

Mary Helen gulped. She might have known. The Mission District was home to many of San Francisco's notables. She could feel the college president warm to the bait.

"Would you like to go?" she asked, trying not to sound as if she had caught the wrong fish.

Cecilia shook her head. "No, thank you. I'd love to, but you know I can't. What would people think if I took a Tuesday morning off? Besides, I have several meetings today and . . ."

Mary Helen didn't hear the rest of the answer. She was trying too hard to suppress a sigh of relief.

"And neither can we!" Eileen rose from the table. "We have responsibilities, too, even if our age entitles us to be legitimately part-time."

"What is the point of being part-time unless we are gone

part of the time?" Mary Helen addressed her friend's fleeting back. "We owe it to them to go. It keeps them honest!"

It took her until nearly ten o'clock to convince Eileen that a ride to Mission Dolores was exactly what the two of them and the system needed.

Fortunately, the convent's green Nova was free and Mary Helen signed it out on the car calendar "till late."

"How late?" Eileen followed her toward the back door.

Mary Helen pretended not to hear. At her age, she could act a little hard of hearing. It worked for Therese, who was a full ten years younger.

As the pair passed the kitchenette just inside the back door, Mary Helen heard voices. It was Therese with a couple in tow.

"Hi, Sisters!" Patricia Boscacci turned quickly and moved across the room, giving them each a big hug.

Mary Helen liked Pat. She had graduated from Mount St. Francis almost twenty years before, but she still could easily have been mistaken for a coed. It was hard to believe that the petite, perky lady with curly honey-brown hair had four children, two of them teenagers.

Behind her stood her husband, Allan, quietly smiling. Allan towered over his wife. He was as calm and contained as she was vivacious and talkative. To Mary Helen they seemed a perfect pair, although she had to admit she sometimes felt a twinge of sympathy for Allan.

The man was the successful head of a large electrical firm somewhere in the city. Although he had a degree in electrical engineering, his wife always considered him an electrician. Pat loved the Sisters and was a very active alumna. Therefore, whenever there was an electrical problem at the college—from a balky socket to the whole heating system—she arrived with Allan.

"What's the problem today?" Mary Helen asked.

"It's the icebox," Therese said, pointing to the refrigerator.

Allan looked at her, wishing, no doubt, that it was an icebox so they could call the iceman and not him.

"The freezing compartment is out of whack," he said, running his fingers through his thick black hair. "But I think it's because the machine is a little off kilter." He pointed to the floor. The tip of a screwdriver stuck out about a fourth of an inch from the side of the box.

"It looks like the work of Luis, the handyman," Mary Helen said, thinking once again that Luis had proven not to be as handy as he might have been.

"I'll send a couple of men over as soon as I can to fix you up," Allan said.

"Where are you two off to?" Pat, who had lost interest in the refrigerator, noticed the car keys.

"We thought we might just sneak away for a little while," Mary Helen said softly, hoping Therese would be too absorbed in the freezing compartment to pay attention. "Today seems like a perfect day for an outing."

Therese rolled her dark eyes. "I would have thought—since some of us have been out and about so much—that a perfect day might be the day we could stay at home!"

* * *

Mary Helen drove quickly down Turk Street and cut over Divisadero to Castro. Even on a Tuesday, Castro Street, the heart of San Francisco's gay community, was crowded. Bumper-to-bumper, Mary Helen edged the Nova toward 18th Street. She knew it was a little out of the way, but it would give her a chance to pass Sanchez and see how close they were to the 400 block.

"Watch out," Eileen shouted. A truck with side panels announcing TINY TOTS DIAPERS—WE'RE CHANGING THE CITY pulled away from the curb. It was followed by two male jaywalkers, hand in hand, who cut in front of the car, giving the hood a friendly pat.

"Are you really sure you want to do this?" Eileen asked, once she had recovered her voice.

"Of course," Mary Helen answered with more confidence than she felt. "The Mission is beautiful." And indeed it was. The whole district was a charming mixture of old Victorian and Edwardian homes, with a few stuccos from the thirties looking as though they had been backed into the narrow lots in between.

Mary Helen found a parking space on 16th and Dolores, right next to the old Notre Dame Academy. Some years back, the massive convent and high school had been converted into a center for the arts.

"It's like a summer's day," Mary Helen said although she had to admit it was not like a summer's day in most of San Francisco. Summer in the City was notoriously foggy. Wasn't it Mark Twain who had said, "The coldest winter I ever spent was a summer in San Francisco"?

He must not have visited the Mission District, sheltered as it was from the ocean, in the lap of Twin Peaks. The weather there was always mild. Why, an island of palm trees ran down the middle of Dolores Street. It could have been Los Angeles!

The two nuns paused for a moment to look at the white-washed adobe Mission San Francisco de Asis, probably the oldest building in the City. Adjacent to it, and at least four times its size, was Mission Dolores Basilica.

In the alcove atop its towering facade, Junipero Serra stood, in full Franciscan habit, looking down. His stone hands were clasped behind his back. Mary Helen wondered crazily what the saintly friar must be thinking about up there, gazing down on all he had started.

Before the light turned green, a Grayline tour bus pulled up to the curb. Japanese tourists, complete with sun hats and cameras, filed off the bus.

"They must have emptied an entire village," Mary Helen murmured to Eileen.

"Do you still want to sightsee, old dear?"

"Why don't we have a little lunch first?" Mary Helen glanced in the general direction of her wristwatch, hoping Eileen was hungry and wouldn't notice that it wasn't yet eleven o'clock. "There are lots of quaint little places in this neighborhood."

Mary Helen drove up 16th a few blocks and turned left on Sanchez. Slowly she cruised the street.

"Where in the name of God are you going?" Eileen turned in the passenger's seat to look at her. "You have passed three delis, two coffee shops, a health-food restaurant, and Just Desserts is right behind us on Church Street."

Her eyes narrowed. "Mary Helen, if it is not too much to ask, what are you up to, exactly?"

"There's where Erma lives." Mary Helen pointed to a small two-story building on the corner. The first floor housed a storefront. Above it were living quarters. A string of carved rosettes ran between the curtained square bay windows. Probably in the twenties, the greengrocer or the butcher and his family had lived there, over their shop. Today, the shop had been converted to a trendy-looking restaurant with ALPHONSO'S BISTRO written in white script on its awning. The top story had probably been divided into apartments.

Eileen folded her arms and stared straight ahead. "I wondered what all this was about," she said. "I should have known. You just could not wait until Erma called."

For a moment Mary Helen was hurt. This wasn't a matter of impatience or even curiosity. This was a matter of genuine concern. While she took several tries at parallel parking, she told Eileen about Caroline's phone call. Eileen followed her across the street, muttering apologies that Mary Helen graciously accepted.

The mailboxes by the front door told them that the upper floor had been divided into two apartments—Erma's and one belonging to an A. Finn. Mary Helen pushed Erma's doorbell and waited. She pushed it again and held it a little longer. Still no answer.

"She's not at home," she said, managing to push A. Finn's bell before Eileen noticed. When A. Finn didn't answer either, Mary Helen walked toward the restaurant's side window.

Inside, everything was dark. Obviously the bistro had not yet opened for lunch. Putting her face to the window, Mary Helen cupped her hands around her eyes. There was a crack of light coming from under a door in the back. Someone was in there. With her car keys she tapped on the plate glass.

"What are you doing?" Eileen had caught up with her.

"There's someone in there," Mary Helen answered without taking her face away from the window. "Maybe he—or she—saw Erma today. Leaving her apartment, or something."

"From the back of the restaurant? With the door closed?"

Ignoring her friend, Mary Helen watched a door at the far corner of the darkened room swing open. A squat man crossed the room, wiping his hands on his spotted butcher's apron.

Frowning, he pointed to the red CLOSED sign still hanging on the glass door.

Mary Helen waved. For a moment the man squinted at her. She could almost see his mind working. Two old ladies in blue tailored suits, no makeup, no jewelry, small crosses on the left lapel.

"Oh, Sister!" He unlocked the glass front door. "Sorry," he said, opening it, "we don't start to serve until eleven-thirty." He glanced at his watch. "About twenty minutes. You want to come in and wait?"

"We're not here to eat, really," Mary Helen said, trying not to stare at the top of the man's head, although it was difficult not to. His pate was bald, yet one long piece of hair had been stretched back and forth in a series of V's across his crown. The top of his head looked for all the world like someone had threaded half a black shoelace, then plastered it all down with brilliantine.

Eileen nudged her. "We were wondering if you had seen Erma Duran this morning. The woman in the apartment above." She pointed.

"Yeah, I know Erma, all right." The man opened the door wide so the nuns could step inside. "She's lived there for years. Since way before Tommy died. In fact, I'm the landlord. Own the whole building. Come on in."

The Sisters stepped farther into the darkened bistro. The delicious smell of sautéing onions was beginning to permeate the whole room. Mary Helen's mouth watered. Inside, small tables covered with white cloths were arranged close together. Napkins, like stiff little bishop's miters, stood at each place. A milk-glass bud vase holding a real carnation and a frond of maidenhair was in the center of each table.

The walls were covered with deep red flocked wallpaper; the burgundy carpet was thick and plush. The whole place looked exactly as Mary Helen imagined a high-class bordello might look. Here and there an imitation hurricane lamp stuck out from the wall. Two or three large ferns in brass planters completed the decor.

"Then you've seen Erma today?" Eileen asked hopefully.

"No, she hasn't been around for the last couple of days. She took off last Saturday, right after she got back from the Big Apple. Leaves me awful shorthanded. Thank God we're closed on Mondays." He wiped his hands on his apron again.

"Erma works for me too," he added, in case the nuns hadn't gathered as much. "She's my hostess. Been doing that since before Tommy died.

"Somebody's been trying to get her all morning too. I can hear her phone ringing, but she's gone. To visit relatives," the man offered before Mary Helen had a chance to ask.

Just as Caroline had said, she thought. And that caller is no doubt Lucy. Poor thing must really be concerned.

"When do you expect her back?" Mary Helen asked.

The man shook his head. Not a hair on it moved. "Don't

know, Sister," he said sadly, "and I really miss her around the place." He brightened. "She said she'd call and let me know."

"Well, thank you. I hope we haven't bothered you, Mr. . . . Mr. . . ." Mary Helen realized belatedly that they hadn't even bothered to introduce themselves.

"Finn. Al Finn." He stuck out his broad hand. "I'm Alphonso, the one on the awning."

"Al for Alphonso." Eileen cocked her head and ended her sentence somewhere between a question and a statement. It was an old Irish trick that had helped her out of many a tight situation.

The man didn't know whether to answer or explain. He chose to explain. "My name is really Alphonsus. My folks were from the old school. You know, name a kid for the saint whose day he was born on. My birthday's the first of August."

"St. Alphonsus Liguori." Eileen beamed. "You were lucky, really. You could have been born on September twenty-ninth."

Finn looked puzzled.

"Feast of St. Michael. How would you like to have gone through life being called Mickey Finn?"

* * *

"How long would you wager the piece of hair across the top of his head is?" Eileen watched Mary Helen unlock the car.

"About a foot." She was abstracted. Al Finn was Erma's boss and landlord. If the name on the mailbox was correct, he was her next-door neighbor too.

Obviously he was also her friend. Otherwise, why would she tell him she was going away and not tell Lucy or her own daughter? Yet she couldn't remember Erma ever mentioning him. Odd!

"Now, see?" Eileen fastened her seat belt. "You worried for nothing. And now I'm really hungry."

"I wonder when she'll call," Mary Helen said.

"Most likely today. Or tonight, when the rates are lower."

Eileen pointed to a deli. "By tomorrow, this whole thing will be cleared up."

Mary Helen nodded her head. Eileen was probably correct. She thought she would give Kate Murphy a call this evening, however, just in case.

* * *

Kate Murphy was in the upstairs bathroom splashing water on her face when she heard the phone ring. Her husband, Jack, answered it on the sixth ring. He must have been waiting for me to pick it up, she thought, checking her eyes in the medicine-cabinet mirror. They didn't look too red, she decided.

"Hon, it's for you," he called up the narrow staircase.

"Thanks." She hoped her voice sounded strong and cheerful. She didn't want him to know she'd been crying.

Wrapping Jack's old flannel robe tightly around her, she padded toward the extension in their bedroom.

The moment Kate heard Mary Helen's voice, she felt teary again. What was wrong with her?

She hardly heard what the old nun was saying. Something about an OWL friend of hers who was missing. At least this time the person was missing, not dead. Kate felt relieved, although she wondered what in the world an OWL was. She didn't have to wonder long.

"Older Women's League," Mary Helen explained. "We are advocates for women's rights."

And a formidable group, I imagine, Kate thought, remembering her previous dealings with the old nun in the Holy Hill murder cases.

"Don't worry, Sister. It's probably nothing," she said, trying hard to put Mary Helen's mind at ease. "All kinds of people disappear for a day or two, then show up unharmed."

There was an awkward silence on the other end of the line. Mary Helen must have suspected Kate of trying to pacify her.

"Why, there was . . ." Oh, help! Kate desperately searched for a good example.

"Agatha Christie?" Good old Mary Helen came to the rescue herself.

"You're absolutely on target, Sister. Agatha Christie," Kate repeated. "And she lived to a ripe old age, didn't she?

"On the other hand, if your OWL friend isn't heard from in a day or two, you call back," she added just before she hung up, "and we'll look into it."

"Is everything all right?" Jack's voice startled her.

"Sister Mary Helen has an OWL friend whom no one has heard from or seen in a couple of days. She's beginning to get concerned," Kate answered without turning around. Her eyes might still be red. "Older Women's League." She anticipated Jack's question.

"You're Homicide; I'm Vice. That sounds like something for Missing Persons. Whew! That lets us both off the hook." She could feel his hands on her shoulders. "Is something wrong, hon?"

"No. Why?" Kate forced a little laugh.

"Your voice sounds funny and you don't seem to want to look at me."

She shrugged her shoulders, not trusting herself to speak.

"And I always figured that you thought I was handsome." She could feel his warm breath in her hair and his strong arms slipping around her waist, pulling her close to him. "It's my three gray hairs, isn't it?" he teased. "Ever since you discovered the first gray hair in my raven locks—"

"Not funny," Kate said.

"If I didn't know better, I'd say you were crying."

"Now what in the world do I have to cry about?" She turned, buried her head in her husband's shoulder, and sobbed.

Poor Jack. She knew he must be bewildered. Yet he stood there holding her, saying nothing, just waiting.

"Actually, it's just your mother," she finally managed. "I called her from work to ask what I could bring for dinner tonight and she said, 'Nothing.' " Kate blew her nose.

Jack stared down at her, frowning. The look on his face was patient but puzzled. "I'll bet poor Ma thought that would make you happy."

"Oh, that's not why I'm unhappy." Kate pushed herself away. "How can men be so thick?"

Jack ran his fingers through his wavy hair. "Did I miss something?"

"I'm not pregnant again this month." Kate plopped down on the corner of their old-fashioned brass bed. The springs creaked and jingled under her weight.

"Can't say we didn't try." Smiling, Jack sat down beside her.

"Both your sisters will be at dinner tonight. And I know your mother is dying to be able to tell them that at least one of her children is giving her a grandchild."

"Did she say that?"

Kate shook her head. "No, but I can just tell."

"I thought we'd already settled that. It's not whether Ma wants a grandchild that's important. It's what you and I want, Kate. Remember?"

"Of course I remember. But you and I do want one. And it's just not happening, Jack. As hard as we try, I just cannot seem to get pregnant."

Jack shook his head in disbelief. "Kate"—he gently kneaded her spine as he spoke—"trying isn't all it takes. Remember those illustrations in your biology book. Those little wiggly-looking things. Or didn't they have that chapter at the girls' school?"

"Don't try to be funny, Jack. This is not funny."

"For chrissake, Kate, we've only been trying since around Christmas: That's not even five months; and February, you remember, is a short one. Relax! Let's give it a chance.

"As a matter of fact, if it would put your mind at ease"—Jack moved closer—"we could give it another try right now, before we go to my mother's."

"You don't suppose God is punishing us?" she asked, pretending not to feel his hand under her loose robe.

"Punishing us for what?"

"For living together all those years before we got married."

"I don't believe you!" Putting his hands on her bare shoulders, Jack turned her toward him.

"Let me take another look. Is this the same wild-eyed feminist I lived with all those years? The one who never wanted to 'ruin our relationship' with marriage? The one I nearly had to club and drag to the altar to give her some respectability?"

Bouncing his eyebrows like Groucho Marx, he ogled her, flicking an imaginary cigar. "Ah ha!" he said. "It looks like the same one."

"You've made your point." Kate closed the front of the flannel robe and hugged it tightly. She pulled her knees up under her chin. "Maybe He's punishing me," she said.

"Punishing you for what? Although I must admit you would try the patience of the ordinary run-of-the-mill saint."

"For not wanting to have a baby at first. Now when I want one, I can't have one."

"Jeez, Kate!" Jack stood up, stuck one hand in his pocket, and held the back of his head with the other one. He walked to the window and stared out at a sea of backyards.

Kate knew from experience that was Jack's ultimate frustration pose. She waited, not daring to say anything until he got hold of himself.

For several moments he just stood there. Finally he turned, came back to the edge of the bed, and sat down. "If that isn't the damnedest, guilt-ridden, Irish-Catholic thing I've ever heard you say." He put his hands back on her shoulders. "And I was worrying about your biology book! I should have been worrying about your theology book. What the hell kind of a God do you believe in?"

"I know you're right." Kate snuggled close to her husband. "But sometimes I just can't help thinking—"

He put his finger over her lips. She could feel his arm squeezing her tight. "Do me a favor, hon"—he rocked her back and forth—"don't think. If it is really worrying you, why not make an appointment with a gynecologist? He . . . or she"—he corrected himself quickly—"can figure out if there is anything physically wrong. That will take care of the biology part, and as for the theology part, ask your friend Mary Helen," he whispered, his mouth close to her ear. "Now, there's a gal who'll really set you straight. I'll bet my badge she could make a Jesuit theologian pale."

*   *   *

The drive from Kate and Jack's house in the Outer Richmond District to Mama Bassetti's in the Sunset District was quiet. Kate enjoyed the silence. It gave her time to compose herself before she got to her mother-in-law's house. She suspected Jack's two younger sisters would be there already. Mama had found a real bargain on roast beef at Petrini's Market, she said, and decided to invite the kids over to enjoy it. At least that was her excuse. Kate marveled at the woman's creativity in thinking up reasons to lure her family to dinner.

Kate was feeling calmer when they entered Golden Gate Park at 43rd and Fulton on the Avenue of Lakes. The area was deserted, except for a few walkers who had braved the early-evening fog creeping up the Avenues from the ocean and two older women who sat bundled up on one of the green wooden benches bordering the lake, gossiping. The pair seemed oblivious of a mallard at their feet, quacking noisily at the brown-paper sack one woman held in her hand.

Jack rolled up the window as they passed downwind behind the Buffalo Paddock. "Even if you can't see them you can smell them," he said, patting Kate's knee.

He stopped the car at the arterial on John F. Kennedy Drive, letting a jogger and a cyclist with an empty baby seat on the back of his bike cross before he took his turn. Looking at the empty seat, Kate could feel a new lump starting in her throat.

"What was it you were telling me about Mary Helen, hon?" Jack asked suddenly.

"What brought that up?" She could hardly speak.

Jack pointed to several elderly women in tennis shoes walking quickly down the path. "Association, I guess."

Twisting a thick lock of her red hair around her index finger, Kate pushed it into a tight curl. "I guess I should have shown a little more concern," she said. "We know from experience that the old girl is no wolf-crier."

"You said a buddy of hers hasn't been heard from for a couple of days?"

"Yes, a woman she goes to OWL meetings with. Another graduate of Mount St. Francis. Way back when."

"And you old alums stick together, right?"

Kate nodded. They drove past a mound bright with blue forget-me-nots. Rhododendrons bordered the lawn. Even though they were past their prime, a few clusters of hot-pink blossoms still clung to the leathery green shrubs.

On their right, set back from the road, a battered sign read BERCUT EQUITATION FIELD. Idly, Kate wondered, as she always did when they passed the spot, if she'd ever seen a horse there. So far, negative.

Suddenly, Jack's last remark registered. "Who's an old alum?" She whacked his leg.

Her husband laughed. "You don't think she suspects foul play, do you?" They turned left on Lincoln Way.

"She always suspects foul play, Jack. And the worst part is, she's usually right on target."

Jack's guffaw startled her. "I know what let's do." He drummed his fingers on the steering wheel. "Let's turn her and

Sister Eileen over to my old pal, Ron Honore, in Missing Persons."

. He turned toward her with an uncharacteristic glint in his eye. Honore was one of the few people she knew who could get under her husband's skin. Jack said it was because of his cockiness. Kate suspected it had more to do with Honore's reputation as a lady-killer.

"And the man is downright ugly," Jack always said.

"Well, the guys don't call him Don Juan Ron for nothing," Kate always answered.

"I've been dying to get the better of that guy since we left the Academy." Jack stopped at the arterial. "If those two gals can't rattle his cage, then nobody can."

May 9

Wednesday of the Fourth Week of Easter

Wednesday morning was just plain gloomy. Mary Helen pulled the collar of her Aran sweater up around her ears, stuck her hands deep into its narrow pockets, and slammed the convent door behind her.

"Overcast, with a slight chance of rain," the radio announcer had said on the early-morning news, but *gloomy* would have been a much more accurate description.

Head down, she started up the hill toward the college. Yesterday had been so beautiful, but this morning the asphalt driveway was shiny and slick. It must have sprinkled during the night.

At the top of the hill, she stopped to catch her breath. Students, late for the first class of the morning, hurried across the nearly deserted campus.

Dark, heavy clouds made the sky seem lower, and in the gloom the lilies of the Nile bordering the circular drive were almost purple.

"Sister Mary Helen, telephone!" The campus loudspeaker startled her. "Sister Mary Helen, telephone!" a nasal voice repeated, crackling the message out over the hill. What the switchboard operator lacked in enunciation, she more than made up for in volume.

Mary Helen checked her watch. It's just after eight o'clock, she thought, hurrying toward the main office. Who in the world would be calling at this hour? She felt a little apprehensive. Early-morning and late-night phone calls always did that to her. It couldn't be Caroline Coughlin already, or could it?

* * *

At eight-twenty sharp, Caroline's root beer–colored Cadillac glided up in front of the convent. Mary Helen barely had time to change her sweater and leave a note for Eileen telling her where she would be.

"Hop in the front with us, Sister." Lucy Lyons shoved the heavy door open and, scooting over toward Caroline, patted the broad white leather seat beside her.

"I couldn't wait another minute," Caroline said as soon as Mary Helen pulled the car door shut.

"To tell you the truth, I couldn't even wait this long," Mary Helen confessed, wondering how Caroline was going to take to being upstaged. "Sister Eileen and I dropped by her apartment building yesterday."

"And did you two find out anything?" Caroline's tone seemed a bit icy, but Lucy studied her with anxious eyes.

Mary Helen pretended not to notice the tone and squeezed Lucy's hand. "Unfortunately, not a thing more than you told me on the phone Monday evening."

Without a word, Caroline drove down the hill and onto Turk Street. "Since none of us heard from Erma yesterday and since no one yet knows her exact whereabouts," she said finally, "I suggest we make every effort to locate her. It is just not like her to leave without saying a word."

The root-beer Cadillac stopped for a light. "Perhaps we can best establish the whereabouts of our mutual friend if we all stick together." Caroline leaned forward and gave Mary Helen her dowager-queen smile.

"That Mr. Finn did say she went to visit relatives." Ignoring the jab, Mary Helen tried to be calm and reasonable. Bickering among themselves wouldn't benefit anyone, especially not Erma Duran.

"And didn't he tell Noelle that he thought they were in St. Louis? Although—I have to agree with you—it is just not like her not to have called someone, if only so we wouldn't worry."

Seemingly appeased, Caroline turned on Divisadero Street and made her way into the heart of the crowded Western Addition.

"Immediately after I called you, I picked Lucy up," she said, as if Lucy weren't present. "She said she never heard Erma speak of any St. Louis relatives."

Mary Helen glanced at the woman sitting between them. Poor Lucy looked exactly as though she had been picked up— *snatched* might be more like it—from right in the middle of whatever she had been doing at eight o'clock in the morning. Her faded violet jogging suit was damp at the knees, and there was mud on the toes of her worn Nikes. Her makeup looked slapdash and her gray braid was badly in need of replaiting. The dark circles under her eyes showed she had spent a sleepless night.

"If anything should happen to Erma because we didn't act, I for one would never forgive myself." Caroline took her eyes off the traffic-clogged street long enough to peer around Lucy. "Isn't that the way you feel, girls?"

"Of course," Mary Helen answered. She wished Caroline would keep her eyes on the road and stop tailgating.

"Please stop saying 'if anything should happen to Erma,' " Lucy snapped with uncharacteristic harshness. "I'm sorry, Caroline," she apologized quickly, "but I really don't even want to begin thinking that way."

They drove for several blocks in an awkward silence. Mary

Helen stared out the window. All their nerves must be on edge. She tried to concentrate on the mixture of stately homes and flats above small storefronts that lined the busy street and think of something to say. She wondered for a moment if she would ever get used to seeing a Victorian, complete with towers, turrets, and Turkish cupolas, atop a Chinese take-out restaurant.

Caroline sailed up the hill, skirting Buena Vista Park. They passed Ralph K. Davies Hospital and picked up Castro Street. Mary Helen couldn't believe that they had crossed the City so quickly.

"So, Lucy, were you jogging already this morning?" she asked, more to break the tension than for any other reason.

"I probably should have been," Lucy responded quickly. Apparently she, too, wanted to smooth things over. "You know what they say: 'Use it or lose it!' What I was actually doing was a little remedial weeding."

Mary Helen was still groaning when they stopped across the street from Alphonso's Bistro at the bottom of the steep Sanchez Street hill. Carefully, Caroline eased the large car into a perpendicular parking space.

What a sight the three of us must make! Mary Helen thought, struggling against gravity to push open the heavy door. Lucy in her jogging outfit, me in my navy-blue nun's suit, and Caroline, crisp in jade linen, complete with gloves and a turbanlike hat that looks as if she had borrowed it from Queen Elizabeth.

Caroline led the trio across the street. If she hadn't known better, Mary Helen would have thought Caroline was on her way to an exclusive garden party in Hillsborough rather than to Erma's apartment over the bistro on 18th and Sanchez. She literally leaned on Al Finn's doorbell.

Considering what the sound must have done to his nerves, Mary Helen thought the man was surprisingly courteous when he cracked open the door. Courteous, but not quite awake.

"I'm dreadfully sorry to have disturbed you, Mr. Finn," Caroline began, ignoring the fact that he was standing bleary-eyed and barefoot in his undershirt and boxer shorts.

Feeling a little like one of the villagers in "The Emperor's New Clothes," Mary Helen looked directly at the man's sleep-creased face. She wondered for a moment where Lucy was looking.

"But we are terribly worried about our friend Erma," Caroline continued, with a flourish of her gloved hand. "May we trouble you for the key to her apartment?"

Finn grunted, shut the door, and left them standing on the stoop. Mary Helen wasn't sure whether he didn't recognize her or was just too sleepy to acknowledge that they had met.

"Did you notice that gentleman's hair?" Caroline whispered.

Lucy couldn't resist. "Did you say *hair* or *bare*?"

Finn reappeared, looking, in Mary Helen's opinion, a lot like an unmade bed. Uneven suspenders held his crumpled pants up over a crumpled shirt. His toe protruded from a gaping hole in one of the socks he had managed to slip over his bare feet.

Without a word, he opened Erma's door and led them up the narrow carpeted staircase. The top step opened into a high-ceilinged, sparsely furnished living room. The wooden banister and stairs formed one wall. French doors on the opposite wall separated it from the combination dining room–kitchen.

Stifling a yawn, Finn shoved his hands into his pockets and leaned against the banister. He shifted uneasily. "I don't know about letting you ladies in here." Apparently, the more awake he became, the more aware he was of what he was doing.

"Nonsense!" Caroline said, leading the other two women down the narrow hallway toward the back room where the apartment abruptly ended. The floor plan looked as if someone had taken a spacious Victorian flat and cut it in half. And Erma had gotten the worse half.

Mary Helen could hear Finn's bare feet padding down the hall behind them. "I ain't so sure this is right," he muttered.

The bedroom door was closed. Caroline grasped the old-fashioned brass knob. Closing her eyes, Mary Helen tried to quell the feeling of dread that shot through her like a sharp pain. She knew it was foolish. Erma's daughter had already been in the apartment. Logically she knew the feeling came from her experience of finding Suzanne.

Despite logic, Erma's face flashed before her—those trusting brown eyes, that ready smile. She held her breath as Caroline turned the handle. Behind that door would they find that familiar round face permanently frozen in terror?

The bedroom door swung back easily. Reluctantly Mary Helen opened her eyes. Empty and undisturbed! She relaxed her shoulders, but it took several moments before her heart slowed down.

Years ago, she remembered, a retreat master had said that a person's bedroom told a great deal about that person. In Erma's case, the remark really rang true.

The room was bright and cheerful. The bedspread, the draperies, a slipper chair were all in flowered print. The sturdy mahogany bed, the matching chest of drawers and nightstand were sturdy and well cared for. Erma had undoubtedly brought them from her parents' home and lovingly polished them for years.

Next to a door, which probably led to the bathroom, stood an old-fashioned dresser with a silver comb-and-brush set carefully arranged on its crocheted runner. Family photographs covered most of the dresser top. Recent snapshots of smiling family and friends were stuck everywhere in the carved mirror frame. Three children's handprints in plaster hung on the wall beside the mirror.

From a corner shelf the shadowless icon of Our Lady of

Perpetual Help shed its radiance on those around. The Madonna smiled sadly and her compassionate eyes embraced the room. A baroque vigil light had been placed before the gilded painting. The votive candle inside was nearly burned out.

Looking around, Mary Helen could feel a lump form in her throat. Please, Lord, she prayed, don't let anything have happened to good old Erma Duran.

"Look in here." Caroline swung the closet door open. Mary Helen felt a little guilty about looking, as though she were invading Erma's privacy.

"Just look," Caroline repeated. A few dresses, a coat, two suits, a couple of blouses, and a worn wool jacket hung in the immaculate closet. Several shoe boxes and a couple of purses occupied the top shelf. Two cardboard boxes were stacked on the bare floor next to a suitcase.

Erma's suitcase . . . That's strange, Mary Helen thought, turning toward Mr. Finn.

Before she had a chance to say anything, Caroline bent over and picked up the paper tag still attached to the handle. "Look at this! She didn't even remove the luggage tag. And none of her clothing seems to be missing. Although, Lucy, you'd know that better than I."

Lucy! Mary Helen realized with a start that the woman had not uttered one word since they'd entered the room. Caroline and Mary Helen turned toward her.

Lucy's small, peaked face was white. Behind her horn-rimmed glasses, her eyes brimmed with tears. "Oh, God," she said, "I was hoping—"

"Hey, ladies!" By now, Finn was fully awake and frowning. "I ain't so sure about you coming in here. People got rights, you know." He stopped, nervously pulled at his loose suspenders. "What if Erma don't want people knowing her business?"

Mary Helen tried to look hurt. "We are not trying to pry into anyone's business, Mr. Finn. We are just concerned about why she went away without notifying anyone."

Finn began to blink nervously. With every blink, the yellow specks in his hazel eyes seemed to jump back and forth. "I probably shouldn't have told you that much—"

"But the suitcase," Caroline interrupted. "It seems inconceivable to me that one would—or could—travel without luggage."

"I wish she'd left a forwarding address or a phone number," Mary Helen said. "Then we could call Erma, find out what was wrong, and settle this matter—whatever it is—once and for all."

"I told you yesterday—she said she'd call." Finn looked at Mary Helen uncomfortably. So he had recognized her!

"I shouldn't have said that much. And I never should have mentioned St. Louis to that other one who called. She don't want her kids to know."

"Know what?" Mary Helen asked, hoping it didn't sound like prying.

"Where she went, Sister. She was trying to get away from them as fast as she could. They were bugging her. She said she'd call when she got settled." Finn swallowed. "To tell you the truth," he said, "I guess the reason I let the cat out of the bag is because I'm getting kinda worried myself."

Lucy wiped her eyes with the back of her hand. "It's worse than I thought." She tried to keep her voice from quivering. "Erma was very upset in New York," she said. "I don't know whether or not you noticed."

Mary Helen nodded. She didn't want Lucy to realize just how much she had noticed.

"Someone had been taking money from her apartment. She was afraid that whoever it was might even have taken her social-security check from her mailbox." Lucy sniffled, feeling her jogging pants for a pocket but found none. "The check was over a week late. She had asked her daughter to pick up the mail for her, bank the check, and give her a ring in New York.

But the check never arrived. Or at least, Ree—that's her daughter—never called."

No wonder Erma had been so upset. Mary Helen dug in her pocket for a Kleenex and handed it to Lucy. "Did she suspect it was one of her children?"

Lucy shook her head. "She just couldn't imagine that one of them would do such a thing." Mary Helen looked over at the three tiny handprints on the wall. It did seem unnatural that any one of those sweet, tiny hands would grow up to steal from his or her own mother. "In fact, she couldn't imagine who would. Do such a thing, I mean.

"I told her I'd help her out. It was only money. But it really upset her. You know Erma. She's a stickler for paying her bills on time. I couldn't convince her that the PG and E wouldn't shut off her gas." Lucy dabbed at her eyes. "I had this funny feeling that something else was bothering her too. I asked, but you know Erma. Never complains, never really lets you in. I just had the feeling that something more than money was wrong. It was almost as if she was afraid of something or somebody." Lucy raised the Kleenex to her eyes and wept.

Putting her arm around the other woman, Caroline patted her shoulder with a gloved hand. "Do you suppose we should call her children? One of them might have an idea where we can begin to look."

"I know Ree's number." Lucy hiccuped. "She's already worried. She may be the best place to start." Wiping her eyes, she wrote the number on a pad of paper Caroline had extracted from her purse.

"And I think I'll give Noelle a buzz first," Caroline said, picking up the pad. "I want to bring her up-to-date."

Finn closed the closet door as if to preserve Erma's privacy. In the background they could hear Caroline dial the phone. From her crisp, businesslike tone and the long pauses, Mary Helen guessed she was talking to Noelle and that the two of them were "organizing, not agonizing."

Caroline reappeared at the bedroom door. "Noelle suggests we set up a meeting with Erma's daughter as soon as possible. Is that all right?"

Lucy and Mary Helen nodded. Only Finn shook his head. "I don't know what you'll be able to get out of Ree. Or out of those two knuckle-headed brothers of hers, either. Nope"—he agreed with himself—"I don't know what you'll be able to get out of any of them. Sure as hell not an honest day's work."

"We'll see, Mr. Finn. We'll see." Mary Helen smiled at the man. "At least it's worth a try." What she really wanted to add was, Never, never, Mr. Finn, not on your longest day, underestimate the "get-out-of-them" power of this group of OWLs! But she thought better of it. Mr. Finn, she was confident, would find that out soon enough.

May 10

Thursday of the Fourth Week of Easter

Right after breakfast on Thursday morning, Sister Mary Helen nabbed Eileen. "We've got to talk," she said.

Sister Eileen turned and perked up, ready to listen.

"Not here." Mary Helen glanced down the long tiled hallway linking the Sisters' dining room with the kitchen and the students' cafeteria. In the background she heard water running and the clang of metal pots. "Someplace private, where we won't be overheard."

"Glory be to God, Mary Helen." Eileen's bushy eyebrows shot up. "What have you been reading? We are on the ground floor of the college building. At this hour, there is no one around but kitchen help."

Despite her objections, Mary Helen motioned Eileen into a storage room across from the kitchen and closed the door. Quickly she brought her friend up-to-date on Erma, her hasty departure, and the fact that the OWLs were going to set up a meeting with the woman's daughter.

Eileen's wrinkled face puckered with empathy. Perfect!

Mary Helen thought as she put a little extra drama into the fact that the New York baggage tag was still attached to the woman's suitcase. If the truth were known, her luggage was still tagged too.

"What do you think we should do?" Eileen frowned.

Mary Helen paused, adjusting her bifocals slowly as though she hadn't really thought about it. "Well, if you're not afraid to get involved again . . ."

Eileen pulled herself up to her full five feet, two inches. "An Irish coward is an uncommon character!" she said.

"Is that an old saying from back home?" Mary Helen was suspicious.

"No, Emperor Francis Joseph I of Austria," her friend admitted, rather reluctantly, Mary Helen thought.

Before the two nuns parted, they agreed to attend the meeting with Erma's daughter whenever and wherever the OWLs could arrange it.

The moment she got back to the convent, Mary Helen called the alumnae office. "I'll be in a little later this morning," she told Lynda, her new secretary.

"I hope you aren't ill, Sister."

"No, not at all." Mary Helen was touched by the young woman's concern. "I have an important meeting, that's all. But I am expecting a call," she added, "from one of the OWLs, probably Mrs. Coughlin. Please just take the message." Carefully, she wanted to add, but didn't. She knew Lynda was always careful.

The old nun put on her wool coat and pulled a knitted scarf from her bottom drawer. It seemed silly to dress so warmly during the second week of May, but the moment she stepped outside she was glad she had.

A strong gust of wind blew her coat open and twisted the ends of her scarf. Quickly, she began to walk down the hill toward the college entrance.

I wonder what Lynda would think if she knew whom I was

meeting, Mary Helen mused, turning her face to avoid the small specks of dust that whirled up from the road.

Head down, she turned left on Parker Avenue. All along the street the west wind howled and bent the young, spindly eucalyptus trees planted near the curb. Even the older, sturdier evergreens bordering the University of San Francisco's ball field swayed with its force.

Fortunately, the wind was also pushing the heavy clouds aside. Vivid patches of blue began to peek among the gray.

Mary Helen squinted. Up ahead on the corner, directly across the street from the massive St. Ignatius Church, was her destination, the adobe-pink Carmelite monastery.

Eyes watering, Sister Mary Helen ducked into the side entrance of the imposing building. Pulling against the wind's force, she opened the chapel door and stepped quickly into the silence. The heavy wooden door closed, leaving her in semi-darkness.

Genuflecting, she slipped into a back pew and closed her eyes. The delicate aroma of incense hung on the air. From somewhere behind the grille to the right of the main altar, she heard the soft, nearly imperceptible, chanting of the cloistered nuns at Divine Office. The peace and otherworldliness of the place was almost palpable.

This was where she was having her meeting—the one she'd mentioned to Lynda. Her meeting was with God. It was one of her secrets. One she had never told anybody, not even Eileen. But for some time now, whenever Mary Helen wanted a serious meeting with God, she'd been coming here. She knew from years of experience that God heard and listened to her anytime and anywhere, but, of late, the Carmelite monastery had become like sacred ground.

The reason might seem foolish to some people, but it made perfect sense to Mary Helen. It had all happened at breakfast one morning. Father Adams, the Jesuit from St. Ignatius who frequently said the early-morning Mass for the Sisters, had stayed for coffee. Someone had asked him if he knew how the poor cloistered Carmelites across the street from the church had managed to build a monastery that was two stories high and nearly half a city block long.

Laughing, Father Adams related the story. An old, shabbily dressed woman who attended St. Ignatius regularly had stopped one of the Jesuit fathers after Mass. She had a little money, she told him, and when she died she wanted to leave it to charity. To whom did he think she should will it?

The priest thought for a moment. He also said Mass for the nuns across the street. He knew the group had come from Spain and were dirt-poor. Their monastery was a shambles. He had heard them praying each day that God would send them a benefactor. The priest figured the woman couldn't have much, but he knew the nuns would be grateful for whatever she left them, no matter how small the amount.

"Why don't you leave it to the Carmelites?" He pointed to the rundown monastery on the corner.

"Will they pray for me when I die?" she asked.

"Praying's their business," the priest answered with a wink.

When the old woman died, she left the Carmelite nuns more than a million dollars.

Since the morning she'd heard that story, whenever she needed serious help Mary Helen had walked down from the college, slipped into the back pew, and offered her intentions with theirs. Praying, after all, was their business, and from the appearance of the monastery, God was into answering them.

Before she left the darkened chapel, Mary Helen looked for the icon of Our Lady of Perpetual Help. Unable to find one, she lit a votive candle before an ornate statue of the Blessed Virgin. Any port in a storm, she thought, letting herself out onto the windswept street.

* * *

As Mary Helen neared the back door of the convent, a red Ferrari rounded the corner and came to a quick stop beside her. She recognized Allan Boscacci.

Rolling down the window, he waved. "Hi, Sister." A shy smile lit up his handsome face. "It's all fixed."

All fixed? Mary Helen thought for a minute. What? Of course, the broken refrigerator. "What was it?" she asked.

"The screwdriver. Iceboxes work better," he said with a wink, "when they are set flat on the ground."

"Thanks, Allan." Mary Helen waved as the sports car rounded the bend. Iceboxes and humans, she thought.

The convent's back door slammed. Amused, Mary Helen watched an irate Sister Therese, waving both hands and a screwdriver, talking nonstop to Luis. Hands in pockets, the handyman simply shrugged and shook his head.

If the poor devil had been smart, Mary Helen thought, deciding to skirt the scene and go directly to her office, he would never have let on that he understood English.

"Here's your message, Sister." Lynda rose and handed her a slip of blue paper. "But it's not from Mrs. Coughlin."

Opening the note, Mary Helen read, "Noelle Thompson called. Meeting at Erma's apartment with her daughter. Ten-thirty tomorrow morning. Expecting you and Sister Eileen."

Not an extra word—so like Noelle. Mary Helen grinned. Clear, efficient, organized. Coincidentally, in keeping with the woman's penchant for blue, Lynda had written the message on blue paper. Noelle had definitely taken charge and, with her running the inquiry, if there was any information to be had, she would certainly unearth it.

Folding the note, she shoved it into the pocket of her coat, went to her inner office, and called Homicide. It was time to bring Kate Murphy up-to-date.

* * *

Inspector Dennis Gallagher answered the phone on the first ring. Kate noticed her partner's face start to turn red, forehead

Pope? Why can't he keep the nuns in the convents where they belong?"

Kate ignored him. "A woman friend of hers hasn't been heard from since the group returned from their convention in New York."

"How long ago?" Gallagher leaned forward.

"A week tomorrow."

"Did they ask relatives, friends, the usual?"

"They're still checking things out. But you know, Denny, I'm beginning to worry."

"Missing Persons is not our department. We got enough homicidal maniacs running around the City to worry about without getting into somebody else's detail." He riffled through the stack of papers on his desk. "See this?" He did it again, and a little cloud of cigar ash from the filled-to-capacity ashtray on his desk scattered across Kate's blotter.

Gallagher blew it onto the floor. "Tell the Sister to call the nearest station. If the guy who gets the call figures something's fishy, he'll contact Missing Persons."

"How can you be so callous, Denny, after all that woman has done for us? Now, really, where would we have been if she hadn't helped us out in both the homicide cases on Holy Hill?"

Gallagher raised his hand. "Don't get me wrong. I appreciate what she did. She was a big help. My point is, this time why can't you let her help out a couple of other guys?"

Kate went to the coffee maker and brought back two steaming mugs of black coffee. "Jack has a plan." She set one cup in front of her partner, watching him blow on it, and hoped the coffee wouldn't end up in the same place the cigar ashes had.

Gallagher looked over the rim, sipping noisily. "What's the plan?"

"He wants me to turn her over to Honore. You know Ron Honore, in Missing Persons?"

"Know him! Sure I know him. What is it they call him?"

"It depends on who the *they* is," Kate answered, knowing

first, then his cheeks, finally, his neck. He loosened his already loose tie.

"What is it?" she mouthed. Poor Gallagher looked almost as though he were in pain. Forestalling her with a raised index finger, he listened intently.

"Yes, 'Ster," he said finally. "Yes, 'Ster. Right here. Hold on."

Pushing the Hold button on the phone, he held out the receiver to Kate. "Jeez, Katie-girl!" He ran his hand across his bald pate. "It's that nun again. Something about a missing owl. I can't make head or tail out of the damn thing. But I warn you, steer clear."

Laughing, Kate removed her right earring and took the phone. "Hi, Sister," she began cheerfully. "So, no word from your friend yet?"

Quickly, Mary Helen brought her up-to-date.

"When are you meeting the daughter?" Kate frowned slightly.

"Tomorrow at ten-thirty."

"Well, that will probably solve the whole thing." Kate tried to sound optimistic. "She'll give you a relative's name; you'll contact your friend; and everyone will sleep easier."

"I hope you're right." Mary Helen didn't sound as convinced as Kate had hoped she would.

"You keep me posted, Sister," Kate said. "And promise me you won't try to do anything on your own."

"What the hell was that all about?" Gallagher asked the moment she hung up. He watched her put her earring back on. "And why don't you get one of them holes in your ears like my kids did?"

"Ugh!" Kate pushed her swivel chair back from her desk. "Sister Mary Helen belongs to a politically active group of older women called OWL—" she began.

"Murder wasn't bad enough," her partner interrupted. "Now the nun is into politics. What the hell is wrong with the full well he was referring to Honore's reputation as a ladies' man.

"Something like Don Juan or Ron Juan." He scratched his bald pate. "Whatever! Those two nuns will slow him down. And if you ask me, it couldn't happen to a nicer guy." Gallagher fumbled around in his jacket pocket, searching for his half-smoked cigar. "What's more, the sooner you do it the better.

"By the way, Katie-girl." He shoved a page of the morning *Chronicle* toward her. "What do you think of this?"

Kate glanced at the paper. It was a full-page ad from Emporium-Capwell's Department Store. "To Mom with Love" was written above a page displaying jewelry, bathrobes, and food processors.

Mother's Day! Oh, my God! Kate had forgotten this coming Sunday was Mother's Day. She hadn't even thought of a present for Jack's mother. And she'd bet even money that Jack hadn't thought of one either.

"What do you think Mrs. G. would like?" Gallagher hitched his trousers up over his paunch. "She's not my mother, I keep telling her, but the one year I forgot, there was hell to pay for the whole week after."

Kate smiled, trying to picture the sweet, accommodating Mrs. G. in a full-blown snit. It didn't even seem possible. She wondered for a moment if Jack would ever forget her on Mother's Day—or whether or not he'd even have the opportunity.

She could feel a familiar lump forming in her throat. This is ridiculous, she told herself. Jack is absolutely right. If it is bothering me this much, I should get it checked out. Find out once and for all if I am going to be—how does the Bible put it? —a "barren wife."

"How about this locket?" Gallagher pointed at the Emporium-Capwell ad. "Or maybe this Cuisinart, huh, Kate? Whatever the hell that is."

Picking up the paper from the desk, Kate hoped Gallagher wouldn't notice her eyes starting to fill as she scanned the page. At the moment nothing seemed appealing for either Mrs. G. or for her mother-in-law.

Kate glanced at her watch, wondering where Jack might be. It was getting close to lunchtime. She'd give him a call and remind him to pick up a present for his mother. Maybe he could do it on his lunch hour. And she'd tell him about Sister Mary Helen and ask him to contact Ron Honore. That would kill two birds with one stone. As soon as she thought it, Kate wished the word *killed* hadn't popped into her mind.

May 11

When Sisters Mary Helen and Eileen arrived at Erma's apartment, the front door was slightly ajar. Quietly they went up the narrow staircase. Caroline and Lucy were already in the living room standing silently beside a couple of armchairs. Finn, this time fully dressed with his long strand of hair plastered neatly in place, stared sullenly out the window.

An unnatural silence filled the whole place. Actually, the scene looked, to Mary Helen's way of thinking, like a wake without a corpse, or refreshments either, for that matter.

"You beat us here." Eileen's cheerful greeting seemed to jar the group into action.

Smiling, Lucy walked toward the Sisters. "That's the trouble with being punctual," she said, attempting to be light. "Nobody's ever there to appreciate it."

Finn turned, nodded his head toward them, but said nothing. His eyes were red-rimmed and blinked nervously as he looked from woman to woman. Probably his bistro hadn't closed until two A.M.

Caroline in a wide-brimmed black straw skimmer began to remove her gloves, one long finger at a time. If Mary Helen hadn't known better, she would have picked Caroline out as the chief mourner.

"Why don't we put your things in the bedroom?" Lucy offered, leading the way.

Mary Helen was laying her coat across the end of Erma's bed when she noticed a black looseleaf binder propped against the leg of the nightstand. Before she even thought about it, she stooped over and picked it up.

"That's our journal," Lucy said. "I guess she left without that too."

Mary Helen must have looked puzzled.

"You remember, Sister. Erma and I started taking that intensive journal-writing workshop at the college. Well, that's the binder they gave us. She must write in it just before she goes to sleep, like I do." Lucy tried to smile, but her chin quivered. "It has all kinds of colored dividers with tabs to record our different experiences."

"And all those experiences are intensely personal," Eileen said, narrowing her eyes at Mary Helen, who immediately put the journal back where she found it.

"I was only going to look at the tabs," she whispered, following Eileen back into the living room.

"Here comes another one," Finn, trying to be helpful, announced from his place at the window.

"It must be Noelle. Good! As soon as Erma's daughter arrives we can get started." Caroline checked her wristwatch. "You did tell her ten-thirty, didn't you?"

Lucy nodded just as Noelle, in a whirl of blue, arrived at the top step. "Sorry I'm late," she said. "Shall we begin by going over the facts we already know?"

She motioned them to sit down. Without a word, everyone, even Finn, followed her into the small dining area and sat down at the table. Noelle, their undisputed leader, took her place at the head.

"Erma's daughter isn't here, I see," Noelle began. "Maybe that's just as well. We can talk more freely among ourselves." She glanced over at Finn. "Thank you, Mr. Finn, for letting us into the apartment this morning. I know it must have been an inconvenience. Please feel free to go about your busy routine. We'll make sure to return the key when we're done."

Finn fidgeted uncomfortably but didn't move. It was obvious that he had something to say but wasn't too sure how to say it. "Look, ladies . . ." he began finally, his jaw, Mary Helen thought, set a little like that of a not-too-friendly bulldog. "Erma's my friend. Besides that, she works for me and this here is my apartment house. I want to be in on whatever happens."

Short, sweet, and very much to the point. Mary Helen watched the look of surprise freeze on Noelle's face.

"I see," their leader responded crisply. "I suppose that's reasonable." Her bright blue eyes jumped from woman to woman, waiting for a comment.

"It would seem to me—"; Eileen cleared her throat. Mary Helen had seen her friend look calmer addressing a crowd of five hundred—"that under the circumstances, Mr. Finn might be a great help."

One look at the man's beaming face and no one had the heart to ask, What circumstances?

"Very well." Noelle's voice brought down the imaginary gavel, and Finn became one of the group.

Mary Helen smiled over at the man. Poor fellow had no idea what he was getting into. She wondered for a moment how he would fit in.

"How shall we proceed?" Noelle was all business.

"This may seem a bit superficial," Eileen said. Mary Helen knew that would never stop her. "But before she gets here, I'd like to know Erma's daughter's real name. It can't be Ree, surely."

The group looked toward Lucy. After all, it was Lucy who knew Erma best and Lucy who had called her "Ree."

Surprisingly, it was Finn who spoke up. "It's Marie. Everyone calls her Ree for short. And the brothers are Junior and Buddy. Thomas and Richard, actually."

Noelle looked a little annoyed. Being part of the group is one thing, her expression said, but taking over, Mr. Finn, is something else again!

Finn must have caught the look. He began to blink nervously, then studied the scuffed toes of his shoes.

Funny fellow, Mary Helen thought, trying not to stare at the man. On the one hand, he was nervous and seemingly shy; on the other, he was tough enough to get his own way. And, although his overall appearance was a bit seedy, he did own a building and operate a successful-looking restaurant. Yes, indeed, he was a hard one to peg! The only thing she felt certain of was that he did care for Erma Duran.

Before she could give the man any more thought, a bang of the front door and a stumbling sound from the bottom of the stairs announced the arrival of Erma's daughter, Ree.

"I'm sorry I'm late. I wasn't feeling too well this morning."

The high, breathless voice floating up the staircase set Mary Helen's nerves on edge. God help us, she thought. A whiner!

"If it isn't her ass, it's her elbow," Mary Helen was almost sure she heard Caroline whisper to Lucy. The astonished look on Finn's face convinced her she had heard correctly.

Lucy rose and went to the banister. The rest of the group turned to watch.

"Come on up, Ree, honey. We just got here." Holding out her short arms, Lucy waited for the young woman to come to the top of the stairs. As soon as she did, she reached up to hug her and kiss both of Ree's dimpled cheeks.

"Aren't you feeling well, honey?" Lucy asked.

Ree shook her head and pulled her full mouth into a pout. "I'm so worried about Mommy."

"Don't worry, honey." Lucy soothed her almost as if she were a small child. "We're all here to help."

Even though Ree wore no makeup and, girllike, had pulled her blond-streaked hair into a ponytail, Mary Helen judged her to be at least thirty-five.

Lucy looked confidently around at the assembled group. "We'll find your mother and bring her home where she belongs."

Mary Helen wished she felt as confident as Lucy sounded. They hadn't even considered the possibility that Erma might not want to be found.

For a moment, Ree, her chubby face still flushed, stood at the edge of the room. She tugged self-consciously at the back of the flowered blouse that hung well over her snug navy pants. The more she tugged, the more the buttonholes down its front pulled away from the tiny buttons.

"Come over, dear. Sit down." Lucy patted the chair next to her. "You've met everyone here, I'm sure, except the nuns."

The look on Noelle's face said, Make the introductions brief. And Lucy did.

"Now, then," Noelle began. "Our job is to locate Erma."

Ree wrinkled her short nose and sniffled. Good night, nurse! Mary Helen squirmed, exasperated. Not only does the woman whine, she sniffles.

"Ree"—Noelle directed her gaze toward Erma's daughter—"Mr. Finn tells us that your mother mentioned going to St. Louis."

"She never said that to me." Ree tugged again at her blouse and focused her large eyes accusingly at Finn. "Why would she tell him if she didn't tell me?"

Finn leaned forward in his chair. For a moment he looked as if he might tell her why.

"That's beside the point," Mary Helen interjected, remembering only too well Finn's opinion of Erma's children. She didn't want to appear rude, but this meeting was too important to let personal animosities disrupt it.

"What we want to know is, have you any idea whom we can phone to get in touch with your mother?"

"I can't imagine who she'd go to see in St. Louis." Ree sniffled again.

"Are there no relatives there, dear?" Caroline's straw skimmer bobbed impatiently.

Her dark eyes filling, Ree shook her head.

"Friends, perhaps?" Caroline probed.

"Poor Mommy. You know her social-security check still hasn't come." Ree, ignoring the question, stared at Finn.

"Friends?" Caroline insisted, despite the growing feeling of tension in the room.

"Only Auntie Barbara."

"Auntie Barbara?" the group repeated in unison.

"Not our real aunt. Just a friend of Mommy's from college way back. But I'm not really sure exactly where in St. Louis she lives."

"Now we're beginning to get someplace." Beside her, Eileen beamed. Mary Helen did not feel quite so optimistic. Something was bothering her. She must have been frowning because Noelle nodded her blue-rinsed head toward the old nun. "What's wrong, Sister?"

"Well . . . I was just wondering about the money. Erma's social-security check hadn't come, and Lucy mentioned to Caroline and me that Erma was worried about money while we were in New York. How could she afford the fare to St. Louis?"

She was just about ready to answer her own question—Visa or MasterCard, of course—when Finn spoke up.

"I lent it to her." He shrugged.

Ree glared at the little man. "You lent it to Mommy? You? Why, you can hardly pay her salary on time."

"I got lucky."

"At the track, I suppose." This time Ree sniffed rather than sniffled. "Just like my father. He—"

All eyes shifted to Finn. Face flushed, he raised his broad hand, as if to stop stones instead of words. "Whoa!" he shouted. "Your father was a good man and a good friend of mine."

The words echoed in the small dining room. Mary Helen could hear the others twisting uncomfortably in their chairs, the way people do who have inadvertently stumbled into a family fight. Several cleared their throats. Eileen, she noticed, was studying a cobweb on the chandelier.

"Ladies and gentlemen," Noelle interrupted quickly.

Mary Helen could sense the relief.

"We are straying from the point. How are we going to proceed with finding our friend Erma?"

Caroline, eager to help her neutralize the situation, raised her index finger. "Let's divide the duties," she suggested, with a nod toward Noelle, "then schedule another meeting."

"Fine." Noelle took a pocket calendar from her navy-blue leather handbag. "We had better not wait too long." She paused briefly, waiting for comments. When there were none, she continued. "Shall we say tomorrow, same time, same place?"

That settled, Caroline went back to dividing. "When we are through here, Lucy, you and I can go back to the college and search through the alumnae records." She tipped her skimmer toward the Sisters for tacit permission. "I'm sure we will be able to unearth a Barbara in Erma's class, or in one close to it, who lives in the vicinity of St. Louis," she said when the Sisters had nodded back. "Between us, we can make the calls.

"Marie, you, of course, should contact your brothers. See if they perhaps know where your mother has gone. Possibly she confided in one of the boys.

"Noelle, you're good with government-type things. Perhaps

you could place calls to the St. Louis Police Department and to hospitals, just in case—and I hate to even mention it—something may have happened to Erma.

"Mr. Finn"—Caroline had clearly thought out her plan—"there must be an organization of restaurant owners or something of that nature in that area . . ."

The man squinted at her as if she had just dropped in from another planet. "You talking about the waitresses' union?"

"I suppose I am." Caroline cleared her throat. "And you, Sisters"—Mary Helen tried not to appear too eager—"you two can do what you do best: pray."

* * *

"Pray, indeed!" Mary Helen muttered, fumbling in her pocketbook for the car keys. On the curb behind her, she could hear Eileen chuckling.

"What's so funny?" she asked without turning around.

"If you could have seen your face, old dear, when Caroline said, 'Pray.' You got so red, I was afraid you might burst."

"I did no such thing." Mary Helen finally unlocked the car door. "I was just surprised, that's all."

"Oh, and what, may I ask, surprised you?"

"That the poor woman does not know that prayer without good works is dead."

"Isn't that faith without good works, old dear?"

"Same difference." Mary Helen adjusted her bifocals, then fastened her seat belt.

She turned the key in the ignition. "And if she thinks for one moment that I'm going to let my prayers die, she has another think coming."

"I could well have predicted that," Eileen muttered, her brogue thickening.

"By the way," Mary Helen asked, eager to change the subject, "what did you make of that little scene between Ree and Mr. Finn just now?"

"I was about to ask you the same question," Eileen said.

"But since you asked me first, I would say that, deep down, those two have a couple of ill-stirred pots about to come to a full boil."

Mary Helen had never heard her say that before. "Is that another of your old sayings from home?"

"No, I just made it up," Eileen said with a complacent smile. "And what do you make of it?"

"Just about the same as you do." Mary Helen checked her wristwatch. "We're in luck," she said. "It's only eleven-thirty. We can surely make it to the Hall of Justice before Kate Murphy goes to lunch."

* * *

Sister Mary Helen was surprised when she and Eileen walked into the Hall of Justice. The police department had erected a plywood barricade across the entire foyer. Well, what can you expect? she asked herself. After all, you haven't been in the building for nearly two years. Things do change.

A security checkpoint, much like that in an airport, had been built at one end. It instructed them ENTER HERE.

"Where are you going, ladies?" the uniformed officer asked, returning their pocketbooks.

"To the Homicide Detail," Mary Helen answered. The policeman looked a little surprised, she thought, but not nearly as surprised as Kate Murphy did when she saw the two of them in the doorway of Room 450. And poor Inspector Gallagher! *Flabbergasted* was the only word that would adequately describe his reaction.

"Hi, Sisters," Kate called.

The crowded detail suddenly became still. One by one the homicide detectives turned their heads toward the doorway. Some smiled, some half rose. O'Connor, whom she remembered from the last time she was here, offered a weak, "Hi, 'Sters!"

The room was much the same as Mary Helen remembered it. If anything, it was more cluttered with more papers. Perhaps an additional wooden desk or two had been shoved together on the cramped floor space.

Suit jackets were slung over the backs of swivel chairs, just the way she remembered. Looking around the room, you would swear that these tall, burly men were nothing more than messy real-estate agents—except, of course, for the gun each one had strapped in his shoulder holster or onto his belt.

Kate crossed the room, smiling, and gave each of the nuns a hug. "So nice to see you," she said.

Mary Helen smiled back. Kate looked wonderful. Married life seemed to really be agreeing with her. If she had changed at all, she was more slim and trim than she had been. Not a speck of gray shone in her red hair. There was a peaceful expression on her open, freckled face. Mary Helen did notice faint shadows under Kate's Wedgwood-blue eyes and wondered, for a moment, what that was all about.

Across the room, Inspector Dennis Gallagher stood by his desk next to a large window, his face flushed. As he struggled to refasten his tie, the man made a feeble attempt to look pleased to see them. Actually, Mary Helen thought, his expression was more like a grimace.

"Come in, come in." Kate ushered the nuns through the maze of phones and filing cabinets and pulled up two chairs next to the pushed-together desks she and Gallagher shared.

"What brings you here today?" Behind her, Mary Helen could hear the quiet room become even quieter. Like one of those old commercials on TV where E. F. Hutton speaks, she thought, amused.

Kate may have looked at Eileen, or perhaps Eileen only thought she did.

"I'll be switched if I can figure it out," she heard her friend whisper, her brogue a bit on the thick side.

"Sister?" Kate smiled, looking first at Mary Helen. Then she looked around the detail, with what the old nun thought could only be described as a glare. Slowly, the typewriters and phone dials began to make noise again.

Gallagher perched his ample bottom on the edge of one desk, hitched up his trouser legs, and leaned forward, ready to listen. "Tell us what's on your mind, 'Ster?"

Clearing her throat, Mary Helen slowly shoved her bifocals up the bridge of her nose and looked from inspector to inspector. "You remember, of course, Kate, my calling you yesterday about my OWL friend, Erma Duran?"

Kate nodded.

"Well, not one of us OWLs has seen or heard from her for almost a week now. We are really becoming very concerned." She paused for effect. It must have worked.

Inspector Gallagher leaned over even farther and began to dig into his pockets, searching, Mary Helen assumed, for his cigar. She spotted it in the full ashtray behind him. Better for his lungs and heart if I let him search, she thought, switching her attention back to Kate.

"Today several of us met with her daughter and her employer. Strangely, neither of them has heard from Erma either."

Kate frowned and began to twist a thick lock of her hair. Good! Mary Helen knew full well that was a sign the girl was thinking.

"A whole week, you say?"

"One week tomorrow, to be exact."

Gallagher found his cigar and scratched a match on the under edge of his desktop. "But no body, huh, 'Ster?" He squinted one eye against the smoke rising from the stub.

Sitting taller in her chair, Mary Helen put on her best schoolmarm face. Gallagher, she suspected, was about to dismiss her as worrying without cause. "As you know, Inspector, finding no body does not necessarily mean that no harm has come to the woman."

Grinning, Gallagher pushed himself off the edge of the desk, put his cigar back in the ashtray, and, with his hands free, tucked his shirt into his pants. "You're absolutely right, 'Ster." He shrugged his shoulder. "But what it does mean is that if there is no body, then there is no case for Homicide."

Mary Helen frowned. In her opinion, Inspector Gallagher looked and sounded entirely too pleased. She wasn't about to be put off so easily. She turned back toward Kate.

"What I think we should do, Sisters"—Kate folded her hands on the desk in front of her and studied her thumbnails —"is turn you over to Missing Persons."

If Mary Helen hadn't known better, she would have suspected from the look on her face that Kate Murphy was a bit too pleased also.

Removing her earring, Kate picked up the phone receiver and dialed.

"Isn't it just down the hallway?" Mary Helen mouthed to Gallagher.

"They moved it." Gallagher stared out the window at the James Lick Freeway. "Missing Persons has gone over with Juvenile, to the old Northern Station on Greenwich. They're moving everything around. Nothing's the same as it used to be."

"Okay, Sisters." Kate slammed down the receiver. "It's all set. That was Inspector Ronald Honore. He's from Missing Persons. Honore is swamped this afternoon, but call him first thing on Monday morning. He'll help you make out a report if you still need one."

Kate scribbled on a scrap of paper. "Here is his name"—she handed the note to Mary Helen—"his phone number, and where you can find him."

As they left the detail, Mary Helen was almost certain she heard Gallagher say, "Hot damn, Katie-girl! Those two couldn't happen to a nicer guy!"

"Why were you so quiet in there?" Mary Helen asked, suddenly realizing that Sister Eileen had said almost nothing while they were in Room 450.

"I just can't seem to get over it." Eileen took a deep breath and stepped into the elevator. "It must be from when I was a girl back home. The garda inhibits me. So many of them all together in that one room."

Mary Helen stared at her friend. "Glory be to God, Eileen. You left Ireland well over fifty years ago. And then you were probably not even twenty years old. Besides which, you lived in the country. How much experience could you have possibly had with the garda? Besides, nothing inhibits you."

Eileen pulled herself up to her full height. "There are some things, Mary Helen, that are part of a person's heritage. Some things you are born to and brought up with that you just don't forget. Some things that are just part and parcel of a person."

Mary Helen narrowed her eyes at her friend. "Eileen, have you been listening to the Clancy Brothers and those Irish rebellion ballads again?"

Her short nose in the air, Sister Eileen walked out of the Hall of Justice several paces ahead of Sister Mary Helen.

Outside, the day was gray and drizzly. A sharp wind whipped down Bryant Street, bowing the sycamores in front of the Hall. The sky looked as though someone had shaded in the whole thing with a number-two pencil. Overhead, one small spot of gray was a little brighter than the rest. Probably the sun trying to break through, although Mary Helen thought the effect was as if someone in heaven had turned on a forty-watt bulb.

When they reached the car, the old nun studied the scrap of paper Kate had given her. It read "Inspector Ron Honore, 2475 Greenwich" and gave the phone number and the extension.

Even though Eileen was fiddling with her own seat belt, she must have noticed what Mary Helen was doing. "Kate said to call the man on Monday." Mary Helen noted the wary edge in her friend's voice. "You are not planning to go in there now?"

"Not *in*"—Mary Helen tried to sound incredulous that Eileen would even think such a thing—"just *by.*"

"Is that a good idea?" Eileen's question hung in the air. Mary Helen didn't answer. It seemed better that way.

The downtown streets around the Hall of Justice always confused her. Some were one-way. Some put you right on the freeway heading to San Jose. And some led you to God knew where.

Trying to be helpful, Eileen peered at the signs and arrows along Harrison Street, reading them aloud. "Let's head for Van Ness," she said finally. "We know for sure that goes across town. From there we can get home."

Mary Helen smiled. Eileen must be confused too. That made her feel a little better. Surely, Van Ness or at least South Van Ness must be around there somewhere. Under the freeway, Mary Helen made a quick right turn.

"Mary Helen! Not here!"

Jerking her foot off the gas pedal, heart pounding, Mary Helen looked both ways, but she couldn't see what she had done wrong.

"What is it, Eileen?" she asked, her knees shaking.

Eileen pointed to the street sign, her gray eyes open in horror. "You turned onto 13th, old dear. Could there be a more unlucky street in all of San Francisco?"

Behind them, horns honked impatiently. Mary Helen could feel her blood pressure rise. "You and your blasted superstitions" was all she had the strength to say, for which she was grateful—not nearly so grateful, however, as Eileen should have been.

Relieved when they finally spotted the sign for South Van Ness, Mary Helen turned right. As they inched their way along the wide boulevard and across the City, Eileen seemed a little sheepish.

She didn't even object, Mary Helen noticed, when they passed the Opera Plaza and Turk Street, where they should have turned for the college. She did grunt when they went by Tommy's Joynt on the corner of Van Ness and Geary. But that was understandable. It was nearly lunchtime, and although buffalo stew might not sound very appealing, the hot turkey sandwich did. At the thought of it, her own stomach growled.

By the time they had passed Hippo's Hamburgers and neared the towering stone edifice of St. Brigid's Church, Sister Eileen had seemingly resigned herself to the inevitable.

Silently the pair zipped past Phillip Mason's Hair Salon and around a parked Muni bus. "The next one's Greenwich," Eileen announced with a little edge on her voice. Apparently she had recovered from feeling sheepish. "And I am starving. So let's make short work of whatever you have in mind. And I dare not even imagine what that might be." She shuddered.

The old Northern Station was sandwiched in the middle of a block of well-kept stucco homes, flats, and modern apartment buildings. The station itself, with its large ornate lanterns over the entrance steps, was a leftover from the Pan American Exposition of 1915.

Only nine years after the earthquake and fire, Mary Helen had read somewhere, the city had filled in land from the Bay, built the magnificent Palace of Fine Arts, and played host to the exposition. The Northern Station at the far end of the landfill had guarded it all.

Mary Helen drove by the building once, turned, and drove by again. "As long as we're here, we may just as well go in, meet the man and say, How do," she said, as if it were a sudden idea.

"I wish I had placed a wager" was Eileen's only comment as she unbuckled her seat belt.

"Can I help you, ladies?" a slight police inspector with thick, curly gray hair greeted them the moment they opened the glass front door. He must have been watching them parallel park. And he would have had plenty of time, Mary Helen figured. It always took her several tries to get close enough to the curb to be legal.

"We were just looking for Inspector Honore." She peeked into the next room, which, from the door at least, looked just as crowded, if not as large, as the Homicide Detail.

"If he's not too busy," Eileen added quickly.

"Honore? He's the big guy over there." The man pointed to the far corner where a computer-made HAPPY ST. PATRICK'S DAY banner still hung on the wall.

"He's the one below the poster. With USF's basketball schedule."

Mary Helen looked toward the corner where the inspector was pointing. A husky back hunched over an old-fashioned typewriter.

"Honore! For you," the man called from the doorway.

"Yo!" Raising his index finger, the fellow stood up and turned toward them.

For a moment, Mary Helen was startled. She adjusted her bifocals just to make sure. Why, standing there, Inspector Honore looked, for all the world, just like a big black Kojak without the hat.

* * *

Separately, Kate and Jack drove up in front of their peaked-roofed home on 34th and Geary at exactly the same time.

When Jack saw her, he circled the block, leaving the parking place in front of the house for Kate. He squeezed into one farther up the hill, almost at 35th. Dripping fog rolling in from the Pacific quickly covered Geary Boulevard like cold steam. In the distance, foghorns bleated.

"Contrary to popular opinion, chivalry is not dead." Jack bounded up the green wooden steps and stood behind her.

Shivering, Kate fumbled to get the key into the dead bolt. "Thanks, pal. First one in turns on the heat." She pushed open the wooden door.

Jack threw on the switch for the thermostat. Kate could hear the ancient furnace in the basement thump on. Side by side, they stood in front of the old-fashioned heating grate in the baseboard.

"Anything new or different?" Jack asked.

"I took your advice," Kate said.

"Now that is new and different! What advice?"

"I made an appointment with the gynecologist. Actually, today I couldn't get away from Gallagher long enough to phone, so I stopped by the office on my way home. Do you have any idea how long it takes to get an appointment?"

"I must admit I don't."

"Six weeks! I can't get in until June twenty-eighth." Kate stared at him, waiting for a reaction. When she didn't get one, she pulled a blue and white pamphlet out of her coat pocket and handed it to Jack. "I picked this up while I was there. It says one thing that causes infertility is stress. We have to do something to lessen our stress."

Blasts of hot air rose from the grate, warming Kate's feet, then shooting up under her skirt to the goosebumps on her legs and thighs.

Jack flipped through the pamphlet, then laid it on the hall table. "No big deal!" He hung up his jacket in the closet and stored his gun on the top shelf. "Let's start by not cooking tonight."

Kate suspected it was Jack's turn to cook.

"It's Friday night. Let's go out to dinner. There's a new Chinese place on Clement."

"I'm serious," Kate said. By now she was warm enough to take off her coat too.

"I'm serious too. Let's just have a relaxing evening together. No cooking, no dishes."

Kate had to admit it sounded like a good place to start. "Why don't we have a drink here first?" She stopped. She couldn't believe those words had come out of her mouth.

That was what her mother had always said. Probably to save money. The suggestion had always struck Kate as tacky. Now here she was, saying the same thing. Not because they couldn't afford it, though, but because it was just cozier to have cocktails at home.

"Swell." Jack went to the kitchen. Kate followed him. "I should probably take a bath before we go."

"Hell, if I have to take a bath, too, let's go out big and romantic." Jack mixed a vodka tonic for Kate and poured himself Scotch on the rocks. He brought the glasses into the small sun room off the kitchen.

"You'll never guess who dropped by the Hall today." Kate followed her husband into the room. They settled back on the overstuffed couch. The flowered chintz made the room seem warm and cheerful despite the dense fog whirling past the windows.

"How many guesses do I get?"

"None. I'll tell you. Our two nun friends, Sister Mary Helen and Sister Eileen."

"About that missing OWL friend of theirs?" Jack hit his forehead with the heel of his hand. "Jeez, I forgot to call Honore about that."

Kate nodded, then sipped her drink. "I gathered as much. Too late now. I put in a call to him this afternoon. Poor unsuspecting slob said to have them call him on Monday."

Jack smiled. "Wait till the guy gets a load of those two."

"Oh, he did. Apparently Mary Helen couldn't wait. The two of them went right over."

"And Honore called you?"

"He nearly came through the phone, shouting 'Why me? You know damn well this should go to cops at the Mission Station.' I guess when I told him I had two older nuns, he thought he could sweet-talk them, calm them down. Charm them, actually. What he expected was sweetness and light."

"And what he got was gangbusters!" Jack snorted.

Kate knew her husband was delighted. Don Juan Ron Honore had finally met his match. Not only would he be unable to charm these two woman, he would hardly be able to control them.

"What did he do with them?"

"What any normal, red-blooded police inspector would do. He gave right in and told them to come back if their friend wasn't located within the next few days."

Chuckling, Jack shook his head. "Damn, I wish I'd been there to see that ugly face!" He rose and took the two glasses for a refill.

"Should we?" Kate asked.

"A bird cannot fly on one wing alone." her husband said and winked. "And that's an Irish saying. A good Irish girl like you should know that and not have to be told by your Eyetalian husband."

"How was your day?" Kate called after him. "And speaking of days," she added before he could answer, "did you pick up something for your mother for Mother's Day? It's Sunday, you know."

"Jeez, no." Jack reappeared in the doorway and handed Kate her glass.

"Do you want to take her out for dinner or a fancy brunch or something like that instead?"

Jack ran his fingers through his thick, curly hair. "That reminds me, hon, Ma called at work today. Wants us to come to dinner at her place on Mother's Day."

"Isn't that a little backwards? Shouldn't the children be giving the party?"

Jack shrugged, then settled back beside her on the couch. "Whatever turns you on! Speaking of which . . ." He kissed her gently on the forehead.

Kate recognized the look on his face, but at the moment she didn't feel a bit romantic. Jack sat back and looked at her. "Why the frown?"

"I was just feeling kind of sorry for your mother. Fixing her own dinner on Mother's Day, and everything."

"She loves it. Nothing makes her happier. Besides, she's never satisfied with anyone else's cooking. You know that."

"Well, it's not right." Kate felt angry and she wasn't sure why.

"What's not right?"

"It just doesn't seem very . . . very"—she sat up straight, searching for the right word—"*appreciative.*" She wondered for a moment whether her children—if and when she ever had any—would appreciate how much she wanted them. "And you're so callous about it." She glared at Jack, suddenly angry with him.

He shook his head. "I can't figure you out. First you can hardly put up with my mother's mothering. Now you're mad because I'm not appreciative enough. Did I miss something?"

Sinking back down on the couch, Kate kicked off her shoes and pulled her legs up beside her. Jack had a point, she knew, and she felt a little foolish. Snuggling closer to him, she put her head on his knee. "Sorry, pal," she said. His strong fingers kneaded her backbone. She had the sudden urge to purr.

"Didn't that pamphlet say we should relax?"

Kate nodded her head.

"Let Dr. Bassetti introduce you to his foolproof method, lady. First let me check your vital signs." His cool hand touched her forehead. "No fever." He felt for her wrist. "Pulse steady." Playfully, he patted her hip. "No apparent deformities. Dr. Bassetti recommends a romantic dinner for two, then plenty of bed rest with the aforementioned doctor."

Kate giggled, then sat up. She felt suddenly warm and lovey. She wasn't sure if it was Jack or the vodka on an empty stomach. "I'm so lucky to have you," she said, pressing her lips against her husband's ear. "And I always take my doctor's advice. I'll be in and out of the tub before you know it."

Eyes closed, Kate felt the warm bath water ooze over her

shoulders and relax them. The faint smell of strawberry bubble bath rose in the steam. Wriggling her toes, she slid farther down into the tub. The water licked at her chin. Without opening her eyes, Kate took a deep breath and let it out slowly. She imagined the tiny ripples it made on the surface of the bath water. She felt drowsy.

"You look like a bubble dancer in the final act."

Kate's eyes shot open. Jack stood by the side of the tub, smiling down at her. He had a glass of wine in each hand.

"What in the world?" Kate sat up in the tub. A few stray bubbles still floated around the sides.

"Dr. Bassetti has done some more research on your problem, lady. Maybe you won't even need to see this busy gynecologist." He set the wineglasses beside the tub. "If we are going to eat romantic, why not start romantic? In the movies the lead and his lady always take a bubble bath together, sip champagne, then send out for pizza."

"And may I ask just how that would solve my problem?"

"Babies come from romance. It always looks real romantic."

"That's in the movies. And you've got wine, not champagne, plus we need a lot more bubbles." Kate watched with trepidation as her husband took off his robe and climbed over the bottom end of the old-fashioned tub.

"I hope these claw feet will support both of us." She eyed the legs holding up the tub.

"Wouldn't that be something?" Facing her, Jack lowered himself into the water. "How about a little more hot water?"

Kate twisted, but couldn't turn around enough to reach the faucet. Feeling his foot beside her hip, she giggled, then twisted some more, making room for his other foot. Now where would she put hers?

Slipping, grunting, and laughing, they both managed to fit into the narrow tub. Kate could feel Jack's toenails against her back.

"Isn't this romantic?" he asked, with a silly grin on his face. He bent over the side of the tub and picked up the two glasses. "People must have been smaller when they built this tub."

Kate tried to sip her wine, but she banged her elbow on his knee. "Or maybe they didn't see the same movies."

By adjusting her hips she moved closer to her husband. She grabbed his waist with her heels. "Now what?" she asked and bent forward to kiss him. All she could reach was his nose.

"Ouch!" He'd cracked his elbow against the edge of the tub. "We better get the hell out of here."

Kate started to laugh. She could feel Jack's foot groping for a place to steady itself. It slipped off her thigh. "Are you afraid the legs are going to go?"

"No, I'm afraid we'll get so stuck in this damn thing that the fire department will have to use jaws to get us out."

Kate was laughing so hard she could hardly speak. "I wonder," she said, "if the boys would also deliver the pizza."

Saturday, May 12

Feast of Sts. Nereus and Achilleus, Martyrs

On Saturday morning Sister Mary Helen awoke feeling uneasy. As far as she could remember she had slept well and had not had any disturbing dreams. Yet the feeling was there and it filled her whole body with the cold, lonely, unsettling squeeze of dread. It was Erma, of course!

Outside, a steady rain now hit against her window. The gutter at the end of the convent building gurgled. Poor Luis had forgotten to clean out the pine needles—again.

She recognized the hum of the vacuum cleaner. It was drifting up from somewhere downstairs. Vacuum cleaner! She must have overslept. Suddenly awake, Mary Helen checked the alarm clock on her bed stand. It had stopped. Fumbling for her glasses, she focused on her wristwatch. Nine o'clock! She sat up, shaken. If she hurried she'd just have time to dress, gulp down some breakfast, and get to Erma's apartment for the ten-thirty meeting.

"Why didn't you wake me up?" She stared accusingly at Eileen the moment she found her. And she spotted her, reading the *Chronicle,* in the coffee room off the college kitchen.

"I thought you could use the extra rest," Eileen answered placidly, looking up over the morning paper. "And I knew I was sure to run into you here if I just stayed put."

"Do you know what time it is? We've got to hurry!" Impatiently, Mary Helen blew on her coffee.

"Not *we,* old dear. *You.*" This time Eileen didn't even look up.

* * *

"When you're in a rush, nothing works right," Mary Helen fussed, sitting in the driver's seat of the convent's Nova. She pushed on the automatic garage-door opener. The thick door didn't budge.

"You try it." She handed the opener to Eileen, who aimed it first at the door, then at the ceiling, and finally halfway in between. Although the overhead motor made a growling sound, the door still did not move.

"Poor Allan Boscacci." Eileen shoved the broken opener into the glove compartment. "Therese will have him on the horn before night falls."

"What do we do now?" At the moment, Mary Helen didn't care about anyone else's problems.

"When in doubt, bail out." With a determined look on her face, Eileen headed for the heavy door.

She must be picking up that corn from Lucy Lyons, Mary Helen thought, following her. Between the two of them, they were able, with much grunting and puffing, to push the door open.

* * *

The nuns arrived at Erma's apartment just in time for the meeting. "As a matter of fact, we are a few minutes early," Eileen remarked, passing their wet raincoats and dripping umbrellas to Lucy. Caroline, Noelle, Mr. Finn, and Erma's daughter stood just inside the dim living room.

"I'll hang these over the bathtub," Lucy said, then grinned. "With all the other drips."

She just can't help herself, Mary Helen thought, hoping Eileen hadn't heard the crack. Yet even she couldn't help smiling at the spry little woman disappearing into Erma's bedroom.

"Everyone is right on time," Noelle began before Lucy returned. She motioned for the group to sit, which they did. All, that is, except Erma's daughter, Ree. The girl stood by the living-room window, sniffling and nervously glancing first at the street below, then toward Noelle, then finally around the living room at the assembled group.

"The boys said they'd be here," she explained, tugging at the back of her overblouse.

"That's fine." Noelle peered over the top of her half glasses. The blue of her silk scarf accented the blue of her eyes and made them even more penetrating.

"Shall we begin?" Without waiting for an answer, she continued, "I trust we were all successful."

Who would dare be otherwise? Mary Helen wanted to ask, but thought better of it.

"Would you like to give the first report, Caroline?"

Caroline, looking pert in her saucy little rain hat, paused until she had everyone's undivided attention. Even Ree, who must have noticed the silence, turned from the window and sat on the sill.

"The college's alumnae office was most helpful," she began, with a smile toward the nuns. Fat chance they wouldn't be, thought Mary Helen, smiling back.

"Lucy and I went though the alumnae records for the late thirties. As you know, that was when Erma graduated." She glanced toward the window to include Ree. "We found your Aunt Barbara."

Drawing in her breath, Caroline swallowed. The silent room grew even more still with expectation. Next to her, Mary Helen could feel Mr. Finn shifting forward. Across the room, she noticed Eileen crossing fingers on both her hands. Her own stomach roiled.

"Unfortunately . . ." Caroline began. Suddenly, the room seemed to deflate. "Barbara—whose maiden name, incidentally, was Barbara Quinn—has not heard from Erma. And, frankly, she is quite upset. She feels that if Erma were in the area, she would surely have called. I'm afraid that rather than solving anything, our investigation has simply upset another person."

Noelle let Caroline's observation ride on the air without comment. "I contacted the St. Louis Police Department, which graciously checked the city's hospitals for me." Noelle paused long enough to light a cigarette. Mary Helen was surprised she had waited this long. "Fortunately, Erma's name was not on any of their lists." She moved an ashtray from the coffee table to the arm of her chair.

"I didn't get nowhere, either, with the union." Blinking his eyes, Finn put his elbows on his knees and clenched his hands together. "I called the waitresses' union and the bartenders', too, just in case.

"Gal on the phone didn't know nothing about Erma. 'No record of her applying for membership here,' she says." Finn's voice cracked and, for a moment, Mary Helen wondered if he was going to cry. Instead, he bent forward, resting his forehead in his hands.

For several seconds, the six women sat staring at the top of his threaded pate. The poor fellow, Mary Helen thought. He really does care for Erma. Funny, Erma had never mentioned him. Relationships, she remembered reading somewhere recently, are a pervading and changing mystery. How true! For the present, the relationship between Erma and Finn surely was a mystery—to her, at least. And that didn't seem to be the only mystery the group had discovered. A sudden chill made Mary Helen hug herself.

"Now, now!" Lucy's voice cut through the gloom. "Let's not get down in the dumps," she said, in what Mary Helen thought must be a superhuman effort to be optimistic, even for

Lucy. "It's not all bad news. After all, Noelle called the police and hospitals. And there was no word of Erma there. So far as we know, nothing bad has happened to her."

Trying to push away apprehension from the edge of her mind, Mary Helen forced herself to nod at Lucy.

Encouraged, Lucy looked hopefully from person to person. "Think positive!" Her voice rose higher. Mary Helen couldn't help but notice the hint of anxiety. "We can't let ourselves even imagine that something has happened to our friend."

Across from her, Mary Helen watched Eileen, who was visibly trying to cheer up. "Lucy is right," she said. "We must have faith that everything will turn out just dandy. We'll get nowhere unless we keep our spirits up."

Lucy picked up steam. "After all, the Sisters have been praying," she said.

Eileen nodded. For a fleeting second, Mary Helen feared the two optimists might break into a duet of "Pack Up Your Troubles."

"Besides"—Lucy's eyes were wide behind her horn-rimmed glasses—"we still have to hear from . . ."

As though on cue, the roar of a motorcycle thundered through the small room. Over the noise, Lucy finished her sentence: "the boys," she shouted.

"What the hell happened to Ma?" A deep voice ricocheted off the walls of the narrow staircase, as heavy footsteps stomped up toward them.

The vision that loomed on the top step was something, Mary Helen imagined, that could have come right out of a B movie about the Hell's Angels. Stunned, the group just stared.

"I asked you guys a question." Hands on hips, the thick-bodied young man glared back at them, his bare chest swelling inside his leather vest. Actually his chest was the only thing about him that was bare. The rest of him was covered with hair and leather and chains and tattoos.

"Where the hell is the old lady?" he shouted at no one in particular.

Recovering from the initial shock, Caroline pulled herself up to her majestic best. "You must be Junior," she said so icily that even Junior froze on the spot. Mary Helen cringed. As if they weren't having enough trouble! All they needed now was a verbal battle. Although if there was to be one, she had no doubt whatsoever about who would win.

"We can fully appreciate your concern for your mother," Caroline continued, bestowing a look of regal understanding on the peasant before her. "And we sympathize. It is plain to see that you care about the old lady, even though, I believe, that is a misnomer. Your concern is further attested to, of course, by the fact that you have immortalized her on your thorax." She pointed a long finger toward his chest.

Junior frowned, puzzled. Mary Helen knew he wasn't quite sure whether he had been complimented or insulted. She swallowed the urge to laugh.

In the uncomfortable silence that filled the room while he was trying to decide, Ree sniffled nervously. "This is my brother," she said, motioning at a young man nearly hidden behind Junior. "This is Buddy."

"Excuse me." Buddy edged his way around the elder Duran and toward Ree.

At first glance, Mary Helen was taken aback. Although he was slight, his resemblance to Erma was uncanny. Like his mother, he was short, curly-haired, and had the same brown eyes and round face. She felt a sudden ache. How she wished good old Erma would walk into the room right now, smile, and give them each that little squeeze of hers.

Buddy kissed Lucy on the cheek, shook Finn's hand, and smiled warmly at the group of women he didn't know.

He was so gentle and polite that, at first, Mary Helen hardly noticed his earrings. To her knowledge, the only men who ever wore an earring were sailors who had crossed the international date line. Recently, she had noticed lots of sailors in San Francisco.

When she mentioned this, Sister Anne had explained they weren't all sailors. Depending on whether the earring was in the right or left ear, Anne had said, it indicated that the wearer was either straight or gay. Although, to save her life, Mary Helen could never remember which was which. But this Buddy had an earring in each ear. She would have to question Anne on that one.

"Buddy is an artist," Lucy announced proudly. "Right now he works part-time as a docent at the De Young Museum. But someday he'll be famous."

Embarrassed, Buddy shrugged. "I'm not really an artist yet," he said.

Regardless, he looked the part—from his sandals to his rose-tinted glasses, earrings, and the wispy tail of hair curling down the scrawny nape of his neck.

"Now that the boys are here we'll get back to business," Noelle said, being very careful, Mary Helen noted, not to ask about Junior's line of work. "If you'll just take a seat, we can proceed."

Junior recovered his voice, but the interval had not improved his manners. "What the hell happened to the old lady?" he shouted, ignoring Noelle's rules of order. "Ree says she's missing." He swaggered toward the center of the room.

"If anything happens to her, you bastard"—he took a menacing step toward Finn—"you've me to answer to. Got that?" He pointed a thick finger at the man's bald head. Mary Helen was startled to see that the nail was gnawed to the quick.

Stiffening, Finn met Junior's dare with hard hazel eyes, the little yellow specks in them quivering. "Is that so, Junior?" Finn clenched his fists, his knuckles turning white. "If I was you, sonny boy, I'd be real careful who I call a bastard and who I'd pick to get tough with."

Taken aback, Mary Helen watched the usually polite, accommodating Mr. Finn rise. She felt the hair on the back of her neck rise with him. A verbal battle was one thing; a real one was something else again!

Deliberately flexing his muscles, Junior glowered at Finn. The *Mother* and heart tattooed on his chest seemed to swell.

Much to Mary Helen's chagrin, Finn didn't back down even an inch. "You, sonny boy, was the one here pestering her the day she took off." He nodded toward the young man with contempt. "You and your lousy motorcycle and your lousy mouth."

Enraged, Junior set his jaw, pulled back his thick right arm, and squared off. Mary Helen was sure he was ready and able to throw the first punch.

Before she realized what she was doing, she was up from her chair and standing between the two.

"That will do!" she said in a voice that had stopped many a school-yard brawl midpunch.

Despite their anger both men stopped, shocked. But neither, Mary Helen was certain, felt as shocked as she did. There are some habits that just don't leave you. Swallowing hard, she met their stares with one of her own.

"I said, That will do!"

Scowling, the men studied her. She wondered for a moment if either one would try to test her.

"Sit down!" she commanded, not bothering to consider what she would do if either one of them didn't.

Just as she suspected, it was Junior who caved in first.

*   *   *

A general sense of relief descended on Erma's living room the moment the boys left. As the roar of the motorcycle faded farther and farther into the distance, the atmosphere became almost festive.

Lucy giggled. "Let me get us all a glass of wine," she offered. "I know exactly where Erma keeps the hooch. She would want us to have one and, God knows, about now we need it!"

"Good heavens, Lucy! It's still morning," Noelle protested, more for appearance than anything else, Mary Helen suspected.

"It's four o'clock somewhere!" Lucy called, clinking bottles in a cupboard under the sink.

"There's an old saying we have back home," Eileen piped up. Mary Helen winced, knowing full well the old saying Eileen had in mind. " 'We may as well be drunk as the way we are!' " Eileen took the stemmed glass from Lucy.

"Here's to our success in locating Erma." Noelle, determined to remain their leader, proposed the toast. Smiling, they all raised their glasses.

"And to Sister Mary Helen who, thank God, did not get her block knocked off!" Lucy added.

Still a little shaken, Sister Mary Helen felt a lump begin to form in her throat. To good old Erma Duran—she thought, trying to smile brightly—wherever she is. And please, Lord, help us to find that out. Fast! Before we have any more mornings like this one.

* * *

Caroline fished in her Louis Vuitton clutch bag for her gloves. "Where do we go from here?" she asked.

As a matter of form, Noelle consulted her peacock-blue pocket calendar. "Tomorrow, as you know, is Sunday and Mother's Day, to boot," she said. "We all have obligations, I am sure, so I propose we meet at the same time on Monday. If no one has heard from Erma by then, I feel we not only could but should report her as a missing person."

"Monday? But Mommy would never be away from us on Mother's Day without calling." Ree's round face was flushed and she looked dangerously close to tears. The strain of the last week was beginning to tell on her.

"Relax, Ree." Finn, who had apparently regained his composure, twirled the stem of his empty wineglass between his fingers. "It's not like we don't know where she said she'd be. Besides"—he stood up and set his glass on the coffee table— "I've got a hunch she'll call tomorrow."

"You and your hunches!" Ree's large eyes narrowed with resentment. She pulled her mouth into a pout but said no more. Mary Helen was glad. She didn't know if her nerves were up to another fight.

Mumbling something about checking on supplies in the kitchen, Finn had the good sense to leave.

Caroline moved to the edge of her chair, poised to go.

"Has anyone anything further to add?" Apparently, Noelle sensed the meeting was getting ready to break up. She glanced in Caroline's direction.

"I have nothing to add." Caroline stood and tilted her beautifully coiffured head of champagne-colored hair. "I would just like to concur with Noelle"—she gazed around the room, innocently batting her eyes—"that if by Monday Erma has not yet been heard from, we should either pee or get off the pot."

She swept from the room and down the stairs, leaving the rest of the group questioning their hearing.

"Thank God she cleaned it up a bit for present company." Noelle gathered up her blue paisley umbrella. "Monday morning, then? Here at ten-thirty," she reiterated, then followed Caroline.

Standing, Mary Helen straightened her skirt and checked her wristwatch. Not even noon, and nothing to do but mark time until Monday. For whatever reason, she felt a little uneasy about the wait. Yet maybe Mr. Finn was right. Maybe Erma would call and they would all feel foolish for having worried. She looked to see if her friend was ready to go.

"Let me get your raincoats." Lucy bustled toward Erma's bedroom with Eileen close behind. Mary Helen followed.

The moment she stepped across the threshhold, a dampness made her shiver. Suddenly lightheaded, she stopped. Although the room was chilly, perspiration broke out on her forehead. Her palms felt clammy. She tried to take a deep breath and pull herself together, but she could barely swallow. The inside of her mouth felt so furry. The room was tilting around her.

Could it be the wine on an almost empty stomach? Or was it something else? Something unseen yet felt in Erma's bedroom? Was it the same foreboding—a premonition perhaps, that had made her so uneasy when she awoke this morning?

Don't be silly, old girl. Those things only happen in your mystery stories, Mary Helen told herself. Yet she could feel her legs begin to tremble. She grabbed for the end of Erma's bed to keep from falling.

"Glory be to God, you look like the wreck of the *Hesperus*." Eileen stood in front of her, a damp raincoat in each hand. "Sit down." She nodded toward the bed. "Quickly!"

Still holding on, Mary Helen stumbled, then sat heavily on the foot of Erma's bed. "All of a sudden, I'm just a little dizzy."

"Put your head between your knees." Lucy was beside Eileen in a moment. "Breathe deeply."

Closing her eyes, Mary Helen did as she was told. The last thing anyone needed this morning was for her to faint.

The dizziness passed slowly. She blinked her eyes open and it was then that she saw it hanging down from under the edge of the bed: a gold chain with a large filigree-edged medal dangling from it. It was caught, caught on a bedspring. Mary Helen's heart gave a jolt. The medal looked familiar. Where had she seen it before? Her mind flashed back to New York, to Bloomingdale's. The mugging! Erma's medal. That's what it was! She could see Erma, her chubby hand covering her throat. Her brown eyes troubled. What had she said? *I don't know what I would do if anything ever happened to this.* Could it be the same—

Crouching down on the floor, Mary Helen dug at the spring from underneath the bed. She couldn't reach it. She tilted her head to take a better look through her bifocals. Kneeling, she lifted the edge of the mattress and stuck her hand into one of the metal spirals.

"Jesus, Mary, and Joseph!" She heard Eileen before she felt her grabbing at her shoulders. "What in the name of God are you doing? What has gotten into you?"

"It's Erma's medal," Mary Helen grunted, short of breath from holding up the mattress. As she spoke the chain came loose.

"Do you remember this?" She stood, medal and chain dangling in front of her. She tried to stop her hand from trembling.

Lucy's horn-rimmed glasses and hazel eyes looked even darker against her pale face. "Erma's Lady of Perpetual Help," she whispered, as if speaking aloud would make the discovery more real. "What can this mean?"

Mary Helen was about to say she wished she knew, when a shrill voice cut through the room: "Mommy's medal!" She had forgotten Ree was still there.

"I knew it! Something has happened to her. She would never leave without that medal. Never, never, never!" With each staccato *never*, Ree's voice rose higher and higher.

One look at her contorted face told Mary Helen that the young woman was nearly out of control. "Your mother may have accidentally left it behind," she said, hoping to calm her down. "Perhaps she doesn't even know it's gone yet," she continued as logically as the hollow feeling in her heart would allow.

"Why don't we just put it on her dresser? When she phones you can tell her it is here." Hoping to distract her, Mary Helen held out the medal and chain toward Ree. She smiled, expecting Ree to take the necklace.

Instead, the woman looked wildly around the room. "Something has happened," she screeched, beating her fist against her breast. "I just feel it here."

Unfortunately, Mary Helen had the same sinking feeling in about the same place, but two of them falling apart wouldn't help to find anyone.

"Something has happened! I knew it! You see, she'd never leave without it! Why doesn't anyone want to help me find Mommy?" Her face darkened as she threw back her head. Twisting her mouth, she let out a piercing cry.

Unexpectedly, she lunged for the medal but caught Mary Helen's forearm instead. Digging her fingers into the flesh, she began to shake her arm. "Never, never, never would she go without her medal! Why won't you believe me?" Her dark eyes blazed.

Good night, nurse! Mary Helen thought, trying hard to keep her balance. What do I do now? She could feel Ree's strong fingers setting her whole body churning.

"Stop it! Stop!" It was Lucy who came to her senses first. She threw her short arms around Ree, or at least as far around as they would go, and wrenched her away. "Come on, sweetie, settle down. Sit a minute," she cooed, trying to lead her toward the bed.

"Let me go!" Flailing, Ree clawed at Lucy's grasp. "I've got to find Mommy! I've got to!"

"Sister Eileen, get some brandy from under the sink." Literally dragging the hysterical woman toward the bed, Lucy pushed her down and held her firmly. "Calm down!" she commanded, struggling against Ree's sudden strength.

Cold water . . . splash her with cold water . . . Mary Helen remembered rushing into the bathroom to moisten a facecloth. Was that for hysteria or temper tantrums? she wondered, flinging the dripping cloth over the woman's anguished face. Whichever, it worked.

Suddenly shocked, Ree caught a sharp breath.

"Here, dear. Sip slowly." Eileen held a glass of brandy close to Ree's lips.

Pushing the glass away, Ree crumpled onto the bed and

buried her pudgy face in the pillow. Shoulders heaving, she began to sob. The three OWLs waited, silently watching.

All at once Mary Helen felt exhausted, as though someone had pulled a stopper and all her energy had run down the drain. No wonder! It had been quite a morning.

She rubbed her sore arm, thankful once again that she did not bruise easily. Although she didn't actually believe in omens the way Eileen did, she should have suspected when she woke this morning with that uneasy feeling that the day was not going to be a good one. So far, it was turning out much worse than she could possibly have predicted.

First no word about Erma. Next Junior and Mr. Finn nearly coming to blows. Then finding Erma's medal. Now Ree's hysteria. And it was barely lunchtime! She would have to check with Eileen to see if there was a full moon!

Sniffling, sobbing, hiccuping, Ree began to calm down. She pulled her tear-streaked face from the pillow, sat up, and reached for the glass of brandy.

"I'm sorry." Her voice was thick. "But I know something awful has happened." Puffy and flushed, she looked helplessly from face to face. "My mother never goes anywhere without that medal."

Much as Mary Helen hated to admit it, Erma's daughter was probably right.

"What should we do?" Ree's swollen eyes were pleading.

Do? If we had any sense, Eileen and I would go straight home and take a nap, Mary Helen thought. We'd let the group handle this thing on Monday. That's what we'd do, if we had any sense. But what good ever comes from being too sensible?

"What should we do?" Ree repeated, then moaned.

Mary Helen's stomach jumped. She wasn't sure she could handle another attack of hysteria. "Do? I know exactly what we should not do," she said.

Straightening her shoulders, she took a deep breath, prayed for fortitude, and pushed her bifocals up the bridge of her nose. "We should not wait until Monday morning. Get your coats, girls. Pull yourself together, Ree. We are going directly to the old Northern Station and report this to Inspector Honore." She sincerely hoped he had drawn weekend duty.

* * *

"Oh, there you are, Inspector," Mary Helen called cheerfully, hoping she didn't sound like a poor imitation of Billie Burke playing the Good Witch of the North. Except for Honore, the large room was deserted. Apparently the Northern Station was closed. Rather than being on call, Inspector Honore may have come in to catch up on some paperwork, Mary Helen suspected.

She couldn't tell from the frozen expression on his face whether he was glad or sorry to see them. She did, however, have her suspicions.

Momentarily she felt a twinge of guilt for upsetting his morning, but only momentarily. Her morning left his in the dust.

Carefully avoiding the old Royal typewriter on a rickety stand, she led her three companions down the narrow aisle to the far end of the station room.

"Don't stand," she said when Honore pushed back his swivel chair. "We'll just sit." She surveyed the room for chairs.

Inspector Honore's mother must have trained him better than that, she surmised, because he stood nevertheless.

"You remember Sister Eileen." Mary Helen pointed to her friend, then felt silly. This man, after all, was in Missing Persons. How could he ever find anyone if he couldn't recognize a nun he'd met yesterday?

He extended his pawlike hand. Mary Helen watched the seams of his jacket strain as Eileen and he shook hands. Apparently he had either done some weight lifting or put on a few pounds since buying the suit.

"This is Mrs. Lucy Lyons, a good friend of the woman I told you about."

Honore gave a hint of a smile. Not even a sphinx could help but smile back at Lucy.

Finally she introduced Ree. Honore, she noticed, did not miss the girl's red face or her puffy eyes.

"What can I do for you, ladies?" He pulled over enough wooden chairs from the surrounding desks for all of them to sit down.

Again, his jacket seams strained as he reached into the inside pocket and extracted a Plen T Pak of Doublemint gum, the kind with seventeen sticks. He reminded her so much of Kojak that she had half expected him to pull out some Tootsie Pops. Inspector Honore offered the half-empty pack to the four women. When they refused, he peeled two sticks and pleated them into his mouth.

"Trying to quit smoking," he explained.

The tight balls of silver foil in his ashtray indicated he was having quite a struggle. Honore cracked the wad in his mouth three times in just one chew.

"We've discovered something that makes us think that Erma Duran did not go to St. Louis. Or if she did, there are some mighty suspicious circumstances," Mary Helen began, not wasting any time. With her nerves as frayed as they were, she wasn't sure how long she'd be able to stand the gum-cracking.

"And what was it you discovered, Sister?" Honore settled back in his chair, rocking slightly.

"My mother's medal and chain." Ree dangled the gold medallion over the desk. Dropping it on top, she pointed despairingly at it. "She'd never leave without that," she said. Her voice had an edge on it.

"You're the daughter, ma'am?"

Obviously not trusting herself to speak, Ree nodded and fumbled in her coat pocket for a handkerchief.

"She's very upset, Inspector," Lucy explained, although Mary Helen was sure the inspector hadn't missed that. "We were all upset when we found it. As Marie said, Erma would never go anywhere without that medal."

"Never," Ree repeated, her large eyes filling with tears.

Popping his gum, Honore rocked back in his chair and looked from woman to woman.

Trying to decide whether we are just being emotional or whether we are on to something that he shouldn't ignore, Mary Helen thought. And we really can't blame him. The gold medal and chain bunched up on his blotter did seem pretty insignificant for such a fuss.

Adjusting her bifocals, Mary Helen tried to look as level-headed and sensible as possible. "That is why," she said, "we have come to file an official missing-person report."

Honore hesitated, as if he were about to say something. Instead, he rummaged through the wire basket on the corner of his desk. Finally he dug out a report form.

"Lots of missing persons turn up, Sister." He foraged through his pencil holder until he located a sharpened one. "Sooner or later, anyway."

Good night, nurse! I hope he's better at finding people than he is at locating his paper and pencil! Impatiently, Mary Helen scooted forward in her chair.

"But let's fill out a report, anyway, ma'am." Honore turned the form sideways toward Ree. His tone said, *If it'll make you feel better.*

Mary Helen strained to see. Her stomach gave a turn when she read SUSPICIOUS CIRCUMSTANCES/FOUL PLAY clearly printed at the top.

Ree answered Inspector Honore's questions calmly, stumbling a little only over waist and bra size, which was understandable. One seldom thinks about those things in reference to one's mother. Also, Mary Helen noticed that Erma's daughter hesitated when he asked, "Probable destination?"

The police officer must have noticed too.

"What makes you think she didn't go to St. Louis, ma'am?" he asked, cracking his gum again.

Mary Helen watched the young woman's lower lip quiver. Oh, no! she thought. If the man even suspects we are being too emotional, one of Ree's scenes will convince him he is right.

"She'd never go without her medal, Officer." The words caught in Ree's throat. "That's what makes me think that something bad has . . ." Poor Ree could go no further.

Again, Honore reached into his jacket pocket for his pack of gum. He peeled a piece and added it to the other two. Mary Helen wondered absently just how many pieces the fellow could chew at one time without his jaw getting sore.

"I know you ladies are worried." He cracked the wad. "But what I'm trying to say is that lots of times older people go away for a while. Take a trip, you know. Their families get all upset, naturally. When they get back, they can't figure out what all the fuss was about."

He paused and grinned. Almost patronizingly, Mary Helen thought.

"They just forget to tell anyone. Maybe on purpose, maybe not. All the *proof* you have that Mrs. Duran has met with foul play is this medal"—with his big hand he turned the medallion over—"and your feelings."

Mary Helen bristled. She could feel her blood pressure rising. The inspector's implication was clear. Erma was an old woman and, therefore, a bit dotty. Not only Erma, but Lucy and Eileen and herself as well. And Ree he had discounted completely! She could understand that their evidence was scanty, but really!

She set her lips. Her dimples must have started to show because she felt Eileen pat her knee with her take-it-easy-old-girl pat.

"Forgot to tell anyone!" Mary Helen said as evenly as she could manage. "Let me tell you something, young man. Erma

Duran is a member of our OWL chapter—Older Women's League, if you are unfamiliar with the acronym.

"Mrs. Duran, who, incidentally, is a college graduate, heads our committee on social-security reform. And, I might add, quite successfully. She has been active in helping welfare mothers, promoting senior-citizen health programs, and coordinating several letter-writing campaigns. In addition, she holds down a job."

And probably keeps her employer and her children from killing one another, she wanted to add, but thought better of it. Old woman, indeed!

She glanced over at her companions. Both Eileen and Lucy were nodding, indignant expressions on their faces. Of the three, only poor Ree looked a bit "spacey," as Sister Anne would say. And that had nothing at all to do with age.

"And as for the medal, Inspector, it is a very precious possession of a very alert and intelligent woman."

Poor Inspector Honore had stopped midchew. Sister Mary Helen suppressed an urge to smile. The big black Kojak looked for all the world as though someone had taken the proverbial wind smack out of his sails.

"Sister, I wasn't implying—" he began.

"I should hope not, Inspector," she said quickly, hoping to spare the fellow the rest of the fib. Mary Helen settled back in the wooden chair. "Now can we get on with the report?"

Looking eager to get their business finished and be rid of them, Inspector Honore thumbed through the wire basket on the corner of his desk and pulled out yet another form.

"Will you sign this, ma'am?" He shoved the paper toward Ree.

Mary Helen winced as she watched Ree's lips move while she read the formal request. It authorized the dentist to release poor, dear old Erma's dental records.

*　*　*

The rain had stopped by the time the four women arrived back at Erma's apartment. Narrow patches of blue were beginning to show in the gray sky. Droplets of water stood out on the waxed hood of Lucy's silver Mercedes. In fact, they had come back to the building so that Lucy could pick up her car.

"See you on Monday morning, Sisters," she said. She turned the key and her heavy engine purred into action. Slowly the automatic window moved down. Mary Helen couldn't help noting the worried frown on Lucy's usually cheerful face.

"It will all work out. You'll see!" she said, feigning good spirits. With a wave, she made a quick U-turn and disappeared up Sanchez Street toward her home.

Watching the silver car disappear, Mary Helen had the sudden urge to go home herself. She'd have a cup of soup, some hot buttered toast, then take a short nap. One look at Eileen and she knew her friend would be open to the suggestion.

Mary Helen turned toward Ree. Much as she would have liked to, she just couldn't leave her standing there on the wet corner. "Can we drop you at your house?"

Ree shook her head, then sniffled. "I was going to go into Mommy's for a minute. There might be something else in there." Those big doe eyes looked pleadingly from nun to nun. Mary Helen knew what was coming before Ree said it. "Will you come with me? I don't want to go in there alone. I won't stay long, I promise."

* * *

Mary Helen felt uncomfortable going through Erma's dresser drawers. Although they were sparse and tidy, a lot tidier than her own, she noticed, she just did not feel right. And she tried to avoid altogether looking at the black loose-leaf binder propped against the nightstand. Not that she would have touched it. Heaven forbid! Going through someone's drawers was bad enough, but to invade another's privacy by reading a journal! Whatever the circumstances, it was unthinkable.

For all they knew, the woman was perfectly safe somewhere and having a wonderful time. She'd be horrified to know that someone had pawed through her things.

Apparently Eileen was having trouble with the search, too, since the moment it started she excused herself to make them all a steaming cup of tea.

Furthermore, Mary Helen didn't have the slightest idea what she should be looking for. These considerations didn't stop Erma's daughter. Ree had taken off her padded jacket and was rummaging through the closet and the nightstand, looking through old letters. Her ponytail swinging, she was generally "invading privacy," as the saying goes.

Then, as if suddenly exhausted, the young woman plopped onto the end of her mother's bed. The springs creaked under her weight.

"I knew it!" she muttered. "I just knew that something's happened."

A cold chill ran up Mary Helen's spine. The fatalism in Ree's voice made the hair on her neck prickle. "What do you mean?" she asked. "How do you know something's happened?"

Letting her double chin sink to her breastbone, Ree wagged her head back and forth. "The check not coming. Bills piling up. Mommy being so worried before she went to the convention in New York. I just knew it!"

Sitting down beside her, Mary Helen put her arm around Ree's chubby shoulders. "Did you ever ask your mother what was troubling her?"

"Yes, I asked her, but Mommy would never say. You know how she was, always wanting to make everyone happy. The most she ever did was point to that." Turning, she stared accusingly at the large picture of Our Lady of Perpetual Help on the shelf in the corner as if the Madonna were somehow to blame. " 'She'll take care of it,' Mommy said. 'And if anything should happen to me, look there.' "

Crossing the bedroom, Mary Helen stood in front of the picture. The large, sorrowful eyes of the Byzantine Madonna stared at her knowingly, sympathetically. The Christ Child in her arms, looking frightened, had one sandal dangling from His small foot. In each of the upper corners, an archangel hovered. One held a pot of hyssop, a sponge, and a spear, the other a large cross—clearly, the instruments of the Child's passion and death.

Was Erma just being pious, or was there something there? The Erma Mary Helen knew may have been pious, but she was also practical. You don't suppose she had taped a note or letter to the back? That only happens in mystery stories, old girl, she reminded herself, but just maybe . . . Mary Helen couldn't resist. She removed the picture and carefully checked it inch by inch, patting the backing for an extra bulge.

Except for a layer of dust, the brown paper back of the picture was absolutely clear and flat. Only a small gold tag said that it had been purchased at Kaufer-Stadler Religious Goods Store on Market Street. Feeling a little foolish, Mary Helen hung the picture back on the hook.

"Right after we drink this, why don't we all go home and take a little rest?" Eileen appeared in the doorway holding a tray. Mary Helen could see the steam rising from the three mugs. The sharp tang of orange filled the room.

"Sister Eileen's right." Mary Helen handed Ree a mug and took one herself.

"For all we know, Mr. Finn's hunch may be correct." Eileen pursed her lips. "Your mother may just call tomorrow."

"That's right." Mary Helen patted the woman's knee. "After all, Sunday is Mother's Day!" As soon as the words left her mouth, she wished she could catch them and push them back in again.

Ree's dark eyes filled immediately and tears ran down her dimpled cheeks.

"Let me take you home." Mary Helen pretended she didn't

notice the tears. "You've had—we've all had—a very hectic morning."

Much to her relief, Ree wiped her cheeks with the back of her hand, sniffled, and stood up. "I live only a couple of blocks away." She tugged at the back of her overblouse.

Silently, Eileen gathered up the cups to rinse. Mary Helen handed Ree her jacket. Without comment she put it on. Looking remarkably like a Chinese pincushion, she walked into the living room and down the stairs.

Alone in the bedroom, Mary Helen snatched up the binder. After all, whatever was troubling Erma could well be written in her journal. From what Ree had just said, it was abundantly clear to Mary Helen that Erma did not want her daughter to know what it was. And with all this going through Erma's things, Mary Helen had no way of telling just how long it would be before Ree discovered the binder.

She flipped through it. To her surprise most of the pages were blank. Erma had written on only a few. Quickly she ripped them out and shoved them into the side compartment of her pocketbook, where they would stay for safekeeping. Knowing Erma would be grateful, she zipped it shut.

* * *

"My house is right down here." Ree pointed to a narrow street, really an alley, off 17th. The street sign read PROSPER. With a felt-tipped pen, some wag had added ITY.

The wooden houses along the short street might have once known prosperity, but no more. Several fronts extended at least six feet above the natural roofs. Mary Helen remembered reading some local history buff's claim that the Italianate fronts were crafted back East, then shipped to the City. When they arrived it was clear that they were six feet too high. Immediately an Eastern extended roof became all the rage.

"The next one." Ree pointed. Mary Helen pulled up to a pink house with long, narrow bay windows and fretwork along the top of its front.

"That's my apartment." Ree pointed again, this time to a door and square window cut into what was once the basement. A flat metal mailbox by the door indicated a bona-fide apartment. Iron-blue hydrangeas bloomed in small patches on either side of the door.

"Aren't those lovely!" Eileen remarked, to make conversation, Mary Helen assumed.

Ree just shrugged.

"Someone once told me he got that color by putting nails in the ground around them." Eileen's voice ended the sentence somewhere between a question and a statement. It was that old Irish trick again. No one commented. What was there to say?

After several tries, Ree struggled out of the backseat. "Thanks for the ride." She slammed the door of the Nova.

"Get some rest," Eileen called after her.

Silently, the two nuns watched her walk up the cement path.

"What do you make of it, old dear?" Eileen asked as soon as the apartment door shut. "She seems suddenly unseasonably calm."

"I don't know what to think. I'm so tired. I hope Allan Boscacci has the garage door fixed because I don't think I have the strength to push it." Carefully, Mary Helen backed out of the alley. "One thing I do know: I am going to take some of your advice."

"And what advice is that?" Eileen looked pleased.

"The part about getting some rest." Mary Helen smiled over at her friend. "After we get some soup, Eileen, let's take a nap."

"Just like a couple of old lassies?" Eileen asked in mock horror.

"Don't be silly! It has absolutely nothing to do with getting old. Anyone—why, even Sister Anne—would be done in by our hectic morning."

*   *   *

Kate Murphy was clearing her desk when her phone rang.

"Just our luck," Dennis Gallagher grumbled, watching her remove an earring. "Bad enough we got the duty on Saturday, but quitting time and we get a damn call."

"You guys about ready to close it up?" Kate was surprised to hear Ron Honore's voice on the other end of the line. Somehow, she would have expected him to be home showering for a heavy date.

She nodded at Gallagher, who was giving her a who-the-hell-is-it? look. "Honore," she mouthed to her partner, who was shifting impatiently.

"We were just about ready to," she said into the phone.

"How about you two meeting me in, say, half an hour at Fahey's? Bring Jack too. I can use all the advice I can get."

Kate hesitated, wondering if either Gallagher or Jack, who had been home cleaning the house all day, had any plans.

"Just for half an hour or so," Honore added.

His voice was so serious Kate began to worry. "Is there something wrong, Ron?"

"Wrong? Not unless you consider meeting Famine, Pestilence, Destruction, and Death something wrong."

"Pardon me?"

"The Four Horsemen of the Apocalypse."

Kate was impressed. She would have thought Honore's Four Horsemen would have been Stuhldreher, Miller, Crowley, and Layden from Notre Dame.

"Or should I say, *horsewomen*?" Honore continued. "Your two nuns pals and two more of their cronies were in today."

So that was it. Kate laughed.

"It isn't funny." Ron sounded offended.

She couldn't resist. "Gee, Ron, I don't know." She paused, baiting him. "It is Saturday night. That's a big night on the town. In fact, I'm surprised a bachelor of your reputation isn't home sprucing up for the evening."

"I promise it won't take long," he said, paying no attention to her jibe. "And, I'm buying."

Kate waited, listening to the phone line click in the silence.

"You did get me into this, you know."

A touch of the old Honore she knew and loved. She cleared her throat, letting him dangle.

"Oh, please, Kate. Give me a break."

"Okay, for a few minutes." Kate wondered for a moment if any sound could be as sweet as the sound of the cocky Inspector Honore begging.

*   *   *

Luckily, Gallagher found a parking space on Taraval Street where the Parkside branch of the library meets McCopp Park, about a block up from Fahey's Saloon. Hands in pockets, he started down toward 24th Avenue. The wind whipping up Taraval pulled at his coat, flung his tie over his shoulder, and pushed his pants legs against his shins.

Shivering, Kate, trying to use her partner's bulk as a windshield, followed half behind him to the corner. Together the pair dashed across the intersection.

"God Almighty, I'll need two straight shots," Gallagher panted, "just to get my blood unfrozen." He held the half door of Fahey's open. "After you."

Inside, the long, narrow bar was warm and cozy. The jukebox near the entrance played softly. On the back wall over the electric scoreboard, a wooden sign announced FAHEY'S SALOON, WHERE THE ELITE MEET!

Kate blinked, letting her eyes adjust to the darkness.

"Well, if it isn't a couple more of San Francisco's finest!" Kate heard the voice of Snooky, the bartender, before she saw him.

"And look who it is too." Snooky put down the glass he was wiping and looked at her over his horn-rimmed glasses. "Although I should have guessed when your better half came in."

Jack waved from a round table in the back. Honore and he

were already there, sitting under the leaping sailfish mounted on the wall.

"Long time no see." Snooky came around the end of the bar and gave Kate a hug. "Marriage seems to be agreeing with you," he said, inspecting her at arm's distance. "You look great!"

Several customers on the bar stools turned to double-check Snooky's opinion.

Kate blushed. "It's good to see you too," she said, and it was. Snooky was like part of the family. His brother was with the sheriff's department and he had an uncle and a cousin or two who were cops.

The tavern was as warm and friendly as Snooky. It was one of those old-fashioned neighborhood bars, the kind San Francisco once had lots of, where people, cops included, could go just to sit, visit, and unwind. As a matter of fact, on any given night, but especially when the 49ers were playing, Fahey's was probably the best-protected tavern in the Parkside District.

"What's your pleasure tonight?" Snooky asked. "It's on the house."

"Not tonight. Honore's paying tonight." Kate winked at the astonished Snooky. "I'll take a rain check on your offer," she said.

"What the hell is this all about?" Gallagher asked Honore as soon as they sat down in the wooden captain's chairs. "Last night I complained that we didn't get fish on Friday anymore, so tonight Mrs. G. is poaching salmon for my dinner. My mouth's been watering for it all day. It better be important."

Honore gave a self-conscious little shrug and asked what they were drinking. Raising his arm, he called their order, three beers and one straight shot, over to Snooky.

Kate noticed the seams of his coat sleeve pull. Honore had put on a little weight since she'd last seen him.

"Given up smoking." He took off his jacket and hung it over

the back of his chair. "Now everything I own is strangling me."

Snooky put the drinks on the table. "And that ain't all. Don Ron here is the only guy I know who drinks beer and chews gum at the same time."

Gallagher looked at his watch. Honore got the hint.

"I appreciate you guys coming over." He studied the ring his beer glass had made on the tabletop.

Being beholden was not going to be easy for Honore, Kate figured. She was tempted to let him squirm, but her curiosity was getting the better of her.

"You said the nuns came by today? What happened?"

"That was my first mistake," he said. "I should never have told you to have them come by at all. I should have sent them right to the local station where they belonged." Honore wagged his head solemnly. "Actually Northern Station was closed today. I was just there for a few hours catching up on some paperwork. God, there's a lot of paperwork in Missing Persons!"

"What happened?" Kate insisted.

"Nothing really happened while they were there," he said. "Nothing I could put my finger on. A lady friend of theirs is a hostess in a restaurant. Nobody's heard from her for a few days. All in all, it was a pretty routine report. One where I'd put out the usual feelers. You know, question people who saw her last, et cetera. Actually, my common sense tells me there's nothing to get excited about. No signs of foul play. The woman probably went away for a couple of days, forgot to tell people or maybe didn't tell them on purpose. Who knows?" Honore shrugged.

"But they were so damn convincing. Especially that older nun, that Sister Mary Helen. I began to doubt my own horse sense."

"That one'll get you every time!" Gallagher mumbled. "And watch out for the sidekick too. Looks innocent as the day is long. But those two gals could sell you your own shoes and make you glad you bought them."

Honore stuck another piece of gum into the wad in his mouth. "The daughter—and if she isn't a lulu!—was with them this time. She brought this gold medal in, see. Dangled it in front of me. Then she claims the missing woman wouldn't go anywhere without it. That's how they all figured out something bad had happened to her. Now that is crazy, I told myself. I'm a policeman, and yet I can get out of my car and forget to take my keys."

Kate stared. Honore must have been affected. He was even suggesting he could have a weakness.

"Not often." He recovered quickly. "But it has happened. Now, that was around noon. The whole thing is a routine matter. Ordinarily, I'd get to it on Monday morning in a routine way."

"I hear a *but* coming." Jack took the last swallow of his beer. Honore held up his hand for a second round.

"But the damn thing's been on my mind ever since they first came in. Like I say, I figured the lady just wanted to get away for a couple of days and they were overreacting. It happens more than you think in my department. It's not like she was senile or anything and wandered away. And it is a free country, you know."

He looked from officer to officer, waiting for someone to disagree. When no one did, he went on. "So, like I say, I played it down. But the more I think about it, the more something just isn't setting right. Nothing I can put my finger on. Just a funny feeling in my gut. Makes me wonder if something really did happen to her."

"Whoa!" Gallagher pushed his shot glass to the middle of the table, ready for Snooky to set down the second. "No you don't, fella! I've had my bellyful of those two nuns."

"That's why I wanted to talk to you guys. I know you've had dealings with them. And I don't know why it is . . ."

Honore's broad finger traced the water ring on the table. Kate sensed he was working up courage.

The man shrugged, a silly smile on his ebony face. "But nuns have always spooked me."

Kate couldn't believe it. The arrogant, smooth-talking Honore had a chink in his armor! Even the glimpse of something vulnerable squirming inside made him instantly a little easier to tolerate. "Why?" she asked. "Aren't you a Catholic?"

"Yeah, I'm a Catholic, all right. Every Creole from New Orleans is Catholic. At least, I was baptized one. But they spooked me even as a kid. Something about the long habits, only their faces and hands showing . . . In New Orleans we had the ones with the white wings on their heads. Coming down the street, the wings flapping like doves . . . I thought it was the goddamn Holy Ghost coming toward me. Scared the hell out of me."

"Oh, for heaven's sake, Ron, you're a grown man! And these Sisters don't wear habits." Kate rubbed it in.

"But they still have those eyes. Like they can look right through you and see if you go to church on Sunday. And the damn thing's been bothering me all day."

"Going to church on Sunday?" Kate couldn't help herself.

"You know damn well what I mean. Do you think they really have an inside track on stuff?"

"Hey, Denny"—Jack slapped Gallagher on the back—"you give him the word. You're our resident expert on nuns."

Gallagher threw back the rest of his shot, wiped his mouth with the palm of his hand, and banged the glass on the table. "Not me, fella. As far as I'm concerned, you're on your own. Yes, sir. They're all yours. I wouldn't touch them again with a ten-foot pole.

"As far as I can see, the whole thing's going to pot. It's beyond me why the Pope can't keep nuns in the convent where they belong." He stood and hitched up his pants. "If you ask me, the whole goddamn Church has gone amuck. Nuns without habits, priests talking English at Mass, altars turned any which way, Sunday Mass on Saturday!

"But you know the worst of it?" Gallagher paused to stick the stub of his cigar into the corner of his mouth. "The worst thing of all was giving up fish on Friday. God, how I loved poached salmon!"

May 13

Fifth Sunday of Easter
Mother's Day

"Looks like Pinelli's Florist made a killing," Jack Bassetti whispered, following Kate up the aisle of St. Thomas's Church. He was right. Nearly every woman at the ten-thirty Mass had a Mother's Day corsage pinned to her lapel.

Most were the traditional five-flower variety: some, carnations with pink ribbon; some, white roses with silver. Here and there Kate spotted an orchid. Even the little old ladies she always saw in church had an added splash of color pinned to their black wool coats.

Waiting for Mass to begin, she noticed some of the young mothers, the ones who usually rushed in late, dragging sniffling, hastily dressed youngsters. This morning they were beaming, looking calm and peaceful. Even the children seemed tidier. Several middle-aged women, whom she could have sworn were widows, today walked down the aisle on the arms of middle-aged husbands.

The entire congregation had a warm, mellow feeling. The

same kind of glow that happens on Christmas Eve and Easter morning. Kate forced herself to smile back at the slim woman who stopped at the edge of her pew. She nudged Jack. The two of them slid over, making room for the woman and three fellows looking like halfbacks in lettermen sweaters stumbling in behind her.

"Happy Mother's Day!" the woman whispered to Kate. Kate wondered for a moment what the Mother's-Day equivalent of "bah, humbug!" might be.

By the time they were ready to go to Mama Bassetti's for dinner, Kate thought her mood would have improved, but it hadn't. Not that Jack didn't try. After Mass he had taken her to a fancy brunch in a quaint new place on Union Street. Several times during the meal he had assured her that Mother's Day was nothing more than a commercial venture started by Hallmark Cards, Inc.

Two billion Chinese, he had reminded her in desperation, didn't even know today was Mother's Day. "Furthermore," he had added, running his fingers through his curly hair, "they don't give a damn!"

But nothing had worked. Much as she hated to admit it, Kate was in a Mother's-Day funk. In the shower she had even shed a few tears, thinking of her own mother, missing her, wishing she were still alive. Kate hadn't done that in years. On the way out the door, she tried hard to conceal the sudden surge of fury she felt when Jack forgot to pick up his mother's gift from the hall table. In the end she had bought it, and he couldn't even remember to take it along.

The ride from their house in the Richmond through Golden Gate Park to Mrs. Bassetti's in the Sunset was short. Too short, Kate thought, staring out the car window, trying to calm down.

She studied all the shades of green along John F. Kennedy Drive. They passed clumps of spring-green bordered by evergreen-green. The pale yellowy-green of the large fern blended with the grasshopper-green of new leaves. Here and there, spinach-green dandelion stems shot up in a marble-green lawn. Green, someone had told her, had a tranquilizing effect on people. Kate hoped that whoever had said it was right.

She was happy to see several family cars already parked in front of her mother-in-law's house. Both of Jack's sisters were there and his cousin Enid with the baby, his uncle Pasquale. Good! By now Kate figured there would be so much talking that no one would even notice her mood.

"Jackie! Kate! Here you are at last, thank God." Mrs. Bassetti flung open the front door before they had a chance to ring the bell. "I was afraid something happened to you."

Even though Kate was beginning to realize Mama Bassetti greeted all her guests that way, she was annoyed. She glanced at her watch. Her mother-in-law had said four. It was only ten past. She looked at Jack, waiting for him to answer.

Jack acted as though he hadn't heard a thing. "Hi, Ma! Happy Mother's Day!" He put his arms around the small woman, picked her up, planted a loud kiss on both her flushed cheeks, then put her down.

"Something smells delicious." Jack handed his mother her gift and took Kate's jacket.

"Italian pot roast. Your favorite," Mama Bassetti said. With her free hand she straightened her shirtmaker dress. The pale blue silk of the dress made her eyes sparkle. Or was it the sight of her only son, Kate wondered.

"Richard at Petrini's saved me a good piece. But come in now." She closed the front door. "Say hello to your sisters, your cousins, your uncle." Mama pointed out each relative as if Jack might have forgotten who they were. "And make me an old-fashioned. My tongue is hanging out."

"Mama won't let anybody else mix her one," Jack's older sister, Angela, began as Kate followed her husband around the room, shaking hands. "Nobody does it like Jackie!" Angela mimicked her mother.

"Oh, for God's sake, Angie!" His younger sister, Gina, blew out a stream of smoke from the thin brown cigarette she was holding. "It's Mother's Day! You're not going to start that Mother-always-loved-you-best routine, are you?"

Fortunately Enid's baby squealed and most of the attention focused on him. Kate glanced toward her mother-in-law. She wondered how the woman was coping with her grown children's squabbling.

Mama seemed engrossed in unwrapping her present, oblivious of the whole scene. Carefully she smoothed out the gift paper, then opened the narrow blue and silver box.

"My God, it's from Tiffany," Angie remarked to no one in particular. "Jackie wouldn't even know how to get there. Kate must have bought it."

Mama Bassetti lifted the delicate chain from the box. An old-fashioned silver locket dangled at the end. She opened the small, hinged case, then looked hopefully at Kate. "Is this telling me I'm going to be a *nonnie*?"

Kate's stomach gave a sudden lurch. A familiar lump, the one she had felt on and off all day, filled her throat. She swallowed. How stupid of her! Of course the woman would think that. How much Kate wished she could announce that she was pregnant. Shaking her head, she blinked her eyes to force back the tears.

"It's Zio," Gina shouted, mercifully changing the subject as the doorbell rang.

Mama put her locket, box, and wrappings on the end table and bustled toward the front door. The old man, whose real name no one had ever told Kate, stood in the doorway smiling, a big black cigar in the corner of his mouth.

"Zio, here you are at last, thank God!" Mrs. Bassetti helped him out of his worn overcoat. "I was afraid something had happened to you. Jackie, make Zio a drink."

Kate chose the moment to escape to the quiet of the back bedroom. "Pull yourself together," she said aloud, glaring at her image in the ornate mirror over the old-fashioned bureau. "You can't go to pieces every time someone mentions motherhood. They'll be putting you away." Taking a deep breath, she dabbed her eyes and blew her nose.

It was that damn pamphlet that was upsetting her. She never should have picked it up in the gynecologist's office. Besides stress, smoking, and poor nutrition, a cursory reading had disclosed at least eight other causes of infertility. Plus, she had discovered the disturbing fact that fifteen percent of all couples cannot conceive. Stalling for a little more time, Kate pulled a comb through her short red hair. Then, although she knew it didn't need it, she freshened her lipstick. Actually, the only ray of hope she had discovered in the whole blasted pamphlet was that couples are not considered infertile until after six months of trying. Jack and she, however, were getting dangerously close.

After thoroughly brushing specks of imaginary dandruff from the shoulder of her cowl-neck sweater, she turned toward the full-length mirror on the closet door to check if her slip was showing below her flared skirt. Instead, she was startled to see her mother-in-law leaning against the doorjamb, studying her.

Her arms were folded; her pudgy face was wrinkled into something between a pucker and a frown.

"So, Kate, whatsa matter?" Mama Bassetti never beat around the bush. "You're upset." Before Kate could decide what to answer, Jack's mother went on. "About my asking about grandkids, right? And I got a feeling right here"—Mama pressed her small, tight fist into the middle of her ample bosom—"that something is wrong."

As her eyes begin to fill again, Kate turned away and sat on the edge of the bed. Before she could get a tissue out of her skirt pocket, her mother-in-law was beside her, a chubby arm around Kate's waist.

"You want to get pregnant and can't. That's what it is, right?"

All Kate trusted herself to do was nod. With one finger she traced the snowflake pattern in the crocheted bedspread.

"That's hard when you're first a young bride, I know. Although, God knows, you two had plenty of practice before you got married."

Kate could feel her face redden. Would her mother-in-law ever let that go?

As though she had never made the remark, Mrs. Bassetti moved her arm up to pat Kate's shoulder.

"When I first married Jackie's father, we tried and tried—but nothing! It was embarrassing. I knew his mother was wondering. My mother was wondering. Lots of times when Jackie's papa had gone to work and I was alone in this empty house, I would cry all morning."

"What happened?" Kate wanted to ask, but the words would not come. Fortunately there was no need. She should have known that when Mrs. Bassetti had something to say, she didn't need prompting.

"My neighbor next door was Mrs. O'Shea. Mrs. O'Shea was right from the old country. Had six kids, all grown. One day, I'm in the backyard hanging out the laundry and crying. Mrs. O'Shea comes to the fence. 'What is it that's troubling you, Mrs. B.?' she says.

"Although I was shy about telling anyone—people didn't talk about those kinds of things then—I blurted it right out and I'm glad I did.

"Mrs. O'Shea went into her house and came back with a bottle of gold-colored liquid. And it turned out to be pure gold." Mama Bassetti paused. Kate could tell that, for a moment, the older woman was deep in memories.

" 'It's St. Gerard oil,' she says to me. 'St. Gerard is the patron saint of expectant mothers and safe births.'

" 'But I'm not expecting—that's my problem,' I says to her, trying hard not to bust out crying again.

" 'No matter,' my neighbor says. 'Let the man stretch himself,' she says. 'What kind of a saint is it that can't go a little out of his way?'

"So, every night after that I rubbed myself with the oil."

"Where?" Kate was fascinated.

"In the middle of my stomach, of course, where the babies come." Mrs. Bassetti frowned, obviously annoyed at a foolish question. "Ten months later Jackie came along. I named him John Gerard for that reason."

Kate had often wondered where Jack's middle name had originated. When she had asked him, he didn't seem to know.

"Twelve months later, Angela, my angel, was born—and fifteen months after that, Gina, my baby. Right after Gina, I put the oil away." Mrs. Bassetti moved toward the bureau drawers.

She pulled out a quilted box hidden deep in the middle drawer and opened it lovingly. "All my special treasures are in here." She lifted the pale green satin lid. "I never let anyone touch them—not the kids, not even my husband. Only Angela tried, said Jackie and Gina put her up to it. I had to use my wooden spoon on all three of them."

Kate nodded, remembering Jack saying that, when it came to discipline, his mother had the fastest wooden spoon in the West.

"After that, nobody touched it—not even Angie." Mama removed a small bottle. On the front the picture of a friar looking piously heavenward had been badly stained. The liquid in the bottle had turned a deep honey color.

"I saved this for a special reason." Mrs. Bassetti handed Kate the container. "This is it. Use it and you'll have a *bambino* in no time."

Kate stared at the bottle in disbelief. The whole notion was preposterous. She knew that the understanding-looking doctor on the cover of her pamphlet would say that it was nothing but pure superstition. Yet she didn't have the heart to tell that to her mother-in-law. Besides, Mama Bassetti would never believe it. Feeling a little foolish, Kate took the bottle and shoved it into her purse.

Mama patted her shoulder. "Babies are such a nice way to start people," she said, her whole face lifting into a smile.

"Where are you, Ma?" Angela's sharp voice cut into the bedroom. "Oh, there you are with that old box. Remember how mad you got when we were kids and I tried to see what was in it? It was Jackie's idea, but I got blamed."

"Oh, for God's sake, when are you going to stop that?" Gina stood behind her sister, clearly exasperated. "We were wondering what happened to you, Ma." Gina took her mother's hand. "The ice in your old-fashioned is melting, and Zio brought you a present. He's dying to have you open it."

"I'll bet it won't be as nice as Jackie's." Angela couldn't seem to stop herself.

Mrs. Bassetti closed her eyes for a moment and sighed just slightly. Opening them, she took Kate's chin in her chubby hand. "Yes, Kate. Babies are a nice way to start people."

Kate just knew that her mother-in-law wanted to add, Even if some of them grow up to be like my Angela.

* * *

Sunday afternoon at Mount St. Francis College was quiet. Many of the nuns who had families in the area had gone home for Mother's Day. Only a skeleton crew remained.

Sister Therese was planning a surprise supper for those at home. Sometime after lunch she had taped a notice on the community room doorjamb: "Something we rarely have," she had written, then underlined "Promptly at six" in red.

"What do you think she has in mind?" Mary Helen asked Sister Eileen who was standing next to her, reading the same note.

"If I were the gambling kind, I'd wager it will be the same

surprise she always fixes." Eileen whispered in case Therese
was within earshot.

"I'm with you." Young Sister Anne came up behind them.
She must have overheard. "I'll bet my new Reeboks"—she
wiggled her toes in her pink tennis shoes—"that it's eggplant
lasagna."

"Yuck!" Mary Helen couldn't help wrinkling her nose.
Somehow, Therese's lasagna always tasted like a cross between
rubber and hot lava. She couldn't imagine what Therese did to
the noodles—or to the eggplant, for that matter.

"If we are having something we rarely get, why not steak?"
she grumbled, then felt guilty. People were starving and she
was complaining about a wholesome meal.

"You do have to admit we rarely have the concoction." Eileen grinned. "Only when Therese gets the urge to surprise us,
which," she added, rolling her eyes, "is mercifully rare."

"Thank God!" Anne had taken the words right out of Mary
Helen's mouth.

* * *

With the business of Erma's apparent disappearance weighing on her mind and Therese's eggplant lasagna in ther imme-
diate future, Mary Helen decided the best thing to do with the
afternoon was to escape for a couple of hours. What better
place than her "thinking spot," the secluded stone bench in a
clearing nestled on the college's hillside. And to aid in her
escape, she'd take along her new detective story. In whodunits,
unlike real-life mysteries, things happen for a reason; violence
is never senseless; and you can count on justice and right being
triumphant. Mary Helen needed to step into that orderly
world, if only for an hour or so.

She stopped by her bedroom to pick up the latest Susan
Dunlap paperback. It was on her desk, neatly tucked into her
plastic prayerbook cover. Beside it was her pocketbook.

She couldn't help noticing the slight bulge of its zippered
compartment. The pages she had snatched to preserve Erma's

privacy, of course, were still there. There were so few of them; yet they might hold some answers or at least give a clue to the answers they so desperately wanted. Under the circumstances —she fiddled with the zipper—it just might be . . .

Unthinkable! Her conscience jumped right in before she finished the idea. No matter what the circumstances, it is absolutely unthinkable to pry, uninvited, into another's intimate thoughts.

Why, wild horses couldn't make me do such a thing! Mary Helen was incensed. Without waiting for her conscience to reply, she grabbed up the paperback.

Lead us not into temptation, she reflected piously, shutting her bedroom door. There was no sense standing there staring at the bulge. How did the old saying go? "I can resist anything but temptation."

Quickly she crossed the deserted campus and took the narrow dirt path jutting off from the main driveway. Yesterday's rain had thoroughly washed the hillside. Mary Helen took a deep breath. The air smelled fresh with the tang of eucalyptus and Scotch pine. The shaded underbrush still had a damp rustle. In its dimness wild flowers and even weeds were blooming in a—a coinage by Hopkins jumped into her mind—in a "May-mess."

She avoided stepping on the rosebud-shaped pine cones that had been blown onto the path, marveling, yet again, that within a few steps of the busy college drive, she felt as if she were in the woods. Several more yards up the hill and she would be as secluded as if she were miles away.

When Mary Helen reached the clearing she was glad to see it flooded with afternoon sun. She touched the bench. It was cold but dry enough to sit on.

Relaxing, she drank in the warmth. Above her was sky. What were those lines from Robert Louis Stevenson? "Under the wide and starry sky, Dig the grave and let me lie."

Such a morbid thought! She shivered. Didn't Eileen have a

saying about a shiver meaning someone was walking on your grave? Pull yourself together, old girl! You came up here to escape. Relieved, she noted that although the sky was wide, it was anything but starry. Billowy white clouds stretched across a canopy of spring-blue.

Wiggling her toes, Mary Helen could feel the dampness in her Sunday shoes. She should have changed them before she walked up the path. The shoes were brand-new and still a little snug. Hoping they weren't ruined, she took them off and put them on the bench beside her.

Lethargically, she circled her toes in the warm sun, yawned, and closed her eyes. She was tired. Who wouldn't be? These last two weeks had been hectic. So much had happened: the wonderful but wearing trip to the convention in New York, and now all this business about Erma.

Time kaleidoscoped and in her mind's eye she saw a young, laughing Erma, with the head of wild, rich brown curls, eagerly researching their long-ago history project. Then, like changing bits of glass, her memory shifted to the same generous Erma who insisted, just weeks ago, that she and Eileen take the trip to New York.

Please, God, don't let anything have happened to her, she prayed silently. Pulling in another deep breath, Mary Helen sighed.

Gradually, the sun warmed her shoulders and she could feel the tension start to ease. She shifted slightly.

What had really been bothering Erma lately? Surely those journal pages, the ones she was determined not to read, held some answers.

Because something was amiss—of that much she was sure—she wished Kate Murphy were on the case. Not that she wanted it to be a homicide—heaven forbid! Maybe she should give Kate a call. Just to see how she and Jack were doing, of course.

"Glory be to God! Get those things off the bench." Eileen's

voice startled her. Mary Helen's eyes shot open and darted from side to side, not knowing what horror—spider, slug, lizard—had crept onto the bench with her.

"The shoes, Mary Helen, the new shoes. It is a terrible omen, new shoes on a bench."

"For heaven's sake, Eileen, is that all?"

"Is that all? Do you know that can mean a death? New shoes, ready for the journey to the netherworld."

Obediently, Mary Helen moved the shoes—not that she was superstitious, but she had enough problems without courting bad luck. The shoes, dry and warm from the sun, felt good when she put them back on.

"Do you feel like taking a quick walk?" Eileen asked. Mary Helen realized her friend must be worrying too. One of Eileen's panaceas for worry was walking. The other was cleaning. On Sundays Eileen always chose walking.

"That's a good idea," Mary Helen said. "Since we are both stewing about Erma we may as well walk and talk. Maybe between us we can come up with some reasonable answers. Then let's stop by the Carmelite monastery for the five-o'clock Benediction."

"You really are disturbed, aren't you?" Eileen's large gray eyes studied Mary Helen. "The Carmelite monastery is always —what should I call it?—your heavy artillery. You do think something has happened to poor Erma, don't you?"

Mary Helen hesitated, surprised that Eileen had discovered her secret. Although she shouldn't have been. Nothing much slipped by her friend. She didn't know what to answer. There was no sense alarming Eileen further about a feeling, however strongly she felt it. Yet in all honesty, she would have to admit that she was afraid for Erma.

Fortunately, before she had to answer Eileen's question, Sister Anne rounded the bend in the path. Her shorts and her "Here today, gone to Maui" T-shirt were soaked. Panting, she bent over. Perspiration dripped from her face.

"What are you up to?" Mary Helen frowned, wondering why anyone would want to get that hot and sweaty on purpose.

"Practicing. Bay-to-Breakers. Next Sunday." Anne was so short of breath she couldn't even answer in whole sentences. "You?"

"We are going to get a little exercise, too, before Therese's shocking supper. *Oops!* I mean surprise supper," Eileen said, reaching into her pocket for a tissue, which she handed to Anne.

Mary Helen couldn't tell from the look on her friend's face whether she had purposely slipped or not. She did, however, have her suspicions.

Wiping her eyes, Anne began to run in place. "Muscles get cold," she puffed.

"You run along." Eileen patted the back of the young nun's damp shirt. "If we are a little late, it will be because we stopped by the Carmelites for Benediction."

For a moment, Anne stared blankly. Mary Helen was afraid that she was going to have to explain to the younger generation that the Benediction is an ancient devotion in which Christ in the Eucharist is exposed and worshipped.

It must have registered. "Say prayer I win race," Anne puffed before she pumped away up the hill.

"We really ought to say a prayer that the poor thing lasts that long." Shading her eyes, Eileen watched the slender young nun disappear around the hill.

"Or maybe we should pray that she survives Therese's eggplant lasagna," Mary Helen added.

The two friends laughed and started down toward the main driveway. Although neither of them said anything, they both knew that what they really would be begging for at the Carmelite monastery this afternoon was their friend Erma's swift and safe return home to San Francisco.

During the evening Sister Mary Helen could not seem to get

her mind off Erma's journal. Even all the bad news on *60 Minutes* didn't help, and Angela Lansbury's sleuthing in *Murder, She Wrote* only fed the flame.

Don't even think about it, old girl, her conscience had chided her. Reading it is definitely out of the question.

Desperate situations warrant desperate solutions, she had argued.

It is the characteristic of wisdom not to do desperate things. Her conscience had quoted Thoreau.

Whoever accused me of being all that wise? she had asked herself.

By the ten-o'clock news, she could no longer resist.

Firmly closing the door of her bedroom, she settled in the reclining chair in the corner and unzipped the side pocket of her purse.

Before her conscience could give her any more trouble, she smoothed out the sheets of binder paper and glanced through them. She was disappointed to see how little was written on each page.

"I feel foolish doing this," the entry began in large, legible handwriting, which Mary Helen recognized as Erma's Palmer.

Not as foolish as I feel reading it, my friend. Mary Helen shifted uneasily.

"But today our instructor told us we should write imaginary letters to people who are important in our lives. We should write what we wish we could tell them in person," Erma continued. "Lucy says she feels silly, too, but that it will probably be good for us, so here goes.

"Dear Junior," the first entry began. "I write to you first because I feel the worst about what I've done to you. You were such a darling, sensitive little boy with blond curly hair."

Mary Helen stared at her bedroom wall, trying to imagine Junior as an adorable toddler, but it was difficult.

"Your father wanted to make a man out of you and you wanted so to please him. He meant well, really he did, but he just did not realize how sensitive you were. Poor man did not know that even your fits of temper were really your way of covering up hurt feelings, but I did. Maybe I should have stepped in more as I did for your brother and sister. But it seemed so important to your father that you turn out to be 'a man.' So I let him handle it. Or maybe, if I was honest I'd have to admit that when I got home after work some nights, I was too tired to fight him. I want you to know how much I loved you then and how much I still love you now."

The letter broke off abruptly, and Mary Helen could feel a lump in her throat.

The entry on the next page was even shorter.

"Dear Marie," it began. "My sweet little girl, my firstborn! How happy your daddy and I were the day we brought you home from the hospital, and how you cried. I should have known then. You were just like your daddy, really. He was high-strung too. How I wish I could have sheltered you from all that happened." Nothing more.

On a third page was written only "My dear little Buddy, You worry me."

Frustrated by the lack of anything concrete that might help and embarrassed about intruding on Erma's private thoughts, for what was proving to be fruitless, Mary Helen began to read the final page.

"Dreams—May 5" was written across the top of the page in Erma's steady hand.

"He was there again. Large, much larger than he really is, with hairy hands and an angry face. For a moment he looked just like Tommy. I was frightened, although I kept telling myself I shouldn't be. He wouldn't harm me. He loves me. He told me again how much he loved me.

" 'Stop!' I begged him. 'Don't hit me!'

"But he just kept coming and crawled into bed next to me like he was a little boy. 'I do love you!' he kept repeating over and over.

"The dream was so real and I was so frightened that when I woke up my heart was pounding, and I couldn't go back to sleep. I know he's been on my mind. He's really worrying me. Nothing I can actually put my finger on except the drinking. And he has been acting strangely these past few days. I can't help wondering if it has anything to do with my money disappearing. But whenever I ask him, he becomes angry. Maybe I should tell Lucy about what I'm feeling. I know I can't tell anyone else. The next time we go to our class, I think I'll ask our instructor what it all means."

Mary Helen checked the date. May 5. Saturday morning! The day Erma disappeared. She must have written this entry when she woke up. Sister Mary Helen felt a sick lurch in the pit of her stomach. Poor old Erma Duran never had had the opportunity to ask what her dream meant. Nor to reveal the identity of the mysterious "he."

Disheartened, she put the crumpled pages back into the side pocket of her purse and zipped it up.

Monday, May 14

Feast of St. Matthias, Apostle

The moment Sister Mary Helen stepped into Erma Duran's living room, she felt the tension. It was more than anxiety over Erma's disappearance or Monday morning letdown. Someone, as the old expression goes, had obviously spilled the beans. She didn't have to wait long to find out who.

"Ree tells us that you have already been to see Inspector Honore in Missing Persons." Noelle's voice was as icy as her blue eyes. Caroline, looking offended, sat next to her.

Taken aback, Mary Helen was fumbling around for an excuse, when she remembered one of her favorite maxims: "The best defense is always a good offense."

"Where were the rest of you when we needed you?" she asked as accusingly as she could manage. "It's a shame that the three of you left in such a hurry." Glancing from Noelle to Caroline to Mr. Finn, she let that sink in. "We really could have used some moral support. Finding Erma's medal was a terrible shock." She moved toward an empty seat on the couch. It was next to Finn. "I've barely recovered from it yet." She squeezed in beside him, making room for Eileen.

"And filling out the missing-person report was really quite an ordeal. One I never want to go through again." Mary Helen paused, satisfied that she had struck just the right martyred tone.

"Sister's right." Much to Mary Helen's relief, Lucy jumped right in.

"We are also sorry we weren't with you. After all, we are all supposed to be in this together," Noelle said, putting a little too much emphasis on the *supposed*. Obviously she was not buying it.

"Oh, what difference does it make who went to the police about Mommy?" Ree sniffled nervously. "We were going to do it today, anyway, if she hadn't called."

"I gather no one has heard from Erma?" Apparently Caroline had recovered. She surveyed the group one by one, stopping very pointedly at Mr. Finn. "No phone call yesterday?"

An awkward silence filled the living room. Finn shrugged, shaking his head. The plastered piece of hair across his crown didn't even budge. The only sound was another of Ree's sniffles.

"Has anyone a suggestion as to what our next step should be?" Caroline asked.

"What can we do?" Noelle lit her cigarette. "The whole affair is now out of our hands and in the hands of the police." Smoke and words came out of her mouth together.

"Not necessarily. In my opinion, there is plenty we can do." Mary Helen didn't want to lose the group. As far as she was concerned, Inspector Honore could use all the help he could get. "You know how busy the police are," she said. "There are a number of questions we can find the answers to that may help them out."

The others looked at her, waiting for her to get more specific.

"For instance, how did Erma get to the airport? And why did she choose to go to St. Louis? Above all, why did she leave so quickly without saying good-bye? That may be the most important question of all. It is just not like Erma to leave without saying something to her family and friends."

Mary Helen paused for breath, hoping she had made her point. Next to her she could feel Finn squirm. She couldn't see the expression on his face, so she wasn't sure exactly what his squirm meant.

"Furthermore, did anyone phone Barbara back?" she continued. "For all we know, Erma may have arrived."

The clear, sharp ring of the telephone made them all jump. Could it be Erma? Speak of the devil, and all. The unspoken question hung on the air, yet no one moved toward the phone. It rang a second time.

"For heaven's sake, Ree, answer it!" Caroline could not contain herself.

Reluctantly Ree edged toward the telephone, which blared out a third time. Mary Helen would have sworn it sounded even louder, more insistent.

"Hello." Ree answered in a small, frightened voice. "Oh, hi, Auntie Barbara . . . No, not yet . . . Yes, I will . . . Okay . . . You too."

Although they had heard only one side of the short conversation, no one needed to ask what had been said.

"She's not there." Ree's tear-filled eyes avoided the group.

"As Sister pointed out, we could all probe a little deeper."

Mary Helen was relieved to hear Noelle's crisp, businesslike voice taking charge.

"And, she has added some important questions to our list," Noelle continued. "Without any further ado, shall we adjourn this morning's meeting and each begin that probing?" Her tone told the rest of the OWLs that her question was rhetorical. She had already flipped open her peacock-blue pocket calendar to May and was apparently scanning the month. "Our regular OWL meeting is this coming Thursday," she announced, as though they didn't know. "That gives us three days to unearth something.

"Let us make every effort to keep each other informed, so there is no duplication of efforts." Obviously she was still piqued about the unscheduled visit to Inspector Honore. "Shall we meet an hour before the large group assembles at ten-thirty?" Her blue eyes canvassed her listeners. "That should give us ample time to report and discuss our progress."

Frowning, Lucy scooted forward on her chair. "What about Ree and Al, here? They aren't OWLs, but they are part of the group."

Al? . . . Al? For a moment, Mary Helen was stumped. She had almost forgotten that Mr. Finn's name was Al.

"Lucy has a point," Noelle said, chewing her lower lip. From the look on the chairwoman's face, Mary Helen had a sneaking suspicion that Noelle had been caught trying to pull a fast one!

"Perhaps we could all meet here at Erma's apartment at nine o'clock," Caroline suggested. "That will give us a full hour and a half before our regular meeting."

"And there's always the possibility that by then Erma will be back." Lucy, ever the optimist, smiled wistfully. "I really do miss her! You know, we talked on the phone almost every morning. I wish she'd hurry back."

Almost as if she were afraid to let any emotions show, Caroline sniffed. "If wishes were horses," she said aristocratically, "we would all be up to our knees in manure!"

After a moment of shocked silence they all quickly agreed on the time and place of their next meeting. A little too quickly for Mary Helen's taste. The group dispersed amicably but hastily.

Watching them hurry out of the apartment, she couldn't help but recall a wisp of a stanza from "The Ancient Mariner."

And having once turned round walks on,
And turns no more his head;
Because he knows a frightful fiend
Doth close behind him tread.

The "frightful fiend," she was sure, was everyone's fear.

Mary Helen stepped out onto Sanchez Street. For a moment the glare of the sun on the cement blinded her.

"Pst!" She turned.

"Pst! Sister, here." It was Mr. Finn just inside the door of his bistro.

She followed him into the darkened restaurant. Cautiously he shut the door.

"I didn't want to say nothing up there in front of Ree," he said, his eyes blinking nervously, "but I don't think we should be looking too hard for Erma."

"Oh!" Mary Helen wondered what the man was leading up to.

"Like I told you before, Erma don't want to be found. Especially by her kids. Remember?"

Mary Helen remembered. She also remembered Mr. Finn had said he was getting a little worried about Erma not calling. She mentioned it.

"Yeah, I am." He rocked on the soles of his feet. "She told me she'd call when she got settled. But like I said, she made me promise not to tell the kids where she was going. I feel bad I let the cat out of the bag."

"That seems so out of character for Erma." Mary Helen was thinking out loud.

Finn shrugged. "Yeah, in a way, the whole thing is, I guess. But, really, you can't blame her. Those three are something else—always hanging around, eating her food, borrowing what little money she had. You know, Sister"—the yellow specks in his hazel eyes vibrated in disbelief—"that youngest kid even brings home his laundry."

Opening the door, Finn checked up and down the street. "I don't want that Ree seeing me talking to you. Mum's the word, Sister." He nodded to indicate that the coast was clear. Quickly he closed the bistro door behind her, leaving Mary Helen with a sudden suspicion that maybe Erma had indeed called and Finn was just not telling.

"Where in the name of God have you been? All of a sudden —*poof!*—you just disappeared." Eileen was standing beside the convent car, which Mary Helen had parked at the foot of the steep Sanchez Street hill.

Ree, whose polyester slacks looked as though they might have shrunk a little in the dryer, leaned against the fender. "I've got to talk to you, Sister." Her voice was agitated.

"Do you want to talk here in the car, or shall we drive you home?"

Ree shook her head. Her ponytail bounced from shoulder to shoulder. She sniffled. "I have to hurry. I don't want him to see me."

"Him?"

She pointed toward the bistro. "He's the one, you know. If anything has happened to Mommy, he's the one who'll know about it."

"First of all, we don't know that anything has happened to your mother, Ree. And Mr. Finn seems like a nice fellow who is genuinely fond of her." Although Mary Helen was well aware of the animosity between Ree and Al Finn, she hoped to interject some logic into the conversation.

"Fond of her? You bet! He follows her around, always stopping in. And h-he"—the woman stuttered, looking for the right word—"leers at her. I've seen him leer. Yes, I swear, Sister, if Mommy left it's because of him."

Mary Helen opened her mouth to speak, but Ree cut her off. "I've got to go before he sees me talking to you. He knows I know." The woman shivered.

Dumbfounded, Mary Helen watched Ree turn the corner and hurry down 18th Street toward Mission.

"What do you make of that?" Eileen's face wrinkled into a frown. "And, by the way, where were you?"

"Mr. Finn stopped me," Mary Helen said absently, once again not really knowing what to make of it herself. "He suggested Erma left to get away from her children."

Eileen shook her head. "And obviously Ree thinks he's to blame. Neither idea makes much sense to me."

"What do you mean?"

"This whole disappearance business is so unlike Erma." Eileen's gray eyes were troubled. "God knows she is not the kind of person to run away from difficulties."

"Or complain about them," Mary Helen added.

"And she's also not the kind anyone would want to harm. Right?"

"Right. But the fact of the matter is, Eileen, that she has disappeared and someone must find out why," Mary Helen said, feeling more frustrated than she had felt in a long time.

* * *

As soon as the pair arrived back at the convent, Mary Helen went straight to the phone. She dialed Inspector Honore at the Northern Station.

"What can I do for you, Sister?" It may have been her imagination, but she thought he sounded a little short.

Quickly she told him about her conversations with Mr. Finn and Ree. She deliberately omitted mentioning that the OWLs were doing a little probing on their own. She shuddered to think what he would say if he knew he was being helped.

When she finished there was a long pause. Mary Helen heard the inspector's gum pop several times, so she knew he was still on the line. She waited impatiently for the man to say something.

"We'll look into it, Sister," he said finally but, in Mary

Helen's opinion, without much heart. "I'll get back to you just as soon as I have something."

Mary Helen sat in the convent phone booth, a receiver in her hand. The impersonal hum infuriated her. After her brief conversation with Inspector Honore she felt even more frustrated than she had before, if such a thing were possible.

Tuesday, May 15

Feast of St. Isidore, Farmer

The wail of an ambulance speeding down Turk Street filled Mary Helen's small bedroom. Its insistent screech as it rounded the corner pierced through her sleep. She awoke with a feeling of urgency. Even in those fuzzy first moments of consciousness, she knew why. Erma! Erma was still missing and someone had to find her. Last night after talking to Inspector Honore, she realized that, as sure as the sun would rise, she had to be that someone.

It only stood to reason, as anyone with an ounce of sense would agree. Why, she and Erma McSweeney Duran went back a long way and although they had kept in touch only on and off over the years, Mary Helen had really enjoyed getting reacquainted. Furthermore, Erma had spent the better part of her life looking after others, maybe even to a fault, trying to make them happy. Now it was high time someone looked after her.

The sooner I get started the better, Mary Helen thought, swinging her feet out of her bed and onto the cold floor. She shivered. The carpetless convent floor was always cold, but this morning it was even colder. In fact her whole room felt chillier than usual. She listened for the low rumble of the central heating, but the room was strangely silent. The furnace must be on the fritz.

"The furnace is broken, Sisters. The furnace is broken." Sister Therese's quick footsteps echoing down the long corridor assured her that she was correct.

Hand on her doorknob, Mary Helen braced herself. To encounter Therese on a Paul-Revere ride any time of day was difficult enough, but before morning coffee it was impossible. Mary Helen climbed back into bed, turned her electric blanket to six, pulled the covers up under her nose, and planned the day's strategy.

She knew Mr. Finn didn't have any love for the two Duran boys. She would go to see them first. She could get their addresses from Lucy Lyons. Ree Duran was suspicious of Finn, who she felt, as the old saying goes, "knew more than his prayers." Next, she would drop by the bistro and have another talk with him. Finn was leery of Ree. She could go by and see Ree, but enough was enough for one day. Maybe tomorrow.

At breakfast after the morning Mass, Mary Helen spotted Eileen. She moved across the Sisters' dining room toward her friend, who was all bundled up and sitting near one of the windows. Both of Eileen's hands were cupped around a coffee mug that said BREWED AWAKENING. It had been a gift from Lucy Lyons.

"Aren't you freezing, old dear?" Eileen moved her feet to where a beam of sun had settled on the parquet floor. "I'll wager it's warmer outside than in." She nodded toward a glistening patch of grass already bright with morning sun.

"Then let's go out." Mary Helen settled down in the chair across from her.

"Out?" Eileen acted surprised. "Now, where would you suggest we go?"

"You know very well what I'm getting at." Mary Helen blew on her coffee.

"Then you haven't given up your determination to find out what has happened to Erma? I thought a good night's sleep might have cleared your thinking."

"I have only become more determined!" Mary Helen banged her cup on the wooden tabletop as if to say Amen!

Eileen rolled her eyes. "If such a thing is possible," Mary Helen was almost sure she heard her say.

Fortunately the convent's Nova was free. Edging down the college driveway, Mary Helen passed Allan Boscacci coming up. His red Ferrari skidded on the turns. His jaw was set and he barely waved when they passed.

"Therese must have awakened the poor fellow." Eileen grimaced. "We'll be lucky if she doesn't drive him right out of his mind."

Mary Helen watched a service truck from Boscacci Electric follow the boss up the hill. "Or at least out of the Church," she said.

Stopping at the college gate, she waited for a break in the Turk Street traffic so she could turn left. On either side, stone eagles atop the pillars kept a sharp eye out against intruders.

"Where are we going?"

Mary Helen was surprised Eileen had waited so long to ask. On the other hand, hurried the way she had been, Eileen hadn't had the chance. She handed over a scrap of paper with the addresses Lucy had given her.

"Let's start with Junior," she said. "He works in a body shop on Divisadero."

* * *

"Hey, what the hell do you think you're doing?" A burly mechanic rolled out from under a car the minute Mary Helen pulled into the garage. "Lady, get that mother . . ." he shouted, then stopped abruptly.

Even under several black smudges, his face reddened.

Maybe he spotted the statue on our dashboard, or maybe our crosses gave us away, she thought, rolling down the window and smiling.

"Excuse me, young man. We would like to speak with Thomas Duran, if we may. We won't take long, I promise. It's about his mother."

"Thomas? You mean Junior?" He wiped his greasy hands on an equally greasy rag. "I didn't know that ba . . ."—he hesitated—"that boy had a mother."

"Hey, Junior," he shouted toward the back of the shop. "Someone to see you." Then, lowering himself onto a wooden square with wheels, the mechanic scooted back under a car.

Junior Duran stuck his bearded face around the back door-jamb and peered cautiously into the garage. Mary Helen had the feeling that if the visitor turned out to be someone he didn't want to see, he was already mounted on his motorcycle.

Three other young men, looking for all the world like carbon copies of Junior, crowded behind him in the doorway. Puffing out his bare chest under a leather vest, Junior swaggered into the garage. The heels of his boots echoed on the oil-stained cement.

"What can I do for you?" he asked, thumbs looped over his thick belt. "You're them nuns that were in my old lady's apartment." He smirked toward the other men, making sure, Mary Helen noticed, that his eyes never met hers. "This is kinda a long way from church, ain't it?"

Mary Helen recognized showing off when she heard it. There was no sense giving him more of an opportunity. She bent forward. "It's about your mother," she said softly. "As you already know, we are very worried about her—as you must be too. I'm trying to piece together some of her actions the day she left. I understand you went to see her?"

Junior's dark eyes shifted toward the men in the doorway, then toward the mechanic who had disappeared under the car. "Let's go outside," he said, "where we can talk private."

Once outside, Mary Helen noticed a change come over the man. With some of the bravado gone, his whole face seemed to soften.

"Yeah, I saw her that day." Folding his tattooed arms, he leaned against the stucco front of the body shop.

"I'm wondering what time that was. And did you notice if she was upset about anything?"

Junior gave a crooked smile. "What are you, some kind of cop?"

"Of course not." All the smart-aleck answers were making Mary Helen a bit impatient. Besides, there was a sharp wind whistling along on Divisadero Street. Before long she and Eileen would freeze to death. "We are simply trying to help locate your mother."

"Hey, don't get mad." His hand touched her jacket sleeve, the tips of his fingers bloody where he had torn at his nails. "It's just that another cop, a black dude, was here already asking questions."

Mary Helen was pleasantly surprised. Perhaps she had rash judged Inspector Honore.

"Like I told him, I want to help. I love my mother." For the first time Junior's dark eyes met hers. If she wasn't mistaken, they were misty.

Another paper tiger, Mary Helen thought, listening to Junior confess about fighting with his mother when she had refused to lend him any more money.

"What time was that?"

"About ten, maybe ten-thirty, Saturday morning."

"Are you sure?"

"Yeah, pretty sure. I remember looking at her clock when I got there and asking her what time she had to be at work. She said she didn't have to go to work on Saturday till they opened for dinner."

"You were very angry with your mother," Mary Helen

stated, then studied his eyes for a reaction. She was trying to pick up any clue she could.

"Yeah, I was damn mad. See, I needed the money bad," he repeated. "I owed some guys. You know how that is."

Mary Helen nodded, although she had no idea how that was or why a grown man would expect his mother to pay his debts.

"I cussed at her. Not bad, just a little. She smacked me on the back of the head, just like she always does when I cuss. I let her. I never would lift a finger to hurt her. I love my mother," he said again.

After a few moments Junior's eyes narrowed, making him look, Mary Helen thought, positively dangerous. "If anyone knows what happened to her," he said, "it's that bastard Finn." He clenched his fist. "If he hurt her, I'll kill him."

* * *

As they pulled away Mary Helen checked the rearview mirror. Junior and his friends were in front of the garage. Unless she was mistaken, they were each holding a can of beer.

"Oh, my, my!" Eileen fastened her seat belt and turned back to look as they merged into Divisadero. "A body wouldn't want to run into those chaps in a dark alley."

"Your body and half the bodies in San Francisco," Mary Helen said, "if you are judging by appearances." She caught herself. You, above all others, old girl, should know better than to judge a book by its cover! She frowned, wondering if Junior's toughness was merely a veneer covering nothing more than soft putty or if it was indeed genuine.

* * *

Buddy Duran lived in a garage apartment on Clayton Street in the heart of the Haight-Ashbury District. The neighborhood, which had been the hippie center of the sixties, had just enough hearts and macramé hangings left dangling in bay windows to remind passersby of the era.

Most of the sturdy old homes, however, had been renovated

and repainted to accentuate the ornate Victorian architecture. Buddy's building was one of them.

Even before the young man opened the narrow front door, Mary Helen smelled what she recognized from a workshop on drugs as the distinctive odor of marijuana. She wondered if Inspector Honore had beat her here too.

"Hi, Sisters," Buddy said, a euphoric look in his unfocused eyes. His flannel shirt was covered with clay dust.

"I hope we're not disturbing you." Mary Helen tried to look concerned.

"No, I've been creating all morning, when I didn't have company." He opened the door just wide enough for the nuns to see into the room and pointed to a lump of clay on a makeshift table. "Right now, I'm just taking a . . . a coffee break." Buddy giggled. "Come in." He threw open the door. "Welcome to my studio apartment."

The room was a mess. Unwashed dishes were stacked helter-skelter in a narrow, stained sink. Beneath it, McDonald's cartons, Chinese-food containers, and a half-empty coffee cup with something growing on the remaining half cluttered the grimy floor. A hot plate held several pots. A few pieces of dirty underwear lay at the foot of an unmade bed.

"Make yourself comfortable." Buddy motioned grandly toward two patched beanbag chairs. "Can I get you something?"

Quickly Mary Helen shook her head. She wasn't quite sure which she wanted to avoid the most: getting in and out of the beanbag chair or discovering what Buddy was prepared to serve them.

"No, thank you, Buddy. We don't want to keep you from your work." She smiled toward the clay. For the first time, she noticed dents pushed in where eyes should be and the beginning of a short nose.

Dreamily, Buddy's eyes followed hers. "Recognize it?" he asked.

Mary Helen didn't want to stunt his creativity by telling him that to her it looked like nothing more than a blob of red clay with a couple of holes in it. "Well, it does look familiar," she said instead.

Beside her, Eileen cocked her head this way and that. "A woman," she said finally, with that Irish lilt that made a statement and a question sound alike. Right or wrong, the inflection would save the artist from hurt feelings and Eileen from embarrassment.

But the pleased smile on Buddy's face told them that Eileen was right on the mark.

"Your mother?"

Mary Helen could tell it was another wild guess.

Buddy nodded and stared at the clay, a silly grin playing on his face. Eileen was batting a thousand.

"Poor Mama." He stared at the clay. Suddenly tears filled his eyes.

"When did you last see her?" Mary Helen put her hand on the young man's bony shoulder, gave it a pat.

He frowned as if he were trying to recall details from a dream. "Saturday—the day Finn said she left."

"I see. What time where you there?"

He frowned, trying to concentrate. "About quarter to eight or so. I had to be at work at the museum by nine."

"May I inquire why you were there so early in the morning?" Mary Helen asked a little hesitantly.

Buddy wasn't the least bit hesitant in answering. "I brought over my laundry. But she never gave it back." He pointed to the shorts on the linoleum floor. "I'm running low."

"You rang her bell at seven forty-five on Saturday morning?" Mary Helen had been a schoolteacher too long. She couldn't help herself. "After she had just come home from an exhausting trip to New York the day before?"

Buddy winced and looked hurt by the tone of her voice. "If

I get there early she fixes my breakfast," he said. "I hope she hurries home."

At that moment, Mary Helen herself felt the urge to kill.

* * *

"Do you know, Mary Helen, if we read it in a novel, we wouldn't believe it." Eileen stared out the car window.

"Read what?" Mary Helen checked the oncoming traffic before turning right onto Oak Street.

"About Erma's two sons, of course." Eileen sounded annoyed. At what, Mary Helen wasn't sure. "No one deserves those two characters!"

"I'm sure Erma loves them." Mary Helen swerved to avoid a car merging from her right. On Oak Street it was hard to take the right-of-way, even if it was legally yours.

"To a fault, if you ask me!" Eileen's Irish was up.

"And in their own strange ways, both of them seem to love her too."

Eileen snorted. "That reminds me of a ditty one of my in-laws from back home used to sing." Her rich contralto filled the small Nova. " 'He held the lantern while his mother chopped the wood. He held the lantern, just like any good boy should.' "

Mary Helen was glad the windows were rolled up.

" 'He . . .' " Eileen stopped midnote. "Something has been pestering me since we left Buddy's and I just realized what it is. His laundry! Do you remember seeing any men's laundry, clean or dirty, in Erma's apartment?"

Mary Helen shook her head.

"What do you suppose that can mean?" Eileen turned in the seat to face her.

"It could mean that someone was in the apartment after Buddy says he was."

"Junior was," Eileen chirped in. "You do remember."

"I have the feeling Junior wasn't in the mood to deliver."

"Oh, dear, Mary Helen, do you suppose Buddy went back

and picked up his laundry and for some reason neglected to tell us?"

Suddenly Mary Helen felt as if she had been laundered and someone had washed out all her starch.

* * *

When they arrived, Alphonso's Bistro was obviously not yet open. The shade on the glass front door was pulled halfway down and a throw-away paper was still in front of it. Inside, the place was pitch-black. Yet the aroma of browning ground meat escaping under the door made Mary Helen's stomach growl. She checked her wristwatch. No wonder. It was already eleven.

Obviously Mr. Finn was in the kitchen. Or one of the cooks. She tapped on the glass and waited. Right after they talked with him, Mary Helen would suggest that Eileen and she could treat themselves to lunch in one of the quaint eateries in the neighborhood. They deserved it. She had read about one place that had North African food, whatever that was. Not giraffe steak or hippopotamus stew, she hoped.

When no one answered her second tap, Sister Mary Helen walked around to the apartment side of the building. She pushed Finn's doorbell and waited but not for long. He opened the door, motioned them in, and hurried back up the stairs to the phone down the hall. Following him up the stairs, the two nuns stood in the entrance way, looking around.

Not that there was much to see. The layout of Finn's apartment looked like half a flat. Apparently Finn or some previous owner had divided the flat into two apartments. He had the front half, Erma the back.

The furnishings in the living room were sparse but clean. Actually, except for a pile of newspapers on a vinyl hassock, the place did not look lived in at all.

Although she couldn't make out the words, Mary Helen could hear Finn mumbling in the hallway.

"Listen!" Eileen whispered, nodding toward the mumbling.

Her hearing was exceptionally keen. In fact, there were days when some swore that she could hear the grass growing in Ireland.

Mary Helen strained, but still nothing was clear.

"He's placing a bet," Eileen mouthed when she realized Mary Helen couldn't hear. "Probably talking to his bookie."

What in the name of God do you know about bookies, Mary Helen wanted to ask, edging closer to the hallway in the hope that she, too, might catch the conversation.

It was too late. Almost immediately Finn reappeared, blinking.

"Morning, Sisters." He wiggled his toes in his stocking feet. "What brings you to this neck of the woods so early?"

"I just can't stop thinking about Erma." Mary Helen suddenly realized how hungry she was. There was no sense wasting time. "If it isn't an imposition, may I look through her apartment again, maybe even have you show me what she did that last day, just in case we missed something?" The detectives in her mystery stories always did that. If it worked for Spenser or Rebecca Schwartz, why not for her?

Wearily Finn shook his head, then sat down to put on his shoes. "It's no trouble but it's no use either. Like I keep telling you, Erma don't want to be found. She left to get away from those lousy kids of hers. Said she'd call when she got settled. So far she ain't . . . called, I mean."

The nuns followed Finn down the stairs to the front door of his apartment. "Let's see now . . . You wanted to see what Erma did that last day. Well, like I told you, it was Saturday. She come down here to tell me she was leaving."

He pointed to the closed bistro door. "Since we're down here already, why don't we look here first?" He fumbled with the key in the single lock. It didn't take much, Mary Helen noticed, to get the place open.

Inside, Alphonso's Bistro smelled even more delicious than

it had from the outside. The cook had obviously added onions to the beef.

"Now what is it you want to look at, exactly?"

Faced with the direct question, Mary Helen wasn't sure. "Just around." She waved vaguely.

Finn shrugged his consent, or at least Mary Helen assumed that was what his shrug meant. Smiling her thanks, she made her way across the darkened room and into the stainless-steel kitchen. Eileen and Finn followed.

A tall Mexican man wearing a high chef's cap was standing over the cast-iron gas range. At a center cutting table another, younger, fellow was chopping. Both glanced over at her, but after a perfunctory smile they went back to their work.

Mary Helen opened several doors that proved to be closets. One held paper goods, another clean linens, yet another cleaning supplies. She tried the door next to the deep sink, one the help probably used for washing heavy pots. Turning the knob, she pulled, but it didn't budge.

"Let me get that." Finn took an old-fashioned key from a hook beside the door. "This door's to the basement," he said. "I keep it locked because the stairs are so steep. Someone falls and—*wham!*"

He swung back the door and felt for the light switch. Mr. Finn was not exaggerating. The stairs were almost vertical. Grabbing the rickety wooden railing, Mary Helen was glad she wasn't subject to vertigo.

"If some bimbo opens this, thinking it's the broom closet and breaks her fool neck, they'd sue the hell out of me."

Pushing her bifocals up the bridge of her nose, Mary Helen peered down into the basement. "Did Erma ever go down there?"

"Yeah, sure, every once in a while. We keep our extra supplies down there."

"How do you get them in?" Mary Helen hoped she sounded like Spenser.

"There's a door at the back of the basement," Finn told her. "Stairs lead down to it from the alley behind the building. Want to take a look?"

Sister Mary Helen ignored his question. "Did Erma go down there the day she disappeared?" she asked, hoping the answer was no. The longer she stood at the top of the steps, the more forbidding they looked.

Finn scratched the bald V's on the top of his head. "Now that you mention it, she did. The cooks were starting to get the dinner going when she came down to tell me she was taking off. As I remember it, one of them ran out of sugar or ice or some damn thing. Everybody had their hands full."

Mary Helen glanced quickly at Eileen, hoping her friend could resist saying, Had his or her hands full.

Fortunately she did, and Finn continued. "One of the cooks asked Erma if she'd go down. Was it you, Chico?"

Chico turned from his skillet. "Yeah, man, and she did. Erma is good people. I miss her around here."

"Are you sure she came back up?" Mary Helen looked hard at Finn.

"Sure, I'm sure. Like I told you, I saw her just before she left for St. Louis."

"What time did you say that was?"

"She took off just before the dinner shift. About three o'clock, I'd say. I told her I'd cover for her."

"Who drove her to the airport?"

Finn's hazel eyes clouded. "I been thinking about that since you said it yesterday. It gets so busy in here I didn't get the chance to look out. Maybe she called a cab."

Mary Helen made a mental note to suggest to Inspector Honore that he check with the taxi companies.

"Do you mind if I look around in the basement?" she asked without the slightest idea why.

"Hell, no. Be my guest. Except there's nothing much down

there to see." Finn shook his head. "I don't know what you'll find down there to help you out."

Neither do I, Mary Helen thought. But she was desperate for a clue, any clue, that could lead them to Erma.

"Are you coming?" she asked Eileen.

Her friend barely repressed a shudder. "I'll stay topside, in case someone has to call 911. And for the love of all that is good and holy, old dear, watch your step!"

Much as Mary Helen hated to admit it, Finn was right. The basement held nothing much worth seeing.

The concrete floor sloped toward the narrow door, which must lead to the alley. The small window at the top of the door was boarded over, probably to protect against vandalism. Mary Helen could hear the rhythmic throbbing of machinery somewhere in the building. Single dusty light bulbs ran down the center of the ceiling, casting deep shadows in the corners of the room.

The whole place smelled of stale dampness and mold. Water-damaged cartons lined wooden shelves against one wall. An old-fashioned ice maker, tilting slightly, took up several square feet of floor.

Adjusting her glasses, Mary Helen looked around, not at all sure what she was looking for. She heard a soft, rustling sound in the corner. Her scalp tingled as she imagined what could be rustling. She stiffened as she wondered how in the world she could get out of the basement gracefully. She wouldn't for a moment want Eileen or Mr. Finn to think she was squeamish.

"Hurry up out of there, Mary Helen," Eileen called down the stairs. "I am a positive wreck wondering what you are into."

"Oh, all right! If you insist!" Mary Helen grabbed the rickety banister. Good old Eileen! You could always count on her in a pinch.

* * *

The moment Sister Mary Helen stepped inside the door of Erma's apartment, she shivered. The air was beginning to hold that nobody-home chill, and a film of dust had settled on the tops of all the furniture. Depressing!

Hands in pockets, Finn rocked on the soles of his feet, blinking nervously at one nun, then at the other. His whole demeanor said that the apartment depressed him too. "Where do you want to look?" he asked.

Mary Helen wasn't at all sure, although she hesitated to admit that to Finn. Or to anyone else, for that matter.

"How about the bedroom closet?" It was the first thought that popped into her mind. On second thought, the closet might be a good place to start. A person packing in a hurry could easily drop something on the floor and never know it. She headed for the back room, Eileen close at her heels.

Finn hung behind. When Mary Helen turned to see if he was coming, he had crumpled onto the couch and was staring into space.

"You haven't forgotten the laundry, have you, old dear?" Eileen suggested in a stage whisper.

"Of course I haven't forgotten it," she said, trying not to sound annoyed. In all fairness, it was Eileen's clue. She was the one who had thought of it. "While I'm looking in the bedroom, why don't you check to see what you can find?"

That was all the encouragement Eileen needed. Her heels clicked on the hardwood as she bustled toward the service porch off the kitchen.

Although everything in Erma's bedroom was the same—the mirror, the dresser top, the icon in the corner—an eerie, abandoned silence hung on the air. The binder that at first Mary Helen had not even noticed now loomed large and black against the nightstand. In fact, she could hardly take her eyes off the thing. Why in the world hadn't Erma written more?

Down on her hands and knees in Erma's closet, Mary Helen spread the clothes apart. She crawled toward the back and began to examine the cedar floor. If Erma had dropped anything, however small, she had no intention of missing it.

She was running her hand around a dark corner when she heard Eileen's voice.

"Come quickly, Mary Helen. I've found it."

Still brushing the dust off the knees of her navy-blue skirt, Mary Helen peered into the old-fashioned Bendix washing machine. Sure enough, she had!

Men's clothes floated in a tub of scummy water. The faint smell of Clorox lingered.

Holding the round machine lid in her hand like a shield, Eileen could only be called triumphant. "I'll wager these are Buddy's clothes." She fished out a flannel shirt. "Didn't he have another one on almost like this when we saw him today?

"And look"—she pointed to where the electric wringer had been pushed over the deep sink—"she must have been getting ready to rinse."

Mary Helen was impressed. "It has been so long since we've seen one of these things, it's a wonder you remember how it works."

"Never underestimate an Irish washerwoman," Eileen said. Looking smug, she replaced the metal lid. "I wonder just what made her stop midwash."

"Maybe this is where we should be looking for clues," Mary Helen scanned the small service porch. Two deep concrete sinks, the old Bendix, a wooden door leading to a small railed landing, a bag of clothespins on the knob, a pulley clothesline strung kitty-corner high above the backyard—everything seemed to be in order.

"Maybe she blew the fuse." She flicked the light switch, but the light went on.

"Perhaps the whole building had a power failure," Eileen suggested.

Mary Helen was just about to ask Mr. Finn, when she heard

the clinking of chains and the tramping of heavy boots coming up the stairs.

"There you are, asshole." Junior's thick voice thundered through the small apartment. "Where'd Ma go, huh?" he demanded. "Tell me!"

"Watch who you're calling names, sonny boy." Like a man nearly out of patience, Finn seemed to strain his words through clenched teeth.

When Sister Mary Helen arrived at the threshold of the front room, Junior, thumbs hooked in his belt, was weaving slightly. Obviously he had been drinking. The air in the room crackled. Mary Helen held her breath, hoping.

All at once Junior plunged at Finn, slamming the palms of his hands against the man's shoulders. His face twisted insolently. He shoved once, twice.

Finn stumbled backward. His head cracked the wall. He grunted with surprise and the color drained from his face.

"Huh, asshole? Answer me!" Junior jeered.

Eyes blazing, Finn bounced off the wall, his muscles taut.

"Huh?" Junior raised his hands to push the man again. Mary Helen's stomach pitched. She saw it coming.

Dipping, Finn's arm snapped back in a blur. He lunged. She heard the slap of flesh against flesh. Junior gasped as Finn drove first one fist, then the other into Junior's naked belly.

Doubling over, Junior staggered forward, gulping in air.

With a lightning-quick rabbit punch, Finn chopped the back of his neck. Junior's body sagged. Finn's knee shot up, hitting him full in the face. Across the room Mary Helen caught the soft, crunching sound of bone breaking.

"Enough!" she shouted, watching the fresh blood from Junior's nose splash on the carpet.

Finn turned, fists clenched, his face ashen. For a moment, he stared blindly as if he didn't recognize her. A shock ran up Mary Helen's spine. It had been a long time since she had seen a look of such cold rage in anyone's eyes.

His body still rigid, Finn backed away from where Junior knelt on the floor.

Eileen hurried in from the bathroom. "You had better go over to Davies' Emergency," she said, pressing a wet wash-cloth to Junior's nose. Clutching onto the edge of the coffee table, he managed to pull himself up.

Glaring, the men circled like two mongrels, snarling, daring each other.

"Really!" Mary Helen snapped. "This is getting us nowhere in trying to find Erma."

"Ask him where she is." The blood was beginning to seep from under the washcloth. "I bet he knows where she is in St. Louis."

His eyes hard, Finn dug into his back pocket and pulled out his wallet. Removing three bills, he threw them at Junior. "Here, smartass, you go to St. Louis. You know so much, you find her."

"Take your goddamn money and shove . . ." Junior, his eyes tearing, stepped menacingly toward Finn.

"That is quite enough!" Eileen appeared with a second cold cloth and exchanged it for the saturated one. "I would suggest, Junior, that you get over to the hospital quickly. In fact, perhaps Mr. Finn should drive you."

As though she were speaking a foreign language, both men turned and stared at her. So did Mary Helen.

Junior was the first to recover. "I can take care of myself. I don't need no help from this—"

"Then you had better," Eileen said crisply, cutting off any further name-calling.

As soon as he heard Junior's motorcycle roar into action, Finn seemed to calm down. Gradually the color returned to his face. Without any reference to the scene, he bent down and picked up his three hundred-dollar bills from Erma's rug.

"You sisters take all the time you need." He rubbed his

knuckles. "If you want me, I'm downstairs. It's lunchtime. Don't worry about anything; I'll lock up later."

Mary Helen went back to Erma's bedroom. If she didn't hear Eileen bustling about, cleaning the blood off the carpet, rinsing out the soiled washcloth, she would have thought she was having a bad dream. Woodenly, she moved a few clothes in the drawers and looked under the bed, but her heart was no longer in the search.

From the corner shelf, the brown eyes of Our Lady of Perpetual Help stared at her. They followed her, full of sadness and sympathy. The Byzantine Madonna clasped the hand of the tiny Christ Child as the Child winced in terror.

"What is it?" Eileen stood in the doorway.

"That picture. Those woeful eyes looking at me as if I should know something, figure out something."

"Don't be too hard on yourself, old dear. I'm sure you will. You always do."

The pair moved toward the living room. "I hope there won't be a stain." Eileen pointed to two wet spots where she had tried to wash out Junior's blood. "They should be dry by the time Mr. Finn finishes with the noon meal and comes to lock up."

"There is really nothing more we can do here," Mary Helen said, leading the way down the stairs.

Yet the two damp spots and the woeful smile of the icon haunted her all the way through their North African lunch.

May 16

Wednesday of the Fifth Week of Easter

When Kate Murphy arrived at the Hall of Justice on Wednesday morning, Inspector Dennis Gallagher was already there. A large paper napkin covered the center of his desk. Several bumps underneath made her suspect that her partner hadn't bothered to move his reports or even his ashtray before spreading it. Two giant-sized Danish pastries oozed raspberry jam onto the white surface. A third one, half eaten, was in his hand.

"Hi, Katie-girl," he mumbled, his mouth nearly full.

"The breakfast of champions, I see." Kate took off her raincoat and hung it on the wooden coat tree. The Avenues had been socked in when she left for work, but south of Market the fog had already started to burn off. She looked out the window. Slits of blue cut through the gray. It was going to be a beautiful day. Eventually.

"Want a piece?" Gallagher pointed to the gooey rolls.

Kate tried not to make a face. "No, thanks," she said. "And for God's sake, Denny, why don't you try eating something nutritious? I can almost hear that stuff clogging up your arteries."

"Don't talk nutritious to me!" He bit into the second Danish. A seedy blob of jam landed dangerously close to the edge of the napkin. "Ever since I gave Mrs. G. that damn Cuisinart for Mother's Day, we've been eating like goddamn rabbits. You never saw anything like it. She's cutting up everything, and none of it any good. Carrots, celery, apples, radishes, cucumbers. I'm afraid of what she'll do if she accidentally gets her hands on one of the kids.

"Last night, she even cut up my potatoes. I like my spuds mashed, so as you can put a hole in the middle and fill it with gravy. Right?" He didn't wait for an answer. "Wrong! Last night she cuts them in that goddamn machine. We have potatoes au gratin—whatever the hell that is.

"This morning was the living limit. Instead of frying bacon and eggs, she's cutting up a fruit salad." He stuffed the sugary end of the Danish into his mouth. " 'Better for you,' she says. By the time I got downtown, I was starved."

"If you're going to insist on eating that crap, why don't you at least get a variety?" Kate picked up her own coffee mug.

"I like raspberry." He looked a little hurt.

Kate was coming back from the coffee urn, when Inspector Ron Honore walked into the detail.

"Hey! It's B. B. Kojak!" O'Connor rose from his desk just inside the door. "This missing-person stuff is really getting to you, huh? You can't even find your own station?"

Honore stopped to shake hands with O'Connor. "Remember who loves you, baby," he said, playing along with the joke.

The two had been at the academy together. B. B. Kojak was O'Connor's own nickname for Honore. For whatever reason— probably pure obstinacy, Kate guessed—he had never switched to calling the fellow Don Ron. The B. B., he had told her, stood for "Big Black." Much as Kate hated to admit O'Connor was right about anything, the nickname fit.

"I've come to see Murphy." Honore made his way across the room.

"We've got to stop meeting like this." Kate offered Honore her cup of coffee. But the man was in no mood to joke.

"This missing OWL business is really getting to me." He pulled up a chair. Leaning forward, he rested his forearm on the two desks. His jacket sleeves stretched as though they might burst.

"Any ideas?" Kate moved her ceramic dish-garden out of his way.

"None, although I spent half of Monday and all day yesterday on it."

"Who'd you talk to?"

"First of all, the Duran woman's two sons, Thomas and Richard, commonly called Junior and Buddy. Junior has a couple of juveniles and a couple of adult arrests for assault and battery, but no convictions. He admits he was there the day his mother was last seen, but the guy claims he has no idea why she left."

Gallagher licked the last of the raspberry jam off his fingers. "What are you telling us for, fella? This isn't our business till you find the body." Crumpling up the napkin, he took a half-smoked cigar from the ashtray Kate had suspected was under it.

"Disgusting habit," Honore said, watching him light it. "Buddy has no record, but when I dropped by his studio—the guy claims he's an artist—it smelled of more than turpentine.

"Also, I stopped by to see the daughter, Marie. I don't know what the hell's wrong with her. Gave me a long song and dance about Finn—that's the mother's employer and landlord. She claims that if anything happened to the mother, we should look to Finn. If you ask me, this Marie lady seems to be dealing without a full deck."

Reaching in his pocket for a stick of gum, he unwrapped it

and pleated it into his mouth. "My last," he said by way of apology for not offering them one.

Gallagher scowled. "What's all this got to do with us?"

"I'm getting to that. I looked into Finn. Nothing. Honest, upright citizen. Even contributes regularly to the Police Athletic League. I went to see the guy. The only odd thing about him is how he pulls this piece of hair back and forth." Honore demonstrated on his own bald head. "Anyway, he gives me an earful about the woman's kids. The whole thing goes around in circles."

"Did you find out anything about the woman herself?" Kate asked before she thought.

"Katie-girl, this here's not our department. Stay out of it." Pretending not to listen, Gallagher stared out the fourth-floor window, apparently totally absorbed in something on the James Lick Freeway.

"Sure did." Honore acted as though he hadn't heard Gallagher. "She, too, is an honest, upright citizen. Pays her bills, goes to church, belongs to a few organizations, including OWL. And that's what's really getting me into trouble—those OWLs."

"I knew it!" Gallagher slammed down his fist. "I knew exactly where this was leading. It's those damn nuns, isn't it? They're on your case, right?"

Looking sheepish, Honore snapped his gum. "Under ordinary circumstances, I'd let the case rest. As you guys know, we got dozens of missing-person reports coming in every week and we're shorthanded. Besides, at the end of this week Kelly's going on maternity leave, and we're going to be even more strapped."

Kate could feel a *but* coming.

"But to tell you the truth, Gallagher's right. That nun's gotten to me. She's so sure something's amiss that I can't help but agree with her. And there are a couple of loose ends."

"Like?"

"Like how did the lady get from Sanchez Street to the airport? No cabs picked up at that address on that afternoon. How come her name is not on the passenger list? Why didn't she go to see the only person she knows in St. Louis?"

Kate grinned. "Those are loose ends, all right. What I don't understand is what you want us to do about it."

"I know it's pushing it a little, but if anything has happened to the woman, it will be your case. So maybe if you guys have a couple of spare hours, you could nose around. See what you can come up with. I could use all the help I can get; and if it does fall in your laps, you'll be ahead."

"You've got to be kidding!" Gallagher shouted so loudly that all the noise in the Homicide Detail stopped instantly. There was an embarrassing silence.

"Hey, Gallagher, we're suppose to solve murders, not perpetrate them," O'Connor called across the room.

"Sorry," Gallagher said and waved. The room went back to normal.

"In case you change your mind, I'll leave this stuff for you." Honore put copies of his reports on Kate's desk. "Nothing formal. No big effort or anything. Just in case you have a couple of hours or stumble onto something."

Gallagher turned to Kate. "Can you believe this guy?" He ran the palm of his hand across his bald crown. "He boggles the mind of the average human being." He stepped close to Honore, scowling. "Get out of here, you bum, before you're a missing person yourself!"

"Don't forget who loves you, baby," Honore called to Gallagher, then quickly left the Homicide Detail.

"The nerve of that guy!" Gallagher took a deep pull on his cigar. "As if we didn't have enough of a load."

Kate picked up the paper he had left. "I wonder . . ." She frowned.

"Don't wonder. Don't even think. As a matter of fact, don't even touch those papers. We are not getting involved."

"Denny, do you think you may be overreacting a little?"

"I don't care what you call it, Kate. Overreacting, under-reacting, whatever. I know one thing for sure—we are not getting involved. No, sir. Not. Period. The end. Do you hear me?"

Kate heard him, but she didn't believe him, not even for one minute.

* * *

The haunting eyes of the Byzantine Madonna were what finally made Mary Helen go to see Marie Duran; the eyes, and the fact that tomorrow was the regularly scheduled meeting of the OWLs.

During Compline on Tuesday night, she had decided to leave the case to Inspector Honore. From what the Duran brothers had indicated, he was on the job, so to speak. Furthermore, Sister Cecilia, the college president, had hinted broadly.

"Well, if it isn't our two absentee ballots," Cecilia had said when she met Mary Helen and Eileen on the way to dinner Tuesday night. The pair had just returned home, still shaken from the scene between Junior and Finn. Mary Helen recognized the statement as one of Cecilia's attempts to be funny, although she couldn't help noticing the president's humor often contained a needle of truth.

The moment they sat down at the dinner table, Eileen flipped through her pocket calendar. "What do you suppose we missed?" She gasped. "No wonder Cecilia was unhappy. Today was the faculty meeting."

"At our age, we are entitled to a few lapses of memory." Mary Helen felt a bit defensive.

"Lapses of memory are one thing, old dear"—Eileen frowned—"but to give the devil her due, we have positively been neglecting our jobs."

"Missing one faculty meeting can hardly be construed as neglecting our jobs. Besides, age should have some privilege.

And the furnace wasn't working," she threw in. She wasn't sure why. "Be reasonable."

But Eileen did not intend to be reasonable. She was having a case of Irish "guilties," and Mary Helen knew there was no stopping her.

"The furnace is working now and, actually, at our age we should be giving a better example. What does it say to the others, if we don't do what we are supposed to do?"

"I'll bet no one missed us, no one except Cecilia."

From the look on her friend's face, Mary Helen could tell that Eileen was about to argue the point. She was relieved when Sister Anne joined them.

"Where have you two been?" the young nun asked, her hazel eyes wide behind her purple-rimmed glasses. "I haven't seen you in days." Anne began to eat her salad. "We sure could have used your input about graduation at this afternoon's meeting."

Talk about saying the wrong thing at the right time! Although she would never admit it, Mary Helen knew Eileen was right. And whatever "input" was, they probably should have been there to give it. To tell the truth, Mary Helen had been so preoccupied with Erma, that finals week and graduation, with all the ceremonies surrounding it, had almost slipped her mind. And summer school? She hadn't given the opening of summer school even a passing thought. Yes, Eileen was right! Her first responsibility was to Mount St. Francis College.

Much as she hated to, she decided to put Erma in the hands of God and the SFPD. After the final blessing at Compline, she told Eileen so.

Yet those sad Madonna eyes had haunted her all night. She had even dreamed about them.

Right after the six-thirty Mass on Wednesday morning, Sister Mary Helen waited for Sister Eileen. "Let's step outside for a minute," she said, watching the nuns file out of the chapel, then start down the hall toward the dining room. She didn't want to be overheard.

Obediently, Eileen followed her. Outside, dawn was just beginning to show over the Oakland hills. "It's going to be a beautiful day." Mary Helen drew in a deep breath. "Look at that sky." She pointed toward downtown, where an aura of peach was beginning to cut through the fog and frame the buildings.

"You didn't pull me out here to discuss the weather," Eileen said. "Furthermore, if you look the other way, old dear, you will see the fog has all but obliterated the Golden Gate as well as the entire Richmond District." Clearly, Eileen's tone of voice was wary. In fact, everything about her was wary.

"Tomorrow is the regular monthly meeting of the OWLs," Mary Helen reminded her.

"And you didn't pull me out here to discuss our appointment schedule either." She narrowed her eyes.

As usual, the direct approach was going to work best with Eileen. "I can't get Erma or the picture of the Madonna and those haunting eyes out of my mind. Just what did Erma mean when she told her daughter, 'If anything happens to me, look there'? The whole thing is such a mystery."

"What kind of shenanigans are you contemplating, Mary Helen? I had the feeling you were being entirely too agreeable and too pious last night."

Mary Helen tried to look a little hurt. She must have succeeded. Eileen's face puckered and she patted Mary Helen's hand.

"Erma and the picture have been on my mind, too, old friend," she said, "and it's high time we did something to take the mystery out of them."

Without much further discussion, the two nuns agreed to meet at ten o'clock in the convent garage. The most logical person for them to see, they decided, was Ree Duran, the most mysterious of Erma's children.

* * *

After several attempts, Mary Helen parallel parked in the narrow alley off 17th Street where Ree lived.

"That's the one." Eileen pointed to a pink house, midblock, with the same Italianate front as its neighbors. "And, remember, that one is her apartment." She indicated the door cut in the basement, with vivid blue hydrangeas on either side of it.

Mary Helen pressed the doorbell of the basement apartment. No one answered. No one seemed to move inside. She stepped back to study the main house. That, too, appeared empty. "Maybe nobody's home." She couldn't help feeling disappointed. "I guess we should have called first."

"I'm sure I hear the television."

Thank God for Eileen's hearing. Mary Helen put her ear to the front door, then rapped. "Maybe the bell is broken."

After several knocks, the door opened a crack. The eyes peering out had trouble focusing at first. A thick brass security chain stretched where a nose should be. Ree grunted and shut the door. Mary Helen could hear her fumbling with the night chain.

Finally, she opened the door just wide enough to let them in. All the blinds in the one-room apartment were drawn. A table lamp and the television set provided the only light. Ree motioned them to sit down on a lumpy couch against one wall. A game-show contestant laughed shrilly.

Turning down the volume on the set, Ree went back to a worn recliner and wrapped herself in an equally worn granny-square afghan. The floor around the chair looked as if Ree had been sitting there for some time.

"I'm not feeling well," she said, sniffling.

It's no wonder, Mary Helen thought. She counted two open boxes of Cheez-Its, a plastic bowl with the melted remnants of chocolate ice cream in the bottom, five wadded candy-bar wrappers, and a plastic liter bottle of diet cola. A cracked bowl with several kernels of unpopped corn was perched next to her on a hassock.

"What is it?" Eileen's eyes were full of concern. "Not that new flu, I hope."

"A cold, I think. Or maybe I'm just depressed." She sniffled again.

"What are you doing for it?" Eileen asked at the same moment that Mary Helen said, "Do you get depressed often?" Their questions intermingled and Ree ignored them both.

Instead, she continued to talk. It was as if she were repeating a familiar story yet another time. Mary Helen had the uncanny feeling that Ree hardly knew they were there.

"I didn't used to get depressed, you know, before it happened. But afterward, I did. It used to worry Mommy. Lots. She didn't say so, but I could tell." Suddenly, Ree reverted to a little girl's voice. "Mommy got me medicine from the doctor. See my medicine?" She thrust the brown plastic pill container toward Mary Helen. "It keeps me happy," she said, pulling the container back before Mary Helen could read exactly what kind of tranquilizers the doctor had prescribed. Ree tucked the brown cylinder beside her in the chair.

"Have you taken some today?" Mary Helen asked, knowing full well what a foolish question it was. One look at the woman's eyes told her she had taken more than one, and probably quite a few.

Ree nodded almost in slow motion. She focused her eyes first on one nun, then on the other, frowning as if she wondered who they were.

"What you really need is something nourishing to eat!" Eileen headed toward the small refrigerator in the portion of the room that served as a kitchen. While she located a pan and set about scrambling eggs and making hot buttered toast, Mary Helen removed the popcorn bowl from the hassock and sat down close to Ree.

"Before what happened?" she asked the young woman.

Closing her eyes, Ree rubbed her forehead. Obviously, it was taking a great effort to think. Her dilated eyes opened and she stared. Suddenly, as though frightened, she clutched the afghan around her body and rocked back and forth.

"Mommy told me not to tell our business to strangers."

"I am hardly a stranger," Mary Helen said soothingly. "And if what you were going to say will help us contact your mother, I'm sure she would want you to tell me."

Ree studied Mary Helen's face, seemingly weighing the words. She continued in her little-girl voice. "Daddy took me and the boys with him to see the horses run. Mr. Finn went too." She shuddered. "They had some beer, Daddy and Mr. Finn. We had soda pop. Daddy went somewhere. He left us with Mr. Finn."

Mary Helen felt as though she were listening to a sleeper recounting a recurring dream. Maybe it was a dream.

"When did all this happen?" she asked.

Tears hung for a moment on the corners of Ree's eyes, then ran down her chubby cheeks. Frowning, she focused on Mary Helen's face. "I don't remember, really. I was just a kid." Although she sniffled, she sounded more like her adult self. "I get mixed up, you know. I remember Mr. Finn was there and my brothers too. I was scared. I remember that. And that it hurt me."

"Who hurt you? Mr. Finn?"

"I can't really remember. But he was there. I remember he was there and he saw. I'm sure he saw. Sometimes when I see his eyes, I think I remember him looking. Sometimes it still scares me . . ."

"Did you ever talk to your mother about it?"

Fishing under the afghan for a Kleenex, Ree stopped to wipe her eyes. "Yes. Mommy said I was just upset. That maybe it was just a bad dream or my imagination playing tricks." The child's voice began to slip in once more. "Mommy said Mr. Finn was a nice man and a friend of Daddy's. She

said she was sure he wouldn't hurt me. And she said my brothers loved me and they wouldn't hurt me either."

Ree blew her nose. "It seemed so real. Mommy said it was
just that I was lost and scared. Mr. Finn was the one who
found me. Daddy came and he was mad. He brought me and
my brothers home."

"Did you ever talk to your father about what happened?"

Again, tears filled Ree's doelike eyes. "Right after it happened I tried a couple of times, but Daddy would get real mad.
Once when I tried to tell him it was Mr. Finn's fault, not mine,
he grabbed me and started to spank me, but Mommy made
him stop. She told him maybe I just had a big imagination or
watched too much TV or maybe I'd had a bad dream. When
Daddy got mad at her for making up excuses, she hollered
back at him and said I was high-strung, just like him.

"Later, when Daddy wasn't there, she told me that he was
mad because Mr. Finn was his good friend and he didn't like
me to say bad things about him. Or about the boys either."

"You said your brothers were there, in this dream?"

Ree shook her head like an animal trying to rid itself of a
buzzing fly. "I think so, but I'm not sure."

"Did anyone hurt them?"

"I don't know. Mr. Finn got ahold of Junior, I think. I get
all mixed up," she repeated. "I was just a kid. You know?"

Mary Helen was quiet, waiting.

"Mommy said the best thing to do was to forget about it,
not talk about it." Ree went on, her little-girl voice returning.
"Then it would go away. Daddy wouldn't get mad at me.
Mommy said everything would work out. But it didn't. I still
get scared sometimes and I feel sad. Sometimes Mommy felt
scared and sad too. Like just before she went away. I could
tell. She told me to look at the picture if anything ever happened to her."

Eileen came across the room with a plate of steaming eggs,
buttered toast, and a mug of tea on a makeshift tray. "Eat up,

dear." She set the tray on Ree's lap. "You'll feel much better with something in your stomach."

Ree ate hungrily, without even looking up. Eileen started to tidy up around the chair, then worked her way over to the kitchen area. At least Eileen's uneasiness was useful. She cleaned.

Mary Helen just sat there staring into space, not knowing what to make of it all. Had Ree been dreaming or had something actually happened long ago at the racetrack? The track part, at least, could be true. It had the ring of authenticity. Maybe the child had been lost. She remembered, right after Erma's disappearance, Ree's angry flare-up about her father and Finn's propensity for the races. On the other hand, all one had to do was talk to Ree for a little while to tell the woman was not completely stable.

Poor Erma. Knowing her, Mary Helen could well imagine how badly she must have wanted everything to work out. How important it must have been to her to keep both her husband and her daughter happy. And how hard she must have tried to do it. Mary Helen fished through her pocketbook, searching for another tissue to hand the sniffling Ree, but the package was empty. Perhaps she had stuck an extra one into the zipped side pocket.

The crumpled pages of Erma's journal caught in the zipper. Struggling to loosen the zipper, Mary Helen was annoyed. Drat! Erma was an intelligent woman. What had she been thinking about? Why hadn't she taken intelligent steps to solve her family's problems? Why hadn't Erma used her head?

"The heart runs away with the head." She remembered that some eighteenth-century Romantic had said that about love. And Erma had loved Tommy Duran. With all his shortcomings, she'd loved him. And her children. Difficult as they appeared to be, she loved them too. She wanted them all to be happy. She wanted everyone to be happy. Erma McSweeney Duran just couldn't help herself.

* * *

That night Kate soaked longer than usual in the bathtub, thinking about, of all things, Ron Honore and the missing OWL. You'd think I didn't have enough cases of my own, she fussed, adding still more hot water to the tub.

"Are you ever coming to bed?" Jack called from their bedroom. "It's dark and lonely in here by myself."

Kate checked the clock on the old-fashioned vanity table. She couldn't believe she'd been in the tub for almost thirty minutes. No wonder the water was cold.

Pulling the plug, she stepped out of the old-fashioned tub and began to dry herself with a soft towel. Her body tingled and soon she felt warm and relaxed all over. With a large feathery puff, she put generous pats of Giorgio dusting powder everywhere. The puff left round, soft white patches on her pink skin.

Self-consciously, Kate opened one of the vanity drawers and took out the small bottle of honey-colored liquid Mama Bassetti had given her. St. Gerard oil, her mother-in-law had called it. For all Kate knew, it could be olive oil from Lucca, straight off the shelf of Petrini's Market. She'd have to ask Sister Mary Helen about St. Gerard and his miraculous powers.

Feeling a little embarrassed even though she was alone, Kate rubbed the oil across the middle of her stomach. What she ought to have been doing, she thought, was taking her temperature as the doctor's brochure suggested.

She studied the friar on the small bottle. His hands were folded and he was looking piously heavenward. *St. Gerard, do your stuff,* she prayed, hoping she wasn't indulging in pure superstition.

"Hurry up, hon." Jack's voice startled her. Quickly she shoved the bottle back into the drawer.

The moment she crawled into bed, Jack reached for her. "You smell delicious," he said, pulling her close. His hands moved smoothly over her thighs, caressing her hips, his touch exciting her.

"Mmm, silky." His hands glided up, seeking her breasts.

"New bath oil," Kate mumbled. As he pressed his body close to hers and eagerly found her lips, she knew bath oil was the last thing on his mind.

May 17

Thursday of the Fifth Week of Easter

"Red sky at morning—sailors take warning." Shivering, Eileen walked down Parker Street toward the Carmelite monastery for the six-thirty Mass.

"I don't care what you say"—Mary Helen could see her own breath—"the moment I read the announcement last night, I knew today was going to be a good day. It was like an omen."

She studied the sky. In fact, red or not, this morning's dawn reminded her of an old-fashioned holy card, the kind you received at Easter, with fluffy white clouds all streaked with gold and rose behind the floating figure of the risen Lord.

"Yes, a very good omen," she declared.

"And s-since when have you b-begun to b-believe in omens?" Eileen was still so cold that Mary Helen could hear her teeth chattering.

"Since I read the announcement about today's Mass. I knew we couldn't go at noon. Because of the OWL meeting, we'd just have to go to the Carmelite monastery. It was as if God were sending us a sign." She smiled at her friend. Sister Eileen had the good grace to simply smile back.

* * *

At nine, when the two nuns arrived at Erma's apartment, Mr. Finn, Lucy, and Caroline were already there.

Caroline, impeccably groomed as usual and obviously impatient, sat twisting her long string of pearls. "I'm glad you're here." She narrowed her eyes at Finn, who was staring out the apartment window. "He says he has something to tell us, but he insists on waiting until everyone arrives."

Apparently deaf to her remark, Finn rocked back and forth on his heels and said nothing.

"Come in, Sisters. Sit down." Lucy, always the hostess, patted the cushion next to her on the sofa. "How have you bean, lima?" she asked brightly. Stifling a groan, Sister Mary Helen sat down where Lucy had patted.

"Here comes the other one. The one with the blue hair," Finn announced.

All that's missing is "Hail to the Chief," Mary Helen thought, watching Noelle sweep into the room. With her usual air of efficiency, she peered over her half glasses, cleared her throat, and prepared to take over the meeting. "Are we all here?" Her bright blue eyes surveyed them.

"But not all there!" Lucy couldn't resist.

Ignoring the remark, Noelle lit her cigarette.

Finn spoke up from his post. "The daughter's not here."

"Oh, she's not coming." Lucy scooted forward. "I talked to her this morning just before Caroline picked me up. The poor child is not feeling well."

"For God's sake, Lucy, the *child,* as you call her, is at least thirty-five years old." Caroline glared. "What is wrong with her now?"

"She has a very bad cold." Lucy sounded defensive.

"That's correct. She was quite a bit under the weather when we saw her yesterday." Sister Eileen jumped in on Lucy's side.

"As I've said a million times, if it isn't her . . ." Caroline pointed a finger.

"Girls, girls. That's neither here nor there."

The room crackled with tension. Mary Helen was glad Noelle spoke up. The discussion had not yet disintegrated into an argument, but it was well on its way. Caroline frowned as if she had something more to say, but refrained.

Erma's disappearance is getting to all our nerves, Mary Helen thought. She watched the women, looking for all the world like three ruffled ducks, settle back in their chairs.

Unabashed, Noelle continued to run her meeting. "We are here this morning to report on anything we may have discovered in the last few days about Erma and her whereabouts, not to discuss her family affairs. Who wants to speak first?" She tilted her head.

Caroline spoke up. "Mr. Finn has something to report." Apparently Ree Duran's health was no longer on her mind. "He promised to tell us as soon as we all were here."

Five pairs of eyes eagerly shifted toward the man. Hands buried deep in his pockets, Finn blinked nervously. Mary Helen didn't blame him. That was quite a battery of eyes for anyone to handle.

He cleared his throat. Mary Helen held her breath. She could feel her stomach begin to flutter with anticipation. Or was it dread?

"Erma called me." Before he could continue, the room burst into an excited chorus of gasps and questions.

Noelle's businesslike voice soared above the rest. "When? And what exactly did she say?"

"Last night. And she . . . she said she was okay. Getting settled and not to worry."

"Did she leave a number where we could reach her?" Lucy moved forward on the sofa. From the smile on her face, Mary Helen knew she was about to go straight to the phone for a nice long talk. Fine! She would be right behind her.

Lucy's smile faded as Finn shook his head. Rats! Mary Helen thought, deflated. Yet she could have predicted his answer. Even if he did know, she was quite certain he wouldn't tell.

The room had settled into a puzzled silence. "Erma said she'd call again. Said she didn't want to talk to anybody till she 'sorted out some stuff,' was the way she put it."

"What stuff?" Lucy's voice quivered. "Didn't she say?"

The man shrugged. "Nope. She didn't say what."

"Then there is nothing more for us to do." Noelle said finally. Mary Helen wasn't sure if it was a question or a statement.

Whichever, Noelle threw the strap of her blue leather purse over her shoulder and studied the group over the top of her half glasses. "At least we know she is safe, ladies." She tried to sound cheerful. "We should be glad for that, anyway."

"You're right, Noelle," Caroline agreed without much enthusiasm. "I suppose tonight we will all get the first real night's sleep any of us has had since this dreadful thing began."

Three *yesses* and an *indeed* supported her supposition. Finn merely grunted.

"Someone should call and inform the police." Noelle shot an it's-all-yours smile at Mary Helen and turned on her blue heel. "And, Caroline, will you give Barbara Quinn a ring? You both should have plenty of time to make your calls and to get over to the OWL meeting."

One by one, the women rose to go. The jumble of feelings in the room was hard to describe: relief, surely, yet confusion; happiness and delight, certainly, yet real bewilderment and perhaps a touch of hurt.

Watching them, Mary Helen couldn't help but think of Easter again. This morning's sky had reminded her of an old holy card portraying Jesus risen. This afternoon Erma's apartment was more like the empty tomb. What had the gospel said about the women who discovered it? "They hurried away, half overjoyed, half fearful . . . to carry the good news." She felt that way herself.

Pushing up from the couch, she knew she should be elated or at least relieved. Oddly, she wasn't either.

Unanswered questions squirmed and jostled in her mind. If anything, Finn's revelation had filled her with an inexplicable sense of uneasiness. The whole episode was so out of character for the Erma she knew. Or maybe she hadn't known the woman half as well as she'd thought.

Above all, she did not want to call Inspector Honore. In fact, she thought she would put it off for a day or two. Who would be the wiser? Besides, now more than ever, it was important that he dig around. He might discover just why Erma Duran had left San Francisco in such a hurry and why she didn't want to be contacted by her old friends, or even by her family.

Gripping the banister, Sister Mary Helen adjusted her bifocals and started down the narrow staircase. There were so many unanswered questions, so many loose ends. Lucy Lyons was just ahead of her. At least she might have the opportunity to have one of her questions answered.

"What exactly is wrong with Marie Duran?" she asked softly enough, she hoped, not to be overheard.

"I'm not really sure," Lucy whispered back. "Some serious health problem, I think."

They were nearing the bottom of the steps. Mary Helen had no time for diplomacy. "Mental?" she asked.

"Erma never said." Lucy tucked a strand of hair back into the gray braid circling her head. "That is, she was never very specific about Ree's problem. Or about her other kids' problems, for that matter. Her home life was very private."

"And you didn't ask?"

Again, Lucy shook her head.

"You've been her best friend all these years, and you never

asked?" Mary Helen was astonished, although she shouldn't have been. Erma did have—how had Eileen put it?—a touch of lace-curtain Irish.

Seemingly just as astonished, Lucy met her stare. "That's why we remained best friends all these years, Sister. Nobody, but nobody, with any sense gets between a mother bear and her cubs."

Impatiently Caroline tooted her car horn. The windshield wipers were moving back and forth. Only then did Mary Helen realize that while they were in the apartment it had started to rain. The soft drizzle wet her face and covered her glasses.

"And we've no umbrella." Eileen fussed in the doorway behind her. "I should have known—with the red sky this morning, and all."

Mary Helen put out her hand. "It's like Shakespeare's 'gentle rain,'" she said. "'It droppeth . . .'" Hoping no one would notice, she switched, midquote, to Matthew, "'On the just and unjust alike.'"

"Except the unjust have all the umbrellas," Lucy quipped, hurrying toward the car. "See you both at the meeting," she called, waving.

"Do you know what else the old bard said?" Eileen smiled. "'All's well that ends well.' Right, old dear?"

"Right." Mary Helen followed her friend to their car parked at the bottom of the Sanchez Street hill. Of course it was right. But if all had ended so well, why did she feel almost as if someone had given her a swift, hard punch in the stomach?

Friday, May 18

Feast of John I, Pope and Martyr

Nothing was going right for Kate Murphy. It might just as well have been Friday the thirteenth. This morning she had been awakened by the eerie wailing of foghorns outside the Gate. Before leaving the house, she had dribbled coffee down the front of her blouse and had had to change it. She'd had the feeling then that this was not going to be her day. As the hours wore on, her pessimism became more and more justified. She and Gallagher had muddled around with rumors and leads that took them nowhere. A complete waste of time.

Now, at five P.M., they sat across from one another in the Homicide Detail, shoving forms around on their respective desks.

"A do-nothing day," Gallagher grumbled, taking the last sip of cold coffee from his mug. "All I've got to show for it is coffee nerves." He grimaced. "This stuff tastes like lye."

Staring into space, Kate nodded. The sharp ring of her phone made her jump. It was Jack. He'd be late getting home, he said. Something was breaking in Vice. There went her Friday night. Kate twisted a strand of her thick red hair. She'd been using Mama Bassetti's St. Gerard oil for a week now—well, five days—and as far as she could tell, still no miracle!

Maybe, as she'd suspected from the start, the stuff was pure superstition or maybe miracles take longer than five days. She'd have to call Sister Mary Helen and invite her and Sister Eileen to dinner. That way she could introduce the topic casually and find out what the two nuns thought about it.

"What's on your mind, Katie-girl?" Gallagher's voice startled her.

"Nothing much, Denny." As close as they were, and even though Gallagher had been on the force with her father and known her since she was a baby, she had no intention of discussing her St. Gerard oil with him. Or with anyone else for that matter, not even with Jack.

"Don't give me that. You're much too quiet and you're twisting." He pointed to her fingers in her hair. "You can tell your old partner. What are you thinking about?"

Kate was feeling so ornery she couldn't resist. "If you must know, my last thought was of your old friend, Sister Mary Helen." She watched Gallagher's face redden.

"Oh, no, you don't!" he exploded with what Kate considered an overreaction, even for him. Obviously the day had frustrated him too.

"You are not dragging me into that one." He pushed back in his swivel chair. "We should be working on our own cases. That one belongs to Honore. Let him worry about it."

Although Honore and his case had been the last thing on her mind, Kate couldn't help goading Gallagher. Deliberately, she batted her eyes. "How could you be so callous, Denny? An old woman is missing. Our nun friends are concerned."

"The city is brimful of murderers and we can't seem to finger any one of them." He leafed through the forms on his desk. "And you want me to worry about one missing person?"

"Not worry, really. Just be concerned."

"Concerned? I am concerned. Look!" Gallagher ran his fingers across the creases on his forehead. "See? Concerned! I'm concerned about all those crazies running loose, killing people."

Laughing, Kate checked her wristwatch. "Quitting time, Denny. Maybe tomorrow will be better." She grabbed her coat off the rack next to the window. "Do you want to go somewhere and drink to it?"

"Not tonight. I'm bushed. Besides, shouldn't you be hurrying home to cook dinner for your husband?"

Kate bristled. Gallagher knew very well that Jack was working late and, although he didn't approve, he was definitely aware that they took turns cooking. He wasn't bushed enough to pass up a chance to needle her! Well, fair is fair.

Refusing to rise to the bait, Kate rummaged through her purse for her car keys, thinking of a way to get back. "Okay, suit yourself."

"Where are you going? Fahey's?"

Kate shook her head. "I think I'll go to Alphonso's Bistro," she said, amazed at her own ingenuity at getting to Gallagher's goat.

"Alphonso's Bistro? Where the hell is that?"

"Over on Sanchez. It's the place where Sister Mary Helen's friend worked. The one who disappeared," Kate added, anticipating with glee the effect it would have on Gallagher.

"You have no damn business going there."

"I'm only going for a drink." Kate tried to sound offended.

"Alone?"

"Of course, alone—if you're too bushed."

"The hell you are," he said, taking her by the elbow. "Your car or mine?"

* * *

"Turn on the heat," Gallagher said the moment Kate started the motor of her car.

"All you'll get is cold air." She shivered. The day had never cleared and now the fog had turned to a cold drizzle. She pulled away from the curb, delighted that Gallagher apparently was too tired to argue when she said she would drive.

The Mission District was home to the City's largest collection of Victorians, and this way she could drive by them without an argument. Maybe the view would improve her disposition. Even as a child, Kate had loved riding by the old Victorians, especially at dusk, like now, when the lights began to show through their bay windows. Over the last few years, many of them had been refurbished and painted in bold colors to bring out the fretwork or the bracketed cornices.

It was still fun to drive slowly along Dolores Street, comparing the houses on the east and on the west. During the earthquake and fire of 1906, her father had told her, the houses on one side of the broad, palm-lined street had been saved, but those on the other side had burned. Driving south, it was easy to see that the houses on her left were postfire, unlike those on her right.

Gallagher, she sensed, was just getting ready to complain about her circuitous route when she pulled up across the street from a forest-green awning announcing, in white script, Alphonso's Bistro. Kate hadn't expected the small storefront restaurant to be quite so trendy.

Even as they walked toward the bistro, Kate knew she shouldn't be here. Gallagher was right, although she would never give him the satisfaction of saying so. This case was Honore's baby. She had no real desire to help him out. Yet, for some reason, she couldn't help pushing Gallagher's buttons. What did Flip Wilson used to say? "The devil made me do it."

She was concerned about the missing woman, of course; and if her probing helped Mary Helen's friend, she thought philosophically, all the better.

Shivering, her partner opened the plate-glass door to the dimly lit bistro. "Are you sure we're in the right place?" he asked as soon as he and Kate had stepped inside and onto the plush carpet.

"What do you mean?"

"The joint looks like a house of ill repute, to put it politely."

Kate took in the red flocked walls, the lush carpet, the imitation hurricane lamps. "Oh? And how do you know?" she asked, then watched him fight to control his temper.

Before he could formulate a calm answer, a short, square, plain-looking man bustled toward them. The only remarkable thing about him was the way he had taken a long strand of hair and stretched it back and forth across the crown of his head. Finn! Kate recognized him immediately from Honore's description. It must have taken a lot of concentration and even more brilliantine for the man to make that series of V's across his bald pate.

"How many?" Blinking nervously, his hazel eyes darted from Kate to Gallagher and back again. Kate knew he was sizing them up. "Cops, right?" he said almost immediately.

Kate flashed her badge. Knowing Homicide had no business asking questions, she hoped he wouldn't look too closely. Fortunately he didn't.

"I can pick you guys out anywhere." The man shrugged good-naturedly. "What can I do for you, Officers?"

Another couple came into the small restaurant and stood behind Kate. "Why don't you take care of these people," she said. "We can wait."

Looking grateful, Finn ushered the pair to a table at the far corner.

"I thought we were coming in here for a drink," Gallagher growled in Kate's ear. "Like I told you, you have no business—" He stopped short. Finn was back.

"I'm Al Finn, the owner. What can I do for you?" He held out a broad hand. "Always glad to cooperate with the police. I contribute to the Police Athletic League, you know." Kate remembered that Honore had mentioned that.

After they had shaken hands and introduced themselves, Kate wasn't sure just what she wanted to ask him. She glanced over at Gallagher, who glared back. Obviously, her partner was going to be of no help at all.

"We are here about your employee, Erma Duran. She's been reported missing."

"Oh, yeah, Erma." He licked his lips. "Another officer, a black guy, was in here asking about her."

A party of five ducked into the restaurant out of the cold. Finn switched his attention to them. "Will you excuse me, Officers, while I seat these people?"

"Sure. May we look around?" Kate asked.

"Be my guests," Finn said, or at least Kate thought he did.

Hands in pockets, Gallagher followed her through the restaurant. He leaned against a stainless-steel sink, folded his arms, and watched her avoid the cooks and poke around the kitchen. Everything about him said he was seething.

Opening a door, Kate peered down a dark flight of stairs.

"Basement," the dark-skinned dishwasher wearing a turban said flatly. Wiping his hands on his apron, he reached around the doorjamb for the light switch. A single bulb lit the steep stairs.

Halfway down the flight, she heard Gallagher close the door behind her. She could tell by the way he stomped down after her that she was about to catch hell. Even though they had been partners for almost four years, he still treated her like one of his daughters. Kate steeled herself. Much as she hated to admit it, sometimes—like now—she reacted as if she were his daughter.

"What do you think you're doing?" he roared.

"Looking around." Kate jutted out her jaw in the same stubborn way she had used to defy her father.

"I know that! I thought we were here for a drink." His eyes blazed.

"We were, but the opportunity just presented itself."

"What opportunity? You know damn well we're out of our jurisdiction. I told you we have no business here. I told you you can't go butting your damn nose into—"

"You told me?" Kate felt her face flush. She stepped closer to Gallagher. "You told me? What right do you have to tell me? You're my partner, not my father."

"Don't bring up your father, God rest him! The guy must have been a goddamn saint not to have wrung your stubborn neck. If you were mine, I'd have been up on charges long ago." Gallagher glowered at her. Kate did her best to glower back.

Neither of them had heard Finn open the door at the top of the basement steps.

"I was wondering where you guys had went," he called.

Hoping he hadn't overheard, Kate began to scan the basement. It was your average San Francisco turn-of-the-century basement: concrete sloping floor, narrow door at the far side leading to an alley probably once used by the coal man, wooden storage shelves along the rough concrete wall, two large laundry tubs streaked with rust. The whole place smelled of dampness and disuse.

Carefully descending the steps, Finn stood next to Gallagher. "What's going on?" he asked.

"Damned if I know," Gallagher barked, then softened, realizing the owner was not at fault. "My partner here is just looking around. Seeing what she can come up with that might give us an idea about the missing woman. Seems some nun friends of hers are pretty worried about her."

"Oh, them. Yeah. I was pretty worried about her myself"— Finn rocked back and forth on the soles of his feet, blinking— "until last night."

"What happened last night?"

"She called."

"She called?" Kate could feel her face redden. Why hadn't anyone told her?

"Yeah. Like I told them all. The day she left she told me

she'd call when she got settled. She didn't want the kids to know where she was. Can't blame her. They were starting to drive her crazy."

Really miffed now, Gallagher glared at Kate. "I can see how kids, anybody's kids, could drive you crazy."

Finn recognized a comrade spirit. "Those three clowns are real crazy-makers," he said. "Couple of days ago, the worst one, in my opinion, drove me to doing something I probably shouldn't have done."

The man sounded so remorseful that for a moment Kate wondered if she should stop him and read him his rights.

"Oh, what was that?" Gallagher was getting interested.

"He made me so damn mad I offered him money—plane fare to St. Louis to see if he could find his mother."

"If you ask me," Gallagher said, "that sounds like you were trying to help."

"Erma wouldn't think so," Finn said, licking his lips and nervously blinking even more.

*   *   *

By the time Jack Bassetti arrived home, Kate was bathed, powdered, St.-Gerard oiled, and in bed. "Did you eat, pal?" She watched him hang up his jacket and loosen his tie.

"Couple of hours ago." His face was pale and drawn. "We sent out for pizza."

"Bad day, huh?"

Nodding, Jack threw his slacks over the back of a chair and climbed into bed. "I'm beat," he said, closing his eyes. "How was your day?"

Kate turned out the bed lamp. "Not so good either." She plumped up her pillow and moved closer to her husband.

Reaching over, he put his hand on her hip. "What happened?"

"Everything! And on top of it, I had a real screaming match with Denny."

Jack grunted.

"But I think we made up. At least, we were speaking by the time we left Alphonso's Bistro." She waited for his reaction.

"Alphonso's?" Jack repeated, without even opening his eyes. "What were you doing there?"

"That's another thing? I'm so damn mad at Honore. Letting me go all the way over to that restaurant, only to hear that the missing woman had been found."

A flash from the headlights of a car parking on 34th Avenue shot across the bedroom ceiling. "Isn't it terrible," she asked, watching it fade into a corner, "to want to get away from your own children?" She moved closer to her husband. "It doesn't seem right, Jack. Erma has three kids she has to escape from, and I want just one baby so badly."

Beside her, Jack's body was warm and firm. She snuggled closer to him. The hair on his bare chest tickled her cheek. Maybe tonight is the night, she thought, feeling her husband's hand slip down her thigh. Only when it landed on the mattress with a thud did she realize that Jack Bassetti was sound asleep.

May 20

On Sunday morning a low, wet fog covered Mount St. Francis College. For once, Sister Mary Helen was glad. Futhermore, she hoped it wouldn't burn off for a good long time. As of last night, Sister Anne was still determined to run in today's Bay-to-Breakers Race. Running was bad enough, Mary Helen thought, without courting the chance of a heat stroke.

About five o'clock this morning, Mary Helen, unable to sleep, had heard the young nun in the convent hallway. She had cracked open her bedroom door to see if everything was all right. Anne was carrying a large glass of orange juice in one hand and a piece of whole-wheat toast in the other.

"Shouldn't you have an egg?" Mary Helen asked before she thought to stop herself. She knew Anne hated to be mothered or, in this case, grandmothered.

"No eggs," Anne mumbled, still a little groggy. "No slowly digestible protein."

"That's right." Mary Helen had read the same article in last

Sunday's paper. On Saturday night, the participants were encouraged to eat a "Last Supper" of spaghetti, French bread, ice cream, and cake—all carbohydrates. Then, three hours before the race, they were to have a light breakfast of "no slowly digestible protein." Whatever that meant.

"Will you and Eileen be there?" Sleepily, Anne pushed her bedroom door open with her foot.

"We wouldn't miss it for anything," Mary Helen answered, knowing for sure that she, at least, wouldn't. The previous Sunday, the *Examiner,* which had sponsored the race since it began in 1912, had put out a special booklet with all kinds of interesting facts and figures. Mary Helen could hardly wait. One hundred thousand runners were expected, the booklet had said, for the seven-and-one-half-mile cross-city race. With that many people in the race, she figured, there could only be a couple of hundred spectators. Eileen and she should have no trouble finding a good place.

* * *

"Where do you suggest we go to watch?" Eileen asked when the two nuns met in the Sisters' dining room as soon as Father Adams had finished the morning Mass. Obviously Eileen was interested in attending. In fact, she sounded downright enthusiastic.

Mary Helen had ripped a map showing good spectator spots from last week's paper. "As far as I'm concerned, the top of the Hayes Street hill is out." She pointed to the spot on the map. The hill rose two hundred feet and "separated the men from the boys," as the saying goes. "I am afraid it will be packed," she said, knowing full well that what she was more afraid of was witnessing a heart attack.

"And the finish line at the beach, there at the Great Highway, probably will be packed too. Plus, we would have to drive —and where would we park?"

Eileen's face puckered. She looked a little disappointed. "If we situated ourselves at the Great Highway, we would have a chance to see the thrill of victory and . . . *de agony of de feet."*

Mary Helen groaned. Lucy Lyons should be quarantined. "Our best bet seems to me to be the Pan Handle." She pointed to the narrow, grassy entrance to Golden Gate Park, which was so named because, to Mary Helen's lasting amazement, it did in fact resemble a pan handle. "And besides, we can walk over there." Quickly Eileen warmed to the suggestion.

At about eight-thirty, the two nuns were elbowing their way to the front line on Fell Street, which bordered the Pan Handle to the north. Mary Helen watched in awe as the serious racers blistered past. Chests heaving, feet pounding the asphalt, they seemed guaranteed to reach the finish line within the hour.

"Get a load of those guys!" A bald-headed man next to Mary Helen pointed to the sweating runners. "Hell, I read in the paper that Bobby Vlught, the first guy to win this thing, would have come in one hundred sixtieth today." He looked at her for a reaction. She tried to look impressed, although she had read the same article herself.

Before long, Eileen waved to a panting Anne. "Here comes our girl," she said. Anne's T-shirt, which read SOLE SISTER, distinguished her from the runners around her.

Quite a few minutes behind Anne, Mary Helen spotted several hand-waving politicians. Next to them were a man with a toddler on his back and two gray-haired women who looked as if they were well into their seventies.

"Glory be to God, look at that!" Nudging Mary Helen, Eileen pointed down the block to a set of human dominoes jogging along next to a life-sized whale, a couple of colored crayons, and the Bank of America team dressed as sheriffs who were chasing three women "bank robbers."

"Go, Jack, go!" Mary Helen recognized a familiar voice. She turned. Sure enough, Kate Murphy was pushing up right behind her.

What a stroke of luck! Mary Helen had been debating all

weekend whether or not to call Kate. Now she was spared having to decide. Meeting the woman in a crowd like this was more than a coincidence or even good luck: it was clearly an act of God.

"Well, you never know who you'll run into." Mary Helen faced Kate and tried not to look or sound too pleased.

"Hi, Sisters." Kate seemed genuinely happy to see them. "There goes Jack!" she shouted, momentarily distracted. "If he ever gets to the finish line, he'll need a week off." The three of them waved as Jack Bassetti, gaining speed, ran steadily toward the entrance to Golden Gate Park.

"I've been meaning to call and tell you how glad I was your friend has been heard from." Kate turned back to the two nuns.

Mary Helen had the feeling Kate was about to say more, but she didn't wait. It would never do for Kate to ask her what Inspector Honore had said when she told him. Nor did she feel like explaining why she had decided to wait until tomorrow to call.

Instead, she launched into the unsettling feelings she had about Erma Duran. She was careful not to leave out a single detail about the missing money, Erma's children, or the animosity between them and Mr. Finn.

Kate seemed sympathetic but, Mary Helen noticed, quite noncommittal, almost uninterested. "Sister, you know I'd help if I could, but this is really not within my jurisdiction. In fact, moving to another city is not against the law. Did you tell Inspector Honore about your feelings?"

"Yes," she said without elaborating. After all, it was true. She had told him about her feelings. Kate did not ask when.

How she wished she could talk to Kate instead, and even to old teddy-bear Gallagher, about the case. Instinctively, she knew that, even if they didn't want to, they couldn't help but give her feelings more credence than Inspector Honore had done.

"I'd better run." Kate checked her wristwatch. "I really mean drive. I parked the car by St. Ignatius and promised Jack I'd meet him at the finish line. After the race he wants to go to the Footstock Festival in the Polo Fields. Poor guy, he still has three miles to go. And from the looks of him, I may have to drive him to the nearest hot bath instead."

Kate Murphy started to move away, then turned. "I mean that about getting together. We haven't had a good visit and I miss it. Don't be surprised if you hear from me real soon."

Sister Mary Helen watched Kate wriggle her way through the cheering crowd. Skillfully avoiding a cluster of runners, she dashed quickly across Fell Street.

"I wonder what is on her mind." Eileen frowned at Mary Helen.

"I don't know, but I'm sure it's not Erma Duran. She didn't even seem interested."

"Of course she's interested. But if someone is not dead or even missing anymore, what on earth can the police do?"

Mary Helen was peeved. All this bureaucracy! The older she became, the less patience she had with it. In fact, it was getting so she agreed with whoever had said, "A committee of one gets things done."

"A woman's life may be at stake! Are we going to allow our friend to disappear in St. Louis without even finding out why?" She glared accusingly at Eileen.

Eileen sighed, her gray eyes wide. "Life, indeed! Aren't you being a bit dramatic? Sure, and we've all tried our best to get in touch with Erma, Mary Helen. You know that. But this is, after all, a free country. If she does not care to be found, there is nothing we can do about it. We are just going to have to accept the fact and be understanding."

As much as she hated to admit it, Mary Helen knew her friend was right. There was nothing more she could do. She would have to accept it, but she would be doggoned if she would ever understand it!

When Kate Murphy finally found Jack in the crowd at the beach, she didn't mention going to the Polo Field. It was obvious that her husband didn't even want to pick up his shirt. All he wanted to do was go home for a hot shower and a stiff drink. Maybe she could talk him into going out for an early supper before he fell asleep.

Watching Jack walk painfully up the narrow stairs toward their bathroom, Kate couldn't resist. "You know something, pal? You're in terrible shape for a policeman."

"Me?" Jack looked shocked. "Why, when I took my last physical, the doctor assured me that I was the envy of the entire medical profession!"

"Will you need any help getting undressed and into the shower?"

When Jack didn't react, Kate knew he was tired.

May 21

Monday of the Sixth Week of Easter

When Sister Mary Helen awoke on Monday morning the entire college was shrouded in rolling fog. Small halos shone around the campus lights. Bundling up in her heavy sweater, she trudged up the hill toward the chapel for the six-thirty Mass. Wisps of fog clung to the lowest branches of the evergreens. Shivering in the dampness, she kicked at a stone in her path.

"Eighty percent of all people hate Monday morning," she muttered aloud, then smiled in spite of herself.

It had been years since she had thought of that little-known statistic. As a matter of fact, it had been the conclusion one of her eighth-grade students had arrived at in his rather novel science project more than twenty-five years ago. She couldn't remember what method the youngster had used to make this judgment or how many people he had surveyed. She wasn't even sure it was true. But the longer she lived, the more inclined she was to attest to its validity.

As soon as she had finished breakfast, Sister Mary Helen left the dining room. Outside, the wet fog made her face tingle and her nose and eyes run. The sides of the hill were so socked in that, if she hadn't known better, she might have thought the City had completely disappeared. Like Erma.

Erma's uncharacteristic disappearance, followed by her equally uncharacteristic phone call, the apartment, the basement of the bistro, her children—all crowded Mary Helen's mind. Nothing jibed, and everything reminded her of the missing woman.

Her common sense told her Erma was fine and, although she wanted to help, apparently Erma was dealing with her problems the way she thought best. Not necessarily the way Mary Helen would deal with them. Why even fifty years ago, she remembered with a smile, the two had differed on something as insignificant as how to approach their history project. Ostensibly the current situation was resolved. She would go right over to the convent and call Inspector Honore. But why did she continue to feel so uneasy?

Sister Mary Helen was the first one to reach the convent after breakfast, so the building was deserted. A foghorn bleated in the distance. She used her key to open the heavy front door. She was determined to place her call to the inspector, go straight to her room, make her bed, and then hurry over to the alumnae office and make up for lost time. To put it bluntly, she would strictly adhere to minding her own business.

That would be the sensible thing to do. But as soon as she stepped inside she knew she wouldn't do the sensible thing. An empty convent, of course, meant an empty phone booth. The temptation was too great. She would contact Inspector Honore, of course, and a phone call or two to the OWLs would certainly be in order and perhaps a short call to Ree. Just to see if they had heard anything more. If they hadn't, nothing was lost. If they had, how much easier it would be to keep her mind on her own business.

Before any of the other nuns appeared, Mary Helen went

into the narrow convent phone booth. The directory was open to B—Boris–Botvin—and Boscacci's number was underlined.

Poor devil. Something else must be broken, she thought, glancing at her watch. It was far too early to call Missing Persons. The OWLs, she knew, would be up. She dialed Caroline's number, letting it ring fourteen times before she admitted to herself that Caroline wasn't home.

Noelle answered on the second ring. No, she hadn't heard anything new. Yes, she would let Mary Helen know the moment she did.

Lucy, too, was home and seemed genuinely glad to hear from Mary Helen. "I've been thinking about our conversation on Thursday," she said, "about Ree's illness. You remember I told you that Erma never said anything directly. Yet there were some things I couldn't help surmising."

"Oh?" Mary Helen could feel her heart quicken.

"You were right about Marie, I think. All weekend I've been mulling over the things Erma did tell me throughout the years. As I said, she never was specific, but I always had the impression that something had happened to Ree when she was a youngster. Something Erma was reticent to talk about, and that after it—whatever *it* was—the poor kid was never quite the same." Lucy paused for breath.

"Do you know anything about Mr. Finn?" Maybe there was some truth in what Ree Duran was saying.

After what seemed like a long time, Lucy answered, "Nothing, really, except that he was a good friend of Erma's husband, and ever since Tommy died he has been very good to her."

"Good in what way?"

"Oh, he kept her working after she should have been retired; he continued to lease her the apartment at the same rent. It is almost . . ."

"Almost what?" Mary Helen asked as Lucy hesitated.

"Almost as if their relationship is . . ." She hesitated again. "Is more than just that of old family friends."

Maybe it is, Mary Helen thought, feeling even more uneasy. "Her children all seem to dislike him, you know. If he's so good to their mother, I wonder why."

"I've often wondered that myself," Lucy said, then added cheerfully, "but none of us chooses her offspring!"

"Speaking of offspring, did you remember anything else?" Mary Helen was fishing. "You mentioned the other kids having problems."

"Oh, the boys? I can't remember exactly what Erma said, but I knew she was concerned about Junior's drinking and Buddy's smoking of funny cigarettes." Mary Helen could hear the telephone lines clicking while Lucy thought.

"Or was it the other way around?" she said finally.

Although it didn't make any sense, Mary Helen dialed Erma's apartment. Suppose we are all worrying about her and she's decided to come home, she thought, listening to the hollow ring. She nearly dropped the receiver when someone answered.

"Hello," a groggy voice said. It took her a moment to realize it was Mr. Finn.

"Excuse me, I must have dialed incorrectly," she said. "I was calling Erma's apartment."

"This is Erma's apartment," he slurred, without any explanation.

"Is she home?" Mary Helen's heart raced expectantly.

"No." There was a long pause. Even in his fuzzy state, Finn must have realized some explanation was due. "I miss her," he said. "I was just here so I'd be near where she was." The phone went dead.

From the hallway Mary Helen could hear the quick, unmistakable slap of Sister Therese pacing. She must be waiting to use the line. If Mary Helen dialed while she was at the end of the hallway, Therese would think it was still the same call.

Quickly, she dialed Ree's number, hoping she'd be talking by the time Therese paced back by the door. Fortunately the woman answered right away.

Feeling as though she had pulled a coup, Mary Helen identified herself. Ree sniffled.

"How are you feeling?" Mary Helen asked, remembering Ree's cold.

"Terrible!" She blew her nose. Right into the receiver, from the sound of it.

"You did hear the good news about your mother?" Mary Helen asked, determined to cheer up Erma's daughter.

"What news?"

"That she called Mr. Finn."

Marie coughed. "I heard it, but I don't believe it."

"Pardon me?" Mary Helen wondered if she'd heard correctly.

"I don't believe it!" Ree shouted without, Mary Helen noticed, a sniffle or a cough. "I've been thinking about it since I heard. Mommy would have called me, not him. She would know how upset I am. Yesterday I called Auntie Barbara. She thinks so, too, and she's worried. She says I should call that policeman and tell him."

In her mind's eye, Mary Helen could see Inspector Honore's face when he received that call. Poor fellow! On the other hand, she didn't blame Barbara Quinn for being worried. The whole episode was so unlike Erma. Furthermore, if two of them expressed their concern to the inspector, he might give it more credence.

Outside the phone booth, she could hear Therese's pacing quicken, her circling narrow. Time was limited. Any moment, Therese would pop her head in the booth, smile stiffly, and ask, "How much longer will you be on the line?"

"Why would Mr. Finn lie to us about the call?" Mary Helen asked, hoping Ree wouldn't have an answer that made any sense. She had called wanting her own uneasiness to be relieved, not heightened.

"I don't know." Ree blew her nose. "All I know is Mommy said to look at the picture of the Madonna."

Replacing the receiver, Mary Helen sat staring at the phone. For a moment she wondered why she'd given in to the temptation to call. To make herself feel better, of course. But if anything, she felt worse. Wasn't it Mark Twain who had said, "It is easier to stay out than to get out"?

How right you were, old boy, she thought, pushing open the phone-booth door.

"At last!" Sister Therese sniffed and swept past her to the phone. Watching her, Mary Helen smiled. She couldn't help thinking of that old expression—how did it go?—"She jumped on it like a duck on a june bug."

Well, if nothing else worthwhile had come of her phone-calling, she had at least given the Boscaccis a twenty-minute reprieve.

"So there you are!" Eileen greeted her in the convent hall-way. "You disappeared in a bit of a hurry."

From the inflection in Eileen's voice, it could be hard for strangers to tell if that was a statement or a question. Knowing Eileen, however, she knew exactly which it was.

"I wanted to make some phone calls." Mary Helen shoved her glasses up the bridge of her nose and stared for effect. "Private phone calls."

Opening her gray eyes wide, Eileen stared back. "I can't get good old Erma Duran off my mind either."

Mary Helen winced. When would she ever learn? Trying to fool Eileen was hopeless. Trying to intimidate her was hopeless squared.

"Did you find out anything new?" she asked.

"A few things," Mary Helen admitted. "For instance, Lucy Lyons led me to believe there could be some truth in what Ree told us last week. Mr. Finn was in Erma's apartment, either asleep or in his cups, or both. And Marie Duran—Ree—thinks Finn is lying about her mother's call."

Eileen pursed her lips and frowned. "Oh, dear!" she said. Suddenly she brightened. "As they say back home, 'bad news comes in threes.'" She counted on her chubby fingers: "Lucy, Finn, and Marie. The next news you hear will be good news!"

"I hope you're right," Mary Helen said. A cold draft whipped down the convent hallway. She shivered.

"Someone must be walking on your grave," Eileen whispered.

Mary Helen scowled. "Someone simply opened the back door. Always-prepared Sister Therese, no doubt, is unlocking it for Allan Boscacci."

"To each her own," she said.

The groan of the foghorn echoed through the building, reminding both nuns that the shoreline had vanished beneath the dense blanket of gray. But Mary Helen assured herself that the shore was there under the shifting fog. Just as the answers to Erma's sudden disappearance were there somewhere under the confusion that surrounded it.

Eileen might be wrong about her shivering, but she hoped her friend was right about the next bit of news being good. Mary Helen had several items on her list of things to do today, but they would just have to wait. Right then and there, she decided to spend the morning in the Hanna Memorial Library. She'd do some research on Erma's Madonna. If the woman had said to look there for answers, perhaps someone should. But first she must phone Inspector Honore and tell him Erma was at least alive.

* * *

Hearing from Don Juan Ron the first thing on Monday morning did nothing to improve Kate Murphy's disposition. "Hey, you don't even have a case here!" She knew she sounded short-tempered, but it had been a bad night. Besides, she was still annoyed with him from last Friday. "And, furthermore, why didn't you tell me you had heard from the lady before I made a fool of myself—"

"Because I just found out this morning," Honore interrupted, "when the Sister called me." She heard him crack his gum. "But the whole thing just doesn't set right."

"Why are you calling me? If you don't have a case, then surely we don't."

"Excuse me!" Honore's mood didn't sound too terrific either. "I just thought since these nuns are friends of yours . . ."

Kate didn't like his tone. In fact, much as she hated to face it, this morning she didn't like anything or anybody. "Listen, Ron," she said as patiently as she could, "I just got here. I still have my coat on. Let me call you back in an hour or so."

"Better yet, Kate"—she could tell that Honore, too, was trying to simmer down—"why don't I get some deli sandwiches and pick you up around noon? We can have lunch out by the Marina. That way we can eat, talk, and envy the way the other half lives."

Despite herself, Kate laughed. Honore pressed his advantage. "I'll even spring for some potato chips, those natural ones," he said, displaying some of the charm that had made him a legend.

"Make them the Hawaiian kind," Kate said, "and you have a date."

"Was that our favorite missing person again? Or did I mistake the vibes?" Gallagher asked when she hung up.

"Let me get a cuppa, Denny. Then we'll talk." Kate walked slowly to the coffee urn at the back of the detail. Relax, relax, she told herself. You can't bring your personal life to the job. But it was pretty hard not to.

Last night she'd realized that the honeymoon was definitely over. After they had come home from the Bay-to-Breakers Race, she and Jack had fought. He'd even raised his voice.

Usually patient Jack had hollered at her! She could feel tears sting her eyes.

"You're taking your goddamn frustration out on me," he had yelled. "And what's even worse, you're making yourself miserable."

She couldn't even remember what had started the quarrel. Although if she were perfectly honest, she knew wanting to be pregnant was at the bottom of it. She also knew, even as she shouted back, that he was right. That didn't make how she felt any easier. If anything, it made it worse. Even this morning there was still a coolness between them.

"Bad weekend?" Gallagher asked when she sat down.

Kate nodded, reluctant to talk about it. The last thing she wanted to do was cry. Careful not to burn her tongue, she took a tiny sip of coffee. She could feel her partner's eyes riveted on her. Doubtless he was debating whether or not to let it lie. She braced herself, sure of what his decision would be.

"You and Jack have a fight?"

"Last night, to be exact. How did you know?" Hastily Kate brushed a tear from her cheek.

"How did I know? I've been married as long as you've been alive. I know the signs." He offered her a piece of the Danish he had in a paper bag. "It happens in the best of families. Couples who don't fight don't make it. That's a well-known fact."

Gallagher stopped to take a bite of the sweet roll, chew, and swallow. "The important part is, did you make up?"

Kate shook her head.

"Oh, you should make up. Making up is the best part of fighting." He licked raspberry off his fingers. "Don't worry. By tonight old Jackie-boy will be full of remorse."

Kate knew her partner said that to make her feel better. Somehow it didn't.

* * *

Inspector Ron Honore picked Kate up promptly at noon. A few minutes later they were parked at the Marina Green. Honore had pulled the car in facing the Bay. Even if they were going to see how the other half lived, he obviously had no intention of staring at their homes while he ate.

Following the time-honored rule that a diet drink cancels out calories, he handed her a poor boy and a diet Pepsi. All morning Kate had been so filled with a dull ache that she hadn't realized how hungry she was. She chewed in silence.

In front of them, joggers and kite flyers, oblivious of the weather, enjoyed the wide apron of lawn around the yacht harbor. Behind them, along Marina Boulevard, were the luxurious two-story stucco homes with their million-dollar views of Alcatraz, Angel Island, and the Golden Gate Bridge. Although today the islands were barely visible and a wall of fog had nearly obliterated the bridge. Only the bright orange tips of the trusses pierced the grayness. Kate wondered foolishly if couples constantly surrounded by such changing beauty ever fought.

"This thing is really starting to bug me, Kate." Honore wiped mayonnaise from the side of his mouth and broke into her thoughts. "According to your friend Sister Mary Helen, Al Finn heard from the missing woman last Thursday."

Kate tried to sound interested. "So what's bugging you? She's no longer missing."

"Technically you're right. This one is solved. That's all I need, you're thinking. But the daughter, Marie, signed the missing-person report. She claims Finn is making it up. In fact, she called me this morning right after the nun did to tell me so."

Kate swallowed the hunk of sourdough roll that she had been chewing. "Why not get the phone number from Finn and just call the woman back?"

"Brilliant! And I thought of that too." Honore wadded up

the paper napkin, dug in the bag, and pulled out another sandwich. "Want half?" he offered.

Mouth full, Kate shook her head. At least the mystery of why the seams in Honore's suit jacket were straining was solved. "So why don't you call?" she asked again.

"Because Finn said the woman wouldn't leave a number."

"Isn't that a little odd?"

"It seemed a lot odd to me, but Finn tells me she doesn't want her kids to find her. My common sense tells me," Honore said, "to forget the whole thing. But in my gut"—he pointed to his belt buckle—"it doesn't feel right."

Kate resisted the urge to say that maybe it was the second poor boy and not the case that was affecting his gut. "That happens," she said instead. "So what can I do for you?"

"Just listen, mostly. Tell me what you think." Honore paused for a large swallow of Pepsi. "Since I last talked to you, I've double-checked. Finn, as far as the computer is concerned, is a good, upstanding citizen. Too good to be called a liar, if you know what I mean. Not married, no dependents. In the neighborhood they tell me he gambles a little at the track —nothing too big. Loses mostly, but the guy can cover his debts. Sometimes slowly, but he covers. Also, I hear he likes women. But the old geezer's entitled, right?"

Kate rewrapped the second half of her sandwich for later. Maybe she wasn't as hungry as she'd thought. "What women?" she asked.

"No mention of the Duran woman, if that's what you're wondering about. If there is anything there at all, the two of them are being very discreet. As far as the computer and the neighbors are concerned, that woman is a solid-gold saint. Pays her bills, keeps appointments, helps people out.

"Now her three kids, on the other hand—they get mixed reviews, all bad. But the daughter is more to be pitied than censured, as the old lyric goes."

"It's no wonder Mama doesn't want to hear from them," Kate said.

"Right, except that the bigger conflict seems to be between Finn and the woman's kids, especially the daughter, this Marie. She is sure he is guilty of something, even if there isn't anything concrete to go on."

"It sounds to me more like a case for a family counselor than for Missing Persons." Kate picked up several crisp brown crumbs that had fallen on the seat of the car and put them in the deli bag.

"You haven't had the chance to see any of these people, I guess." Honore wadded up his second napkin.

"As a matter of fact, I did meet Finn. Gallagher and I stopped by after work the other night."

"That's what you meant this morning by making a fool of yourself." Honore looked so pleased that for a moment Kate was afraid he was going to hug her. "Well, what did you think?"

"To tell you the truth, the guy seemed nice enough. Cooperative, et cetera."

"Did you have a chance to look around?" Honore stopped. "Of course not. How could you? What excuse would you use to go nosing through the guy's restaurant?"

"He didn't ask for any, so we didn't give any."

This time Honore did reach over and hug her. It was warm and hard and so unexpected that Kate was too startled to resist.

"Sorry," Honore said, suddenly aware of what he was doing. He ran his hand over his bald head. "I hope you don't think . . ."

Kate shook her head, debating whether or not to tell him that the only thing she did think was, I wish you were Jack. She decided to spare his ego.

Regaining his practiced cool, Honore cleared his throat. "Kate, you're a real pal," he said. "Did you find anything?"

"Nothing significant." Kate, too, was all business. "Only that Finn's bistro has a fairly clean kitchen, a damp basement, and that he offered to give one of Erma's sons enough money to go to St. Louis to look for his mother. Or so he said."

Deep in thought, the two stared out over the Marina. Dozens of blue and white yachts bobbed gently in their berths. Hungry gulls circled the masts, then, wheeling over the grass, landed on the piers, impatient for the chilly lunchtime crowd to go back to work.

Several silent walkers bundled up against the cold clip-clopped along the broad sidewalk. Watching a sweatsuited mother pushing a toddler in a stroller, Kate felt a twinge of envy and an urge to phone Jack.

"What do you think?" Honore asked finally.

"I think I had better get back to work," she said, her tone brisk.

"No, about this case, I mean." He offered her a piece of gum, which she declined. Honore had changed flavors. Kate couldn't imagine that Juicy Fruit would taste any better on top of salami and mortadella than spearmint. It might be even worse!

"I don't think there is any case, Ron. Unless you found something in the Duran woman's apartment to indicate that she left under duress."

Honore shook his head and shoved a stick of gum into his mouth. "I was in the apartment. Nothing there. No signs of a struggle. Everything in order, neat as a pin. In fact, that's the funny part. She didn't even unpack from her trip to New York or take any clothes with her to St. Louis, according to the daughter anyway. Everything is there, including that medal the nun found. Much as I hate to admit it, I'm beginning to agree with the kid, and I use the term lightly. Something is out of sync."

"I agree." Despite herself, Kate was getting interested. She began to twist a thick lock of hair. "A woman who is exact about paying bills, keeping appointments, whose apartment is as neat as a pin, would not go off without putting her affairs in order. And no woman in her right mind would go away without putting some clothes and makeup in a suitcase."

"Unless something spooked her and she ran." Honore hit the steering wheel with the palm of his hand. "But strictly speaking, that's not a police matter. Apparently she isn't missing. Or harmed."

"True. I guess the only thing you can do, Ron, is let it go."

"I wish that daughter would stop calling me to talk about some damn picture."

"What picture?"

"You haven't seen the apartment, have you?" Honore checked his watch. "I could get you there and back to the Hall in forty minutes."

"I'd need to make a phone call first."

"I'll stop at the Safeway." He motioned vaguely toward Gas House Cove. "I know they have a pay phone in their parking lot."

Honore looked so eager that Kate didn't have the heart to turn him down. Her phone call was quick. Jack, his office said, was out.

* * *

"It's only Our Lady of Perpetual Help." Kate stood next to Honore in Erma's icy bedroom. Finn had been most accommodating about letting them in. "There's an icon like that in almost every Catholic church in the City. What did the daughter say about it?"

"She said the secret to her mother's disappearance is in that picture. Now what the hell do you think that means?"

Kate shrugged. "Could she be a religious nut?"

"Beats me. Why?"

"They can be the worst kind." Despite her skepticism, Kate couldn't help taking the picture off its shelf in the corner. It was your ordinary, run-of-the-mill religious-goods store print backed with brown paper. Nothing fancy about the frame either.

"I've already taken it apart and checked for messages, if that's what you're thinking," Honore said, watching her run her hand over the paper backing.

"Maybe there is something in these Greek letters." She pointed to the characters in each of the upper corners.

Honore shook his head. "I called the priest in my parish to check. The writing is only the abbreviations for the four figures in the picture. It stands for"—he fumbled in his jacket pocket for a slip of paper—"Jesus Christ, Mother of God, and the two archangels, Michael and Gabriel." Popping his gum, he slid the paper back into his pocket.

"Hm," Kate replied, only because she couldn't think of anything else to say. The eyes of the Madonna clasping the hand of the Child gazed at her sympathetically. Or was it her imagination? Inexplicably, her scalp prickled. All at once the empty room seemed hollow and damp. The tomblike silence was shattered by a car backfiring. Kate jumped.

"Steady, girl." Honore studied her face. "You look pale. Feeling okay?"

"Maybe it's the salami," she said. "Or maybe it's a guilty conscience." She checked her wristwatch. "I've got to get back to the Hall, or Gallagher will be reporting me as missing."

To satisfy Honore, Kate did a cursory search of the bedroom, closet, and drawers. She even looked under the bed.

"What's this?" she asked, flipping through a black binder she found leaning against the leg of the nightstand.

"Looks to me like some kind of diary or journal." Honore shrugged. "But nothing seems to be written in it."

"Unless," Kate said, noticing the dustlike traces of paper, "someone has torn the pages out."

* * *

"Where the hell have you been?" Gallagher growled the moment Kate walked into the Homicide Detail.

"Here comes Miss Popularity now," O'Connor called from the corner.

Although she had no idea what he meant, Kate shot him a dirty look on general principle.

"You know very well where I've been, Denny," Kate said. "Did something happen?"

"Did something happen?" He ran his hand across his bald crown. "We had a goddamn chocolate chip in here dancing. Left you that bag." He pointed to a polka-dot bag of cookies perched on the corner of her desk.

"Then the goddamn florist delivered that." A long, narrow white box tied with red satin ribbon lay across her desk blotter.

"What's this all for?" Kate fumbled with the small envelope from the florist.

"Since I know it's not your birthday or your anniversary"—Gallagher rose, hitched up his belt, and moved toward the cookie bag—"all I can figure is that must have been some fight you guys had. I think it means your hubby is sorry."

Turning her back to the detail, Kate slipped the enclosure card out of the envelope. "If you want to make up, I have some ideas," it read. "For more details, meet me at the yellow peaked-roof house, corner of 34th and Geary, 5:30 sharp. Love Jack."

Kate could hardly wait!

* * *

One peek through the beveled glass door of the Hanna Memorial Library and Mary Helen knew finals week at Mount St. Francis College had begun in earnest. The place bulged with students hunched over long, narrow wooden tables that were punctuated with brass reading lamps. At summer school nearly fifty years ago, she and Erma McSweeney had hunched over those same tables, Mary Helen thought with an unexpected pang of nostalgia. Diligently they had studied in the light cast by those same brass reading lamps.

From the far end of the main reading room, a bigger-than-life portrait of Archbishop Edward Hanna kept a watchful eye on the scene. Hanna had been the archbishop of San Francisco when the college was founded in the 1930s. From the looks of things, the library, named in his honor, had not changed much since.

Elaborately decorated bullet-shaped lights hung from the high-arched ceilings. Rare books, many of them bequeathed by the archbishop himself, lined the walls on dark walnut shelves. Some of the original leather-back chairs studded with brass were being occupied by young women in faded denim designer overalls. At least Sister Anne had called them designer overalls and explained that the fading was deliberate. To Mary Helen *designer* and *overalls,* even those in full color, seemed like a contradiction in terms.

At the other end of the oblong room was the circulation desk. Behind it Sister Eileen was busily stamping out books. A line of weary-looking students queued up in front of her.

Waving at her friend, Mary Helen headed for the reference section. A loud *pst* made her turn. Wildly, Eileen was motioning her to come over.

"What is it?" Mary Helen asked in a stage whisper. She knew Eileen took her position as head librarian very seriously.

"When you told me you'd be over to do some research I figured what it would be," Eileen whispered back. "I could find only one reference, so I removed the book from the shelf before anyone else took it. Not that there's much call for this particular volume of the *Catholic Encyclopedia,* but one never knows."

She patted the thick black book on the desk beside her. "P," she said, "for Perpetual Succor, Our Lady of. In some places called 'Perpetual Help.'" Mary Helen noticed she had even stuck a small piece of paper in to mark the page.

"How did you know that's what I had in mind?" Mary Helen asked, then felt foolish. The two of them had been fast friends for more than fifty years. You can't know a person that long without having some insight into the way she thinks. Particularly if you are also her pinochle partner.

"Just a lucky guess." Eileen turned back to the stack of books in front of her and resumed her stamping.

Mary Helen found a comfortable, well-lighted carrel along a sidewall of the library. Quickly she opened the volume of *Catholic Encyclopedia* to the article she hoped would shed light on Erma's mysterious picture. She was disappointed to see how short it was.

She read carefully, hoping to stumble upon some pertinent information. Then she skimmed, still hoping something would jump out at her. Nothing did.

The article was interesting enough. It described the Byzantine Madonna and told the significance of all the figures in the picture. It gave a little history: "Fifteenth century . . . picture brought to Rome by pious merchant . . . Man died there . . . specified picture be venerated . . . For three hundred years crowds flocked to Church of San Matteo, where it was exposed.

"Augustinians served the church . . . also sheltered the Irish escaping persecution . . . In 1812, the French invaded Rome . . . destroyed church . . . Picture disappeared . . . lost for over forty years . . . Discovered in 1865 in an Augustinian oratory.

"As a boy, Pope Pius IX prayed before the picture in San Matteo . . . became interested in its discovery . . . Wrote a letter to the Father General of the Redemptorist convent . . . built over the ruins of San Matteo . . . Picture enshrined there."

The article went on to tell about the Pope's great devotion to the picture and to Our Lady under this title and his fixing a feast day and approving a special Mass and Office for the Redemptorist Congregation. The Pope was also among the first to visit the new shrine. Facsimiles of the picture, the article concluded, had been sent from Rome to every part of the world.

Mary Helen read the article yet a third time. Currently, she reminded herself, the feast of Our Lady of Perpetual Help is observed on June twenty-seventh. Even at third reading, none of the facts seemed to give any indication of what Erma could possibly have meant. At least they gave no indication to Sister Mary Helen.

"Any luck?" Eileen asked when Mary Helen returned the encyclopedia to the circulation desk.

"None," she said.

"To tell you the truth, I read it before you arrived and I couldn't make head or tail of it myself."

"That at least makes me feel a little better."

Eileen looked sympathetic. "From the looks of you, you couldn't be feeling much worse," she said.

* * *

Outside, the day was still damp and dreary. Leaning against one of the stone lions guarding the entrance to the college building, Mary Helen surveyed the scene. The benches and lawns surrounding the building were deserted; it was too cold to sit outdoors. Students pulling heavy sweaters tightly around themselves hurried along, eager to get inside. A brisk wind picked up small scraps of paper and spun them like minitornados across the deserted campus.

Only the hot pink petunias bordering the driveway seemed unaffected by the weather. The flowers looked as perky and cheerful as if the spring sun were shining.

Kicking at a loose piece of gravel in the entranceway, Mary Helen heard the pebble without really seeing it bounce down the steps in front of her. Her mind was preoccupied with Erma. Maybe a brisk walk around the grounds is what I need, she decided. Oxygen to the brain—good for the thinking. Right now her brain needed all the oxygen it could absorb.

Hands buried deep in her sweater pockets, she started along

a walkway. Look to the picture, Erma had said. What in the world had she meant? Names? Perhaps.

There were Jesus and Mary, of course, and the two archangels Gabriel and Michael. Could she have meant to look for someone named Gabriel or Michael? Sister Mary Helen racked her brain, but no one and nothing surfaced.

Breathing deeply, she went over the other names connected with the Madonna: the Church of San Matteo . . . was there a Matthew? The Augustinians . . . maybe somebody named Augustine? Pope Pius IX. What was his real name? She'd have to look it up.

Then, of course, there was Marie, a derivation of Mary. But the very idea of Marie harming her mother was preposterous. She was obviously devoted to Erma and very dependent on her —actually too dependent. Although Mary Helen had to admit that Marie Duran was puzzling. Why did the woman keep insisting Finn had harmed her mother? Even when he had offered money to the brother to go to St. Louis. Even—and more puzzling—after he announced that the mother had called . . . Marie Duran couldn't seem to get him out of her craw. Mary Helen listened to the gravel crunch under her feet and wondered why.

Did Ree know something none of them knew? Or was she really mentally ill and unable to face the reality that Mama had finally been driven to leave home? Was she just looking for someone like Finn to take the blame?

And this picture business! What had Erma really said? Or had she said anything? After all, they had only Ree's word for it. Maybe she had fantasized the entire conversation. But if so, why? If there was a reason, what in the name of all that was good and holy could it be?

How she wished Erma had left a phone number! Then she could "reach out and touch someone," as the phone company frequently suggested, and clear up the whole mess.

"Hi, Sister." Pat Boscacci's voice startled her. The petite

young woman had the two youngest of her four daughters
trailing behind her. "Allan's here somewhere." She gave Sister
Mary Helen a squeeze. "Sister Therese called him. The girls
and I have come to pick him up."

Two shining little faces smiled up at her.

"The girls had the day off. A teachers' meeting or some such
thing," Pat said, winking at the one closer, "and we're on our
way to spend the day in Golden Gate Park. We haven't done
that in years."

"Your poor husband," Mary Helen said, ushering the little
brood of Boscaccis toward the convent, where they could get
out of the cold.

Two final bangs as soon as she opened the back door were a
sure sign that Allan was finishing up. They came from the
laundry room.

"Hi." He smiled as soon as he saw them. Immediately Mary
Helen noticed a large tattered and discolored rag on top of the
avocado-green Maytag. Avocado-green appliances had been
the last convent buyer's idea of chic.

"That's the culprit." Allan pointed to what had probably
once been a lovely bathmat. "Somebody must have dropped it
behind the washer, then pushed the machine back on top of it,
which messed up the balance."

"Are you finished already?" Sister Therese swept down the
hallway. "And here are those darling little girls. You must be
frozen." She bent toward them. "Come, come! Let me get you
some hot chocolate with marshmallows floating on top."

"No, thank you, Sister." Pat took the girls' hands. "We're
on our way to the park."

"And the Japanese Tea Garden," the younger one piped up.

Leaving the Boscaccis and Sister Therese arguing about the
relative merits of hot chocolate in a warm convent versus Japanese tea in a windy garden, Mary Helen walked down the
hall.

"Telephone for you, Mary Helen." Sister Anne's voice made her jump.

As she neared the phone booth, Anne pointed to the blinking light. "It's Kate Murphy and she sounds wonderful."

Kate did sound wonderful, if a little rushed. When they met at the Bay-to-Breakers, she had said she would call soon. But Mary Helen never expected it would be this soon. Something in Kate's tone made her suspect that this was more than a friendly call. Kate had something on her mind.

What could it be? Maybe she had rash judged her last Sunday, as Eileen suggested. Perhaps she really was concerned about Erma and had uncovered something important. Could this be the good news Eileen had predicted early this morning?

"Is there something you have to tell me?" The question was blunt, but at the moment Mary Helen's hope overcame her finesse.

"Ask you," Kate said.

Mary Helen was surprised and delighted when Kate invited Eileen and herself to dinner on Wednesday night. She was not nearly so delighted when Kate promised they wouldn't say a single word about police work.

She could have sworn Kate had something important on her mind. Maybe she was losing her touch.

May 23

Wednesday of the Sixth Week of Easter

"Why don't you come about seven o'clock?" Kate had said. "That sounds like a nice, fashionable hour to dine. Furthermore, it will give Jack and me time to get home from work and get dinner ready."

"And for the two of us to have a snack, so we won't be starving to death," Eileen had said when Mary Helen relayed the message.

Since they received Kate's invitation on Monday afternoon, Mary Helen had been wrestling with how best to get Kate interested in her growing uneasiness about Erma's whereabouts.

"It's not against the law to move," Kate had told her.

It's also not against the law to find out why a person needed to do it so quickly, she reassured herself.

She might even mention that strange dream entry she had discovered in her friend's journal. But how could she bring that up without letting on that she had ripped out the pages and read them? As hard as she tried, she could not figure out a way.

On the dot of seven, the Sisters arrived in front of the yellow peaked-roof house on Geary Boulevard. Mary Helen was surprised to see a white Camaro parked in her usual spot.

"She never mentioned other company," she said. "I wonder who . . ." It didn't take her long to find out.

"Sisters, Sisters, come in." Mary Helen recognized Mrs. Bassetti's voice immediately. "It's so good to see you! And right on time. Jackie, it's the Sisters. Don't just stand there, take their coats."

Well, well! she thought, realizing now who the driver of the Camaro was. There's lots of zip left in us old girls yet. If the opportunity arose, she must invite Mrs. Bassetti to join OWL.

The Murphy-Bassetti living room was warm and cozy. Outside, the fog hadn't lifted all day. Mary Helen settled down in front of the roaring fire. Actually, as far as she was concerned, the fog hadn't lifted—literally or figuratively—all week long. Not in the neighborhood and certainly not about Erma Duran. The living-room fire was so bright and welcoming. Tonight might just be the night. She moved over on the sofa to make room for Eileen and waited for the first opportunity to talk about Erma.

"What can I get you, Sisters?" Jack returned from hanging up their coats.

"Tell them what you have." His mother settled next to the Sisters. "That's not the way I raised him," she apologized.

Patiently, Jack reeled off a long list of spirits. Both Eileen and Mary Helen settled on beer.

"He's a good boy." Mrs. Bassetti beamed, watching her son leave the room.

"He surely is," Eileen agreed. "That reminds me of an old saying we had back home."

Mary Helen frowned. For the life of her, she couldn't imagine which one.

" 'Three things are always ready in a decent man's house.' "

Eileen looked around, smiling, " 'A beer, a bath, and a good fire.' "

Both Mrs. Bassetti and Mary Helen stared. For a split second, Mary Helen feared Mrs. Bassetti was about to run the tub.

Jack reentered with the drinks. Now might be her chance. Kate, who had been sitting quietly, passed around a platter of crisp vegetables and creamy dillweed dip. Mary Helen was amazed to see how much more patient the young woman had become, especially with her mother-in-law.

You could do well with some of that patience yourself, old girl, she thought, trying to stay calm. Erma and her predicament would come up in its own good time.

The five chatted pleasantly about everything and nothing, until Mary Helen was nearly convinced that the evening would turn out to be purely social. Try as she might, there was no polite way to introduce Erma Duran into the conversation. Mary Helen was beginning to seriously consider impolite ways.

As they finished their second drinks, Jack excused himself. "Dinner will be served," he announced, "just as soon as I finish the gravy."

"Aren't you going to help him?" Mrs. Bassetti frowned at her daughter-in-law.

"He hates it when I help him," Kate answered. "Besides, he's getting to be a much better cook than I am."

Unable to restrain herself, Mrs. Bassetti rose and bustled toward the kitchen. "Jackie," they heard her say, "don't use a fork. Here, let me do that. Get me a wooden spoon. God help us, you've got company and there's nothing worse than lumpy gravy."

As soon as Mrs. Bassetti was out of earshot, Kate moved over and sat on the couch with the Sisters. "Poor Mama Bassetti." She twisted a thick piece of her red hair. "She can't get used to a liberated woman."

"And how are you, Ms. Liberated Woman?" Mary Helen asked.

"Just fine, really, except"—Kate cut the chitchat short—"there is something I wanted to ask you about before my mother-in-law comes back."

Aha! So there was a hidden agenda, after all! Mary Helen felt suddenly warm inside. She would have sworn that Kate had something on her mind when she called last Monday, and she was right. The old touch was still right on target.

"I want to ask you about getting pregnant."

Mary Helen hoped her expression didn't give her away. She had been so sure Kate was going to talk about Erma that it took her several blinks to rearrange her thoughts and several more to adjust her face.

She didn't want to appear disappointed, nor did she want to appear astonished, when she realized what the topic was.

"Pardon me?" Eileen's voice rose. Obviously she was not fretting over appearances.

The two listened attentively while Kate told of her desire to conceive and her failure so far. At least Mary Helen was as attentive as she could possibly be, wondering all the while what in the world Kate was getting at.

"Then she"—Kate pointed toward the kitchen—"gave me some St. Gerard oil. She was given it by a neighbor and claims it works miracles." Kate quickly related the story. "What do you know about it?" she asked.

So that was the point! Mary Helen racked her memory. "Nothing," she said finally. "Nothing at all."

To be brutally truthful, she had never heard of St. Gerard oil, and she seriously doubted that St. Gerard had either. Perhaps Eileen knew something about it. That kind of thing was more up her alley. She looked questioningly at her friend.

Equally baffled, Eileen shook her head. "I have never heard of it either." Kate looked so deflated that Eileen couldn't resist adding, "But that doesn't mean it doesn't exist," she said. "After all"—her eyes twinkled—"neither of us has ever had any call to use it."

"I suppose not," Kate said absently.

"I'll tell you what I'll do," Mary Helen offered. Obviously, in her present mood, the girl needed a straw to grasp. "First thing tomorrow morning, as soon as Eileen's library opens, I'll look it up and give you a call. If your mother-in-law attributes three children to having used it, someone must have heard of it."

That settled, maybe now she could mention Erma.

But Mrs. Bassetti, her face flushed, reappeared in the doorway. "Come to the table. Quick! While it's hot. *Mangia! Mangia!*" She wiped her hands on the corner of an oversized butcher apron, which must have been her son's.

Jack's leg of lamb was delicious and the gravy lumpless. The dinner conversation flowed from current events to life at the college. Mary Helen waited for the lull. She was just about to fill it when Mama Bassetti beat her to it. She regaled them with several charming stories about Jack as a youngster. Although he fidgeted in his chair, Jack seemed to take them good-naturedly enough.

The evening passed pleasantly and quickly, although several times Mary Helen found herself distracted. Erma Duran hung on the edge of her mind like a heavy weight. Something bothered her and, whatever it was, hovered just out of reach, evading her grasp. She felt like a person awakening after a vivid dream, aware of it yet unable to remember the details.

When the old-fashioned clock on the mantel struck ten, Mary Helen was shocked. High time they went home. Everyone should be starting to droop. Besides, their hosts had to go to work tomorrow. For that matter, so did Eileen and she. Mary Helen glanced around the table. Actually, the only one who looked droopy was Jack. But then, poor dear, he had been bending over a hot stove. With his mother "helping."

About ten-thirty, they finally rose to go. Jack walked them

to the car and Kate waved from the open doorway. Mrs. Bassetti was already in the kitchen, attacking the dishes no doubt, in case it was also Jack's turn to clean up.

"Congratulations, old dear." Eileen said as soon as Mary Helen turned on the ignition.

Great waves of fog billowed down Geary Boulevard, obscuring her vision. She hit the defrost and the windshield wipers simultaneously. "Congratulations for what?"

"For spending an entire evening with two police officers and not bringing up Erma Duran, not even once!"

"It's not that I didn't want to bring her up." Mary Helen edged carefully away from the curb, watching for approaching headlights cutting through the swirling fog.

Eileen's gray eyes opened wide. "Then why didn't you?" she asked.

"Because I really could never find a way to fit it in."

"Which in itself is a miracle of sorts," both nuns said in unison.

May 24

Ascension Thursday

"Are you with us this morning," Sister Cecilia asked, "or have you 'ascended' above the conversation?"

The question startled Sister Mary Helen. It was the first thing she'd really heard during the entire breakfast and it was Cecilia's idea of an Ascension-Thursday pun. If there was anyone worse at puns than Lucy, it had to be Cecilia.

Mary Helen looked around. All eyes were on her. "Sorry. I guess I'm a little preoccupied this morning."

"Or perhaps a little tired. You were out quite late last night." Therese sniffed.

Smarting but feigning deafness, Mary Helen wondered what exactly had been addressed to her. Whatever it was, it couldn't have been as important as the questions whirling around in her own mind.

She had awakened puzzling and had been puzzling ever since. In fact, she was so distracted during the morning Mass that only a look at her watch made her sure the celebrant had been Father Adams. He was the one priest who could say

Mass in twenty-five minutes, three readings and a homily included—not that she had heard one word of his sermon. Her mind had begun to wander during the first reading.

Luke's account of the Ascension was vivid: the Apostles, gaping open-mouthed; Jesus' bare, pierced feet hovering just above their heads; their total bewilderment as they watched Him being lifted up into a cloud.

She couldn't help but identify with them. Gazing into an empty sky, they must have wondered about the man they thought they had known so well. Fortunately for them, two men in white flowing robes appeared to explain. At the moment, she wished someone would appear and explain a few things to her, white gowns optional.

Yet despite her distractions at Mass, Mary Helen had felt God's closeness. Who else but He could be urging her to probe and pick until she discovered truth? Only then, she knew, would He fill her with a sense of peace.

Give me a hint! Mary Helen prayed silently, picking up her breakfast tray. *Or give me a break!*

She excused herself from the table. Only Eileen seemed to stare at her curiously. She wondered for a moment if her lips had been moving.

Back in her bedroom, Sister Mary Helen stared at her neatly made bed, frowning. She couldn't even remember having made it. Now, that is distracted! she scolded herself. She hated bed-making. It always seemed like such a waste of time. You just have to unmake it to get back in.

How she wished she had used the opportunity to talk to Kate Murphy last night about Erma. How she wished she could talk to her right now.

Of course! she thought, brushing her teeth, St. Gerard Majella! She paused, brush in hand. What a perfect excuse to call Kate first thing this morning.

Pulling her Aran sweater from the closet, Mary Helen hurried through the convent halls. Sounds of tidying up and getting ready for school came from each small room. Therese emerged with a dust mop, a dustcloth, and a determined look on her face, prepared to give them both a good shaking.

Downstairs, the washing machine sloshed rhythmically. Beside it the dryer hummed its monotonous hum. Everything was so normal, so right, so slow. The contrast only served to heighten Mary Helen's sense of unrest and urgency.

The Hanna Memorial Library was nearly deserted when she arrived. Wonder of wonders, she had even beaten Eileen. Good! Mary Helen hurried over to the reference shelves.

Butler's *Lives of the Saints* would have what she needed. But before she looked into it, she had better check the *Catholic Encyclopedia* for the real name of Pope Pius IX. Maybe his name would provide a clue to what Erma meant when she had said, Look to the picture.

The pope's real name was Giovanni Maria Mastai-Ferretti. Mary Helen searched her mind. She couldn't think of one John, one Mastai-Ferretti, or, for that matter, even one Italian that figured into the whole case.

In Butler's *Lives,* volume IV, page 131, she found the life of Gerard Majella. Scanning the entry, she searched for a mention of St. Gerard oil, but found none. The saint had been an Italian, born in 1726. The son of a tailor, he had become one himself. Gerard had tried religious life, been rejected, and worked as a servant in the bishop's house. Finally, he was received into the Redemptorist Order by its founder, St. Alphonsus Liguori. His life was simple—if you didn't count miracles, bilocation, and ecstatic flights, Mary Helen thought. But as young Sister Anne would say, Who's counting? "His feast day is celebrated on October sixteenth, and he is patron of childbearing," she read.

In the whole account, Sister Mary Helen found no mention of any oil. Obviously Mrs. Bassetti's neighbor had made it up. It was Mrs. Bassetti's faith that had made it work.

Although she had suspected she wouldn't find anything,

Mary Helen couldn't help feeling disappointed. Doubting Kate wanted to believe so badly, and nobody—certainly not Mary Helen—likes to be the bearer of bad news.

Definitely the young woman wanted children. Who wouldn't? The shining face of the two Boscacci youngsters flashed through Mary Helen's mind. Then Gerard Majella, the Pope, the Madonna, the washing machine, Erma, the "he" in her journal all tumbled in on themselves, banging together like so many bouncing Ping-Pong balls in the lottery spin.

Quickly, one by one, the ideas shot out and lined up, making perfect sense. Mary Helen slammed Butler's *Lives* shut. She rechecked the *Catholic Encyclopedia.* Of course she was right! Only one thing remained to double-check. Just to make certain.

Picking up her sweater, she dashed across the quiet room. No one seemed to look up. She didn't even notice Eileen watching her, nor did she see the worried look on her friend's face as she let the beveled door swing shut behind her.

* * *

When Sister Mary Helen parked the car, the corner of 18th and Sanchez was virtually deserted. Several houses up on Sanchez, a small black mongrel stopped, stared, but went right back to sniffing. Apparently she didn't even look suspicious enough to bark at.

Good! she thought, making her way to the apartment building. Crossing town, Mary Helen had formulated a hasty plan. First, she would make sure whether or not Mr. Finn was at home. She leaned heavily on his doorbell. So heavily, in fact, that she could hear it ring from outside. When he didn't answer, she rang again.

Satisfied that Mr. Finn must have stepped out, she went to the bistro door and rapped on the window. No one appeared. She rapped again. Probably not even the cooks would arrive for at least another hour or so. The lock, she remembered, looked easy to pi—open. All right, then—pick!

Fishing in her pocketbook, she pulled out the unsolicited credit card the phone company had sent. Maybe the changes in the company weren't all bad, she thought as she ran the card along the doorjamb. Although she had read often about the procedure in her mysteries and had seen the new Mike Hammer do it on television, Mary Helen was genuinely surprised when the front door popped open.

Carefully the old nun made her way across the darkened room, avoiding tables and pulled-out chairs. In the deserted kitchen the smell of stale grease hung on the air. Only the *drip, drip,* of water on the stainless-steel sink broke the heavy silence.

Taking the old key from its hook on the wall, she unlocked the basement door and flipped on the light. Holding tight to the rickety banister, she began to descend the steps. They creaked. She stopped, listened, making sure she was alone. Adjusting her bifocals, she continued.

Cautiously, Mary Helen peered around the dim basement. Good night, nurse! She had left the college so quickly she had forgotten all about bringing a flashlight. The single bulbs running across the center of the ceiling threw heavy shadows into the corners. She made her way across the room.

Against one wall the concrete sinks were filled with grime. Water had made narrow rivulets of mud down their centers. Dusty cartons marked "toilet tissue" were stacked against a rough wall. The gray paint on the alley door had begun to peel.

From outside, she could hear the muffled sound of traffic: the rattle of a pick-up truck, the dull roar of a passing motorcycle. Yet inside, the basement had a tomblike silence.

With a sense of dread, Mary Helen approached the ice maker near the middle of the basement. She touched its motor. Cold. She opened the ice-storage lid. It was empty except for a puddle of nearly stagnant water covering the bottom. Bending over, Mary Helen studied the concrete floor surrounding it.

Her stomach dropped. Her mouth was suddenly so dry she could hardly swallow. Just as she had suspected: new cement. Kate Murphy, she thought straightening up. I must phone Kate Murphy. Immediately!

Suddenly the floor overhead creaked. Was it really a creak? Or simply her imagination? A second creak followed. Frozen, Mary Helen listened. It was the unmistakable sound of someone walking lightly, cautiously, across the kitchen floor. Someone who did not want to be heard. Someone who was heading toward the basement.

Hardly breathing, Mary Helen crept toward the alley door. Its window was covered with dust. Perhaps that was why she didn't notice, until she ran her hand along the wooden surface, that someone had removed the inside handle. That same someone had recently nailed a two-by-four to the door to make sure it was securely shut.

As she backed toward the corner, the rough wall snagged her sweater. She crouched in the shadows. Cobwebs brushed her face. Mary Helen shuddered, but refused to imagine what else might be with her in the corner. Her muscles cramped, yet she waited, not moving, too terrified to even breathe. Dust tickled her nostrils, tempting her to sneeze.

Straining, she heard the footsteps stop, the door to the basement grate open. For a long moment all she could hear was the sound of her own heart beating. A stair creaked, then another. She watched as the figure outlined by the glow of the kitchen light carefully descended the steps.

Midway, it stopped, listened for noise, descended again. She was surprised to see that the figure was clutching a large pillow.

* * *

Kate Murphy yawned and checked her wristwatch. Not even noon and she felt ready for a nap. Or maybe she wasn't awake yet. Stretching, she looked out the window of the Hall of Justice. Outside, it was that kind of day—gray and cold and sleepy. She checked her watch again.

"A minute later, right?" Dennis Gallagher must have been watching her.

"Right," she said. Then, unable to resist, Kate stuck out her tongue. Whoever invented sticking your tongue out was a master psychologist, she thought. It made her feel a little foolish but a lot better.

"Did you guys have a rough night?" Obviously Gallagher had chosen to ignore her reaction. "You look bushed. Still making up?"

Kate could feel her face flush. "For your dirty mind's information," she said, "what we did was have the nuns over for dinner last night."

"The nuns?"

"After we made up," she added, to satisfy the incredulous look on Gallagher's face.

He was about to comment when Kate's phone rang. She was surprised to hear Sister Eileen's voice, although at first the nun's brogue was so thick Kate could barely understand her.

"Slow down, Sister," she said.

"Speak of the devil." Gallagher pushed back in his swivel chair to listen.

"Is there something wrong, Sister Eileen?"

"Something is always wrong," Gallagher muttered. With her free hand, Kate shushed him.

"Glory be to God, I'm not sure, but I'm afraid so. I know how busy you are, Kate dear, and I would not think of bothering you ordinarily, but Sister Mary Helen took out of here about eight-thirty this morning like the devil himself was on her tail."

For the third time in a matter of minutes, Kate checked her wristwatch. "That wasn't even two hours ago."

"You haven't the ghost of an idea the amount of devilment the woman can get into in two hours. Or maybe you do. Anyway, she left without telling anyone where she was going and, what is worse, she had that look on her face."

"What look?"

" 'Tis difficult to describe unless you've seen it." Eileen paused. " 'Tis a cross between Joan of Arc and Miss Marple," she said, "and it leads to only one thing—trouble!"

"Are you sure?" Kate tried to speak calmly and reasonably, but it was no use.

"Surr-re, I am surr-re." Eileen was rolling her r's. "I have been friends with the old dear for over fifty years, and I know that look when I see it. Besides, Kate, I have had a turrible eerie feeling all over since the moment I saw her leaving."

Kate needed more to go on than faces and feelings. "Have you any idea of where—"

Eileen interrupted. "I have an idea, all right. A good idea that it has something to do with Erma Duran's disappearance. And furthermore, I would wager all the books in Hanna Memorial, the rare ones included, that she is over there right now, poking around."

"Perhaps she had another appointment."

"Sure as the sun will rr-ise"—her r's were really rolling now —"I know she's into this Erma business. And don't ask me if I called around. Sister Anne and I have called her office, her dentist, her eye doctor—anyplace we thought she might have an appointment. And the other OWLs as well. No one has any idea where she might be."

"You realize, Sister, that, strictly speaking, this is not my case. It's Inspector Honore's."

"Sister Anne is on the horn this minute, trying to get through to the Inspector." Obviously Eileen had thought of everything. Kate was undoubtedly her last hope.

"What exactly is it you want me to do?" she asked and braced herself for the answer.

For the first time there was a long pause on the other end of the line. "I really do not know," Eileen said. Kate noticed a slight quiver in her voice. "I just know my dear friend could be in some danger. And I cannot possibly sit by and let it happen."

"I understand how you're feeling, Sister." Kate had picked that phrase up in a communications workshop, although she wasn't at all sure she did understand. Sister Eileen must be frantic. She had never heard the round, jovial woman sounding so distraught. "But I really don't know what it is you want me to do." There was another long pause. "Sister, are you all right?"

For several seconds there was no answer. "Sister?" Kate repeated.

Apparently Sister Eileen was mulling over something. "Just fine, dear," she said, suddenly calm. "I realize, as you say, that this is not your case, so there is really nothing you can do. Thank you for listening." Abruptly she hung up.

Kate stared at the dead receiver. "Damn!" She began to thumb through the phone book, looking for the number of the Sisters' Residence.

"What happened?" Gallagher asked.

"I'll tell you in a minute." Kate dialed. The phone rang twenty times before someone finally answered.

"Sister Eileen is in the library," a polite voice answered. "Would you like that number?"

By the time the voice found the number, gave it to Kate, and she redialed, Sister Eileen had just left.

"Double damn!" Kate slammed down the receiver.

"What was that all about?" Gallagher stood up.

"Let's go, Denny." Kate grabbed her coat. "I'll explain on the way to the bistro."

"The bistro? Why the bistro?" Apparently Gallagher wasn't moving until he had some sort of explanation.

"Because that seems to be the only logical place Sister Eileen would go, and she was suddenly too calm for comfort—my comfort."

"Sister Eileen?" Gallagher sat back down. "One's bad enough; now we got the second one. And we have no damn business at all with either of them nuns. I told you not to get involved. It's not our case. Stick to your own business."

"Suit yourself." Kate took her purse from her bottom drawer. "And I know you're right, Denny, but I have the uneasy feeling that sticking to my own business may have caused Sister Eileen to make our business hers. Frankly, I couldn't live with myself if I went by the book and let something happen to the old dears."

Kate crossed the detail, heels clicking. Behind her she heard a familiar grunting noise. Gallagher!

"I thought you weren't coming." She pushed the Down button on the elevator and tried not to smile.

"Goddamn it! Get that smirk off your face." Gallagher paused to light the stub of his cigar. "By rights, we should let those nuns get themselves killed. Serve them right! But you say you couldn't live with yourself. What about me, huh? What do you think, that the younger generation's got an edge on this guilt business?" He pointed his finger at her. "Hey, I could tell you stories about guilt, Katie-girl, that you wouldn't believe!"

* * *

The moment Mary Helen heard the voice, she recognized it. She was not surprised. A little saddened maybe, but not surprised.

"I know you're in here somewhere."

From her corner, she watched him squinting, trying to adjust his eyes to the dimness of the basement.

How long would it take him to spot her?

"There's no way out, you know," the voice rasped.

Mind whirling, she crouched more deeply into the shadows. Think calmly! she told herself, ignoring the trickle of perspiration that ran down her back.

"I'll find you. Why don't you just come out?" Finn coaxed. He was moving slowly toward the center of the room.

She watched him peer around the old ice machine. Her hand groped along the rough wall, searching to grasp something—anything. If only she could find a board, an old wrench, something she could hit him with. That always happened in her mystery stories. But there was nothing. Not even a loose board! Her heart jolted.

Mary Helen's legs began to cramp. She shifted her weight and tried to think, but the only thing she could think about was the sound of her own heart hammering in her ears. She pulled in a deep breath to slow it down.

"Where are you? I know you're here." Finn moved closer. Mary Helen closed her eyes, clenched her damp hands more tightly, and tried to shrink into an invisible ball that the man would overlook.

Whether it was from cold or from fear, now her teeth were threatening to chatter. Her legs began to tremble. Mary Helen wasn't sure how much longer she could stay crouched in the corner, waiting for death. Or even if she should.

What had Eileen said? "An Irish coward is an uncommon character!" If it was her time to go, by God, she would go with dignity, not quailing in some dusty corner. Squaring her shoulders, she steadied herself. Then, wondering briefly if she had more bravado than brains, she rose.

God, help me! she prayed, swallowing hard to keep her throat from closing. She knew from their long-standing relationship, He most certainly would.

"Here I am!" She hardly recognized her own forced voice.

Finn looked over, blinking. "Oh, it's you," he said, not unkindly. "I'm sorry it's you."

For a moment the pair studied each other. The dim light from the bulb bounced off the bald V's Finn's hair outlined on the top of his head.

"I rang your apartment bell when I came," Mary Helen said, as if trespassing were the problem.

"I guess that's what woke me up." Finn shifted the pillow.

"I was taking a nap upstairs on Erma's bed. Makes me feel closer to her now that she's gone." Mary Helen remained silent.

"I'm sorry it's you," he repeated, "but I should have known it would be. That business about the phone call didn't put you off, did it?"

Woodenly, Mary Helen shook her head, wishing momentarily that it had. "I was sorry when I realized it was you too," she said slowly. "What stumps me, however, is *why,* Mr. Finn. I always had the feeling that you loved Erma."

"I did. I still do." Finn blinked. "And I miss her. It was an accident. It really was. I didn't mean to hurt her. I never would have hurt her on purpose."

"What kind of an accident?"

"I lost my temper." Perspiration broke out on Finn's forehead. "She fell and cracked her head against the bed and . . . I didn't mean to." He rocked nervously on the soles of his feet.

Mary Helen inched over, determined not to glance at the open door leading up to the kitchen. If she could just keep him talking, keep inching over, maybe, just maybe, she could make a dash for it before . . . No! She refused to think about the pillow hanging limply from his hands.

"What could Erma possibly have done to make you lose your temper?" She cleared her throat. "She always seems . . . seemed so accommodating."

"Yeah." Finn glared at her. "Especially with those kids of hers. She was goofy about those kids. You know her checks had been missing."

He stopped, waiting for Mary Helen to nod.

"She blamed me. Me! Just because I had a few gambling debts."

"And you didn't take them?"

His nostrils flared. "Of course I didn't. That's what started the argument. I told her it was Buddy. She was shocked. She tells me Buddy wouldn't do such a thing. The little twirp!"

Finn's eyes narrowed. "I told her all her kids were nuts. Then we really started to fight. Erma brought up an old story about me doing something to Ree when she was a kid."

Keep him talking, Mary Helen thought, shifting her feet ever so slightly. "Ree told me as much." She kept her voice even. "And you're saying you didn't?"

He stared at her in amazement. "Damn right, I didn't! Actually it was Junior who knocked his sister down. I thought the kids were lost, so I went looking for them. He was on top of her by the time I got there. Buddy was looking on. I'm sure she didn't tell you that part.

"I got him off her. Tommy came around the corner. When she sees him, Ree says I was the one who knocked her down." He shrugged. "We never could figure out just what happened or whose fault it was or exactly what the kid had in mind. I never seen Tommy so mad. He walloped the daylights out of Junior right there at the track. Smacked the sister good and hard a couple of times, too, just in case."

"Did you explain that to Erma?"

"She never wanted to talk about it. Tommy—I know he was ready to kill both kids! Somehow Erma blamed that on me too." He shook his head. "You know, when she was around she never let him lay a hand on Ree or the little guy. And that Buddy sure could have used it. If you ask me, that's why the poor guy drank." He stopped to catch his breath.

"Yet I couldn't help loving her. But she wouldn't marry me after Tom died. Her kids, especially the daughter, didn't like seeing me with their mother. And so Erma said she hated my temper and my drinking, but I know the kids had a lot to do with it." Finn shifted the pillow.

Watching him, Mary Helen's stomach roiled. She wasn't even a foot closer to the door. "Do you have a hard time controlling your temper?" It was the only question that came to her, although she had witnessed the answer.

Finn looked and sounded puzzled, almost as if he were talking about someone else. "It happens when I'm drinking, mostly. I can't seem to help it. Something just happens in my head. I only hit her once or twice, I guess, in all the years I've known her. And that was in these last few years. I been drinking more." Finn's eyes were blinking almost uncontrollably. "I told her I was sorry. I tried to make it up to her. I let her live here, work in my place. I tell you, I loved the woman."

"I'm sure you did." Mary Helen tried to soothe the man and not look shocked. No wonder the subtle mention of the picture to Ree. Erma didn't want to upset her daughter. Good old Erma didn't want to upset anyone. After all, Finn was her security; yet she must have feared that someday Finn's drinking, coupled with his unbridled rage, would cause her harm.

"What made you come back here?" It was Finn's turn to ask questions.

"The picture, really." Suddenly her mouth was so dry, she was having trouble getting it around the words. "Erma said that if anything happened to her, we should look to the picture." She stopped to swallow. "At first, I couldn't make anything of it. This week I was doing some research and I remembered you telling us your name is Alphonsus after Alphonsus Liguori, founder of the Redemptorists. Our Lady of Perpetual Help is a special devotion of the Redemptorists. The picture was enshrined at their convent. It was the only connection that made any sense. But there was something else," she added as he made a movement.

"The fact that I remembered your ice machine was leaning. Allan Boscacci, a fellow who fixes our electrical problems, says machines should be flat." Mary Helen knew she was babbling. From the look hardening in Finn's eyes, she realized her time was limited.

She shifted a few inches closer to the staircase and tried to stall. "Always, always, they should be flat, Allan said. And I was just checking and, sure enough . . ." Edging over, she pointed toward the new concrete square beneath the ice maker. "It seems unlikely that you would put a new piece of floor in crooked unless you were in a very big hurry.

"Won't the cook be coming soon?" she asked, anxious to change the subject.

"I locked the front door and turned the CLOSED sign out." The voice was cold, detached.

Mary Helen looked over at Finn. His eyes slid from the concrete floor up to her face.

The movement was so swift that Mary Helen was shocked to feel the pillow over her face. She gasped, sucking in air, fighting against the pressure backing her up, forcing her against the rough basement wall. Grunting, she moved her head from side to side, struggling to escape the softness covering her mouth, pushing her glasses into the bridge of her nose.

"Do not go gentle . . . Old age should burn and rave . . . Rage, rage against the dying of the light." Crazily, the words popped into her mind as she clawed at Finn's strong hands. She could feel his flesh under her nails. Desperately she tried to push against the blackness that was smothering her.

Slowly consciousness began to slip away. Her limbs felt limp and tingly, unable to support her. Her ears were ringing. So this is what dying is like, she thought, hardly feeling the wall behind her.

A moment of passing and she would awaken to lightness and peace, where all mysteries would be solved. *O Christ, Christ, come quickly! . . . Jesu, hearts light . . .* She couldn't help smiling as she slipped into the whirling blackness.

High-pitched shouts, the scuffling of feet, the thud of blows, and Caroline swearing like a stevedore convinced Mary Helen she had not yet entered paradise. Her head throbbed. Beneath her the floor was cold and hard.

Painfully she opened her eyes. Through cracked glasses she could see Noelle, Lucy, Caroline, all pulling and kicking a cowering Mr. Finn. Sister Anne held tight to his shirttails, and dear Eileen had a firm grip on his one long, thin piece of hair.

"Freeze!" Kate, crouched in shooting position, barked from the top of the stairs. Gallagher and Honore flanked her.

"I said *Freeze!* Before you kill the guy!" Mary Helen heard her shout. Closing her eyes, she surrendered once again to the swirling dark.

Friday, May 25

Feast of Venerable Bede, Priest and Doctor

Even before she opened her eyes, Sister Mary Helen knew where she was. The Lysol smell, the slippery feel of a plastic sheet on a hard mattress, the sound of crepe soles on waxed floors. Although she hadn't been in the hospital since she'd had her gall-bladder attack thirty years before, the earmarks were unmistakable and unforgettable.

What was she doing here? Then she remembered—Erma, the basement, Mr. Finn, the pillow. God help me! she thought, aware that indeed He had. She lay quietly for several moments, telling Him just how grateful she was. And although she was sorely tempted, she made no rash promises to reform. God and she had been friends too long for either of them to be fooled.

As her mind cleared she realized that her head throbbed and her neck was stiff and sore. Her eyelids felt stuck together. Slowly she forced them open. Morning sun flooded the room. Eileen, the rosary beads still in her hands, dozed in a hardback chair. Anne, her back to the bed, stared out between the vene-

tian blinds, apparently studying the commuter traffic in the
street below.

"Where am I?" Mary Helen said, only because it seemed
like the right thing to say.

Both nuns rushed to her bedside, smiling, squeezing her
hands. Poor Eileen's face was pale and she looked exhausted.
"Jesus, Mary, and Joseph!" she said, tears in her eyes. "Don't
ever give us a scare like that again!"

"She's awake," Anne called down the hallway. Suddenly the
antiseptic room was alive with people, all talking at once.

"Thank goodness the Sisters called us." Noelle, dressed in
sailor-boy blue, sounded more like the admiral of the fleet.

"We were so worried about you." Several strands of gray
had escaped from Lucy's braid. "But we shouldn't have been."
She grinned. "When the going gets tough, the tough . . ." She
stopped searching for an ending that fit.

"Pray like hell," Caroline added, her wide-brimmed hat dipping toward Mary Helen.

At least Mary Helen thought it dipped. Everything looked a
little fuzzy.

"Your spectacles, Sister dear," Therese piped up then and
fitted them over her ears. Good old efficient Therese had discovered the spare pair of glasses in her nightstand. Mary
Helen cringed, momentarily picturing the drawer full of paperback mysteries Therese must also have discovered.

"They were on top of your desk, with this." Sister Cecilia
winked reassuringly. The college president handed her what
looked like—for those who didn't know better—a prayerbook
in a plastic prayerbook cover.

"Thank you," Mary Helen said indistinctly. Her mouth was
suddenly dry and her eyelids heavy.

"It must be the medication," she heard Eileen say as she
drifted back into sleep.

*   *   *

When Mary Helen awoke again, her room was empty. The afternoon sun cast warm slits of light through the venetian blinds and across her white top sheet. Quietly her door opened a few inches. She recognized the top of Eileen's head and her gray eyes peeking in.

"Sleeping Beauty has awakened," Eileen announced, pushing the door back.

By the time Mary Helen had put on her bifocals, Kate Murphy was at her side. Inspector Gallagher and Inspector Honore fidgeted uncomfortably at the foot of the bed. Gallagher, she noticed, kept his eyes anyplace but on her. Poor devil had probably never seen a nun in bed before, she mused. But then again, few people had.

"We're so glad you're safe." Kate's blue eyes were concerned. "When you're feeling better we'll have to talk seriously about—"

"And thanks to you three, Mr. Finn is safe too," Mary Helen interrupted, hoping Kate would attribute her rudeness to ill health. She did not want to hear the end of Kate's sentence.

Kate laughed. "I have the feeling he was the happiest person in the whole basement to see us. I knew you'd be curious about the outcome."

Mary Helen nodded, then wished she hadn't. Her head pounded.

"Finn confessed," Kate said. "He admits killing Mrs. Duran. By accident, or so he claims. Apparently the man has a hair-trigger temper. He wanted to marry her, but she kept refusing him again and again.

"What he said about her coming down to the bistro was true. She did come down to tell him she was leaving, leaving the apartment for good. Finn went upstairs. They argued bitterly about the kids. He must have followed her around the apartment, begging her to change her mind. She only became more determined to go.

"When she ignored his pleading and went out to the back porch to finish Buddy's laundry, something in Finn must have snapped.

"Mrs. Duran apparently ran into her bedroom to escape his rage. Unable to control himself, Finn ran after her and knocked her down. She rolled under the bed, trying to get away from him."

"That's how the medal got stuck"—Mary Helen thought aloud—"and why the laundry was half done."

Kate nodded. "He pulled her out, slapped her several times —once with such force that she tumbled backward and hit the end of the bedstead just the wrong way. According to Finn, that's what killed her."

Mary Helen winced.

"That's his story, anyway." Honore snapped his gum. "We'll have to wait for an autopsy."

"Then you found her? She was buried in the basement?"

"Yes, Sister." Kate patted her hand. "As soon as he realized she was dead, Finn panicked. He had to bury her somewhere. As far as we can figure, this all happened Saturday afternoon. He must have buried her in the early hours of Sunday morning. After they finally closed up Saturday, he shoved the ice machine aside. Dug like the devil himself was after him. Buried the body, refilled the hole, and moved the machine back. He had time, since the bistro doesn't open until dinner on Sundays."

"That's who she meant by the *he* who was worrying her." The moment the sentence left her mouth, Mary Helen wished it hadn't.

Kate's eyes narrowed. "You weren't by any chance doing a little private investigating, were you? You know, Sister, I found a black binder alongside the bed. It looked surprisingly like someone had torn some pages out."

Mary Helen groaned and put her hand up to the lump on her head.

"Maybe this isn't the right time, Sister," Kate began. "Or maybe while your head still aches, it is. You gave us quite a scare, you know. You really shouldn't be dabbling in police work. It's much too dangerous! Why didn't you call us instead of going over there by yourself?"

"I fully intended to," Mary Helen said. "In fact, I was in the library looking up St. Gerard oil when the whole thing tumbled together."

Kate's blue eyes studied her. She bent forward. Obviously she didn't want the other two inspectors to hear. "What did you find out about it?" she whispered.

She looked so eager, so hopeful, Mary Helen didn't have the heart to tell her the truth. Not right now, anyway. Instead she closed her eyes.

"She must have drifted off, poor dear." She heard Kate whisper.

"She had a close one." Mary Helen recognized Honore's low voice. "She'd better watch herself after this, before something really happens to her."

"Watch herself, hell!" Gallagher growled. "Nothing's going to happen to her. That nun leads a charmed life. What's going to happen, goddamn it, is that the old gal's going to end up being the death of me!"

Wednesday, June 27

Feast of Our Lady of Perpetual Help

Over a month later, on the Feast of Our Lady of Perpetual Help, Sister Mary Helen organized a Memorial Mass for Erma Duran. The day seemed appropriate, not only because of Erma's devotion to Mary under this title but because the picture had been a tremendous help in solving the case.

And to Mary Helen's way of thinking, the Carmelite monastery seemed like just the place to hold it. Who knew how much help their prayers had been? Therefore, she was thrilled when Mother Virginia, the Carmelite prioress, and Father Adams both agreed.

"My campus ministry group will do the music," Sister Anne volunteered. "Our new guitarist is just great!"

"Who are you inviting?" Sister Eileen asked.

"Our OWL chapter and Erma's children, of course," Mary Helen said. "And I'll let Kate Murphy know. Maybe she and a few of the policemen would like to attend."

By ten o'clock the Carmelite chapel was full. Sister Mary Helen was delighted to see that Mother Virginia had arranged for a large print of the Byzantine Madonna to be placed on a side altar. Several vigil lights and a large bouquet of home-grown roses surrounded the icon.

From behind the iron grille at the side of the main altar she could hear the rustle of the cloistered nuns assembling. Several of the OWLs peered curiously, hoping in vain to catch a glimpse of them.

Next to Lucy Lyons, Erma Duran's three children sat in reserved seats, looking dutiful if totally out of place. Junior, thank God, had found a shirt to wear under his leather jacket. Marie had changed her polyester slacks for a skirt and, from a distance, it seemed Buddy had come *sans* earrings.

The clang of a bell signaled Father Adams's entrance onto the ornate main altar. The congregation rose. Mary Helen was happy to see Kate Murphy slip into a side pew. Gallagher, Honore, and Jack Bassetti followed her.

The familiar ritual lulled Mary Helen into a brown study: Erma Duran, her goodness, the circumstances of her death. The woman, God rest her—and Mary Helen was sure He was doing just that—had been the salt of the earth. But even salt can lose a bit of its savor. Nobody's perfect; everyone has an Achilles' heel.

Mary Helen's eyes slid toward Erma's children, her Achilles' heel. Certainly the Byzantine Madonna to whom she was so devoted would understand that. In the picture, Mary's own eyes were filled with sadness over her Child. Mary Helen could imagine the two mothers chatting now.

Sadly she wondered if Erma's three children would ever realize the parts they'd played in their mother's death. She wondered, too, what would happen to Alphonsus Liguori Finn.

Father Adams had just finished reading the gospel for the Feast, when Mary Helen noticed Kate Murphy dash out. The young woman's face was pasty.

Slipping out behind her, Mary Helen found Kate in the vestibule, a Kleenex over her mouth, retching.

"Quickly! Over here!" The old nun shepherded her to a small restroom and closed the door just in time to muffle Kate's gagging. "Are you all right?" Mary Helen called. The flushing of the toilet drowned out the answer.

Clammy and shaken, Kate opened the door. She wiped her mouth with a damp paper towel.

"Are you okay, hon?" Jack Bassetti stood behind Mary Helen.

Leaning against the vestibule wall, eyes closed, Kate nodded her head.

"Has she been sick?" Mary Helen asked.

"For the last week or so. At first I thought she had a touch of the flu." Jack put his arm around his wife. "It's going around the Hall. But it's the funniest kind of flu. She's only sick in the morning. By the afternoon she seems to be fine."

Kate, who had recovered, patted her lips with the damp towel.

Mary Helen couldn't help smiling. "A fine detective you are, Jack Bassetti!" she said. Maybe there was something to St. Gerard and this oil business, after all. "It sounds to me as if what your wife has is not a touch of the flu. It's a touch of pregnant!"

"Pregnant?" Jack shouted.

"Shh." Mary Helen wondered just how much the congregation was overhearing.

"Yes, indeed," she said. She shoved her bifocals up the bridge of her nose to study the couple. "I will bet you dollars to doughnuts that Kate's flu bug turns out to be nothing more than a classic case of morning sickness." She patted her friend's hand.

Kate beamed at her husband. "I was hoping to surprise you. Tomorrow is my doctor's appointment. Then I'll know for sure. Isn't it great?" She hugged him. "Same doctor, different reason!"

At the moment, Mary Helen could not remember when she'd seen the thought of a trip to the doctor bring such a look of radiance and joy to anyone's face.